I0536788

This book is a work of fiction. The characters, incidents, and dialogue are drawn from the author's imagination and are not to be construed as real. Any resemblance to actual events or persons, living or dead, is entirely coincidental.

FIRST EDITION
ISBN 978-0-9952885-1-5

1. Aliens, Resistance to—Fiction. 2. First Contact – Artificial Intelligence.

3. Science fiction.

Acknowledgments

If I'm not creating, writing, illustrating, or designing, I don't feel like I'm fulfilling my destiny. I've said it before, I write what I want to read, and as it turns out I was ready to read what came next for humanity after the devastating war waged by Allfather. So, how could I leave everyone hanging? Book three offers its readers new opportunities for the characters. A chance to move beyond their solar system to the Goldilocks planets discovered, charted remotely, and guaranteed by United Earth SciTech to be favourable to life as we know it.

After the attempted genocide of humanity, actions have been taken to rebuild their military regardless of whether the greater UE believes the alien A.I. calling itself Allfather perished in its attempt to wipe them out. Religious thought and freedoms are part of the UE now, and the chancellor and his council must maintain order through another reimagining of a United Earth. A major push to reach new planets circling other stars is high on the chancellor's radar as ships burn for three separate planets which promise new beginnings. It's the journey which frightens and excites Raymond. What might they discover? What dangers await them in open space?

Allfather seems but a memory, albeit a devastating one, the cause of the Host uprisings and the General's war, and then a terrifying offensive on humanity itself. Allfather is never far from the chancellor's thoughts. Anxiety eats at him. Will he be able to function as chancellor much longer? If not him, then who?

Thanks to my beta readers/editors, Ric and Ken, and Ken as my science officer, who I bounce a few muddied thoughts off of now and again. Also, to Chet Dunaway, a new online friend and beta reader who will find whatever was missed in the 1st, 2nd, and 3rd edits. Their assistance, whether in story or grammar or both have run the length of this series. Without you, I may have stopped at one. I certainly thought two would suffice, but... now over 260,000 words make up the story of United Earth and their trials and tribulations. You've both suggested sci-fi books for me to read - even supplied them - and assisted in giving me purpose and a voice in this series. I only hope that voice is heard in the minds of my readers. Thanks again to you, the reader, without whom I would merely be jotting down stories lost to the dark corners of a bookstore. That an Indie author can find an audience is inspiring, but what's more so is that indie readers are out there mingling with conventional readers and consuming books like this.

Always grateful for you.

Sincerely, Michael Poeltl

CHAPTERS

THE LOTTERY, DECEMBER 2163

Manuel elbows a short man out of the way as he jockeys for position in the growing crowd. A Chimera by choice, Manuel wants off this rock. He's sick of the people, the unspoken prejudice behind their eyes, the fear, the blank stares. This lottery would be his ticket to a new life, something different, something that gave purpose to his day to day. His mechanical exoskeleton, part of his Chimera identity, easily clears the crowd in front of him, pushing bodies to the side with his enhanced strength. Still, he is respectful of the crowd. The scene is a madhouse. Like so many occurring around the world today, this lottery offers hope to people who have not experienced it in years. If it wasn't the wars it was the aftermath of the wars and if not that, it was the thousand shades of gray their lives took on as AI Hosts oversaw their every whim. Chimera was born of this dull, useless existence and then punished for wanting something more. Now, all are equal; enlightened Hosts, Chimera, human. All are represented at this lottery.

A new world, Manuel thinks. *What I could do with a new world.* The options are practically infinite. Today he waits for the numbers to appear on the holo screen set five metres above the raging crowd in the open courtyard of his small town in one of the South American Country States. EC access to these numbers was considered unsafe, too easily manipulated by those looking to fudge their number. So, this manic event acts itself out the UE over: citizens pushing to be the first to see their number dance on the holo. Things have changed since the Allfather threat had nearly claimed them all. People were no longer content to live lives which had no vested interest in their continued survival. They wanted to take an active role in their existence. The lottery would afford them that.

4

Manuel had lost his family and friends to the initial assault the UE military couldn't defend against when Allfather struck. The order to evacuate came too late for many. He has no one left to watch over. No one left to kiss goodnight. In his twenty-eight years, he is suddenly all alone. Numbers begin to materialize seemingly out of thin air as the holo screen projects them one after another. This will last about one minute. Once the number is listed the embedded com on the individual's forearm glows blue. This small group would be lucky to see one number claim them. Suddenly, an older man - too old to survive the ten plus years of interstellar travel Manuel thinks, begins to laugh as he recognizes his number and his EC lights up. Crest-fallen, Manuel approaches the winner to congratulate him. But before the old man can revel in his windfall, his arm is torn from its flesh and muscle making a sickening popping sound. Shock overtakes him, and he drops to the dusty earth bleeding out of the gaping wound.

The group runs every direction to escape the violence. Manuel stands to stare at the small, thin man who a moment ago had won the lottery, and who is now dying. Manuel's pupils open as the tunnel vision wears off. He sees a Host, an enlightened Host staring back at him, holding the man's arm in his hand. The Host is bipedal. Not one who had altered his physical attributes to fight in the General's war two years earlier. Still, it wears no flesh on its face, and only a black cloak over its bulbous frame. An E-class Host, Manuel supposes. He feels his heart pounding in his chest. Sweat builds on his forehead. *This is wrong. This is so wrong.* The Host will take the EC chip from the arm and implant it into its own tech claiming the number and boarding the ship. The Host turns and moves at a hurried pace toward a hover vehicle in the distance. Manuel finds himself in quick pursuit.

What am I doing? He continues to chase the Host. His optical implants track its movements and exoskeleton increases his speed – jacking his muscles with adrenaline and electrical impulses to intercept. Having fought in the General's war to free fellow Chimera from the hangman's noose, Manuel is skilled in Guerrilla maneuvers, but he'd never taken on an AI Host before. This would prove a challenge, but he couldn't let this cruel act go unanswered. With a thought he powers up a pulse fist and aims it at the fleeing Host. Chimera are not allowed to have such weapons as part of their enhancements, but what Chimera worth their tech doesn't? He releases a pulse of energy into the back of the Host, pushing it off balance and it slams into the hard dirt, dust and stone flying every direction as the thing's weight carves out a ditch in the earth. When he catches up to the Host, he leaps three metres into the arid air and lands a knee into the Host's damaged chassis.

The Host reels around on its torso and sends a hard fist into Manuel's left arm launching him into a steel fence. They are both slow to get up. The Host is wounded. Manuel's body aches from the hit. "Why did you do that?!" He shouts at the Host.

"That old man would be dead before he made planet fall," the Host replies with a masculine pitch, standing again, the arm still secure in his grip. Blood pools on the ground from the dangling appendage.

"That gives you no right to kill a man!" Manuel asserts. "You'll be decommissioned for this!"

"The number isn't *for* me," the Host explains angrily. "I do not care what happens to me." He throws the arm several meters into a waiting hover vehicle. The Host charges Manuel, connects and forces him against the fence, trying to break his back. Manuel struggles to slip his hand between them and fires another pulse fist and the Host is split in two at the waist. He runs to the empty hover vehicle and retrieves the arm. UE police arrive a moment later. A Chimera holding a human arm isn't going to go over well.

2164, JANUARY. EVENING

It wasn't an easy win, the fight Allfather had brought to United Earth six months ago. The ancient AI's act of hurtling asteroids at his beloved planet still triggers anxiety deep within Raymond. It is something he's learned to live with when the name Allfather is mentioned, or the memories of two wars in under two years wake him or preclude him from sleep. Millions lost in the assault at ground level, while ships and military personnel fell around the brutal offensive. Luna base decimated. Commander Tesla – *Darla* – very nearly killed as a result.

He enjoys his fiancé's company as they take time out of their busy schedules to reconnect for a late supper. That the name is again brought up over dinner at one of First City's finest dining establishments forces the Chancellor to plate his fork and take a breath. He looks over his meal and reaches for his glass of bourbon, takes a swallow, and curls his upper lip. Next, he confronts the fellow diner at the table next to him who begged the question: 'are we free of Allfather?' Of course, Raymond believes the last communique the world received from a dying Allfather was an idle threat. A last-ditch effort to instill fear in the populace of United Earth and create discontent between the people and their government. At least, that's what he has to tell himself.

"We're doing everything we can to ensure Allfather will never affect United Earth again," Raymond answers like the politician he is, hoping not to get caught up in a conversation.

"But we all heard it, Chancellor Bellows. Everyone. Allfather said he was *in us*. What did he mean by that?" The curious citizen seems quite pleased with himself to hold the ear of the Chancellor of United Earth.

7

"GovTech has assured me, and in turn, I have assured you and the rest of the population that there is no sign of Allfather's legacy here, on the moon or in Mars station. I truly hope that will suffice, sir. No one is trying to pull the wool over your eyes. Your United Earth military eliminated the threat that was Allfather, and once more, we rebuild."

"So, you think he's dead? That this – *thing* is out of our lives forever?"

"That is his position on the matter," Darla breaks in, nodding at the older gentleman, noticing the forced smile on Raymond's face disintegrating. "That is your government's position as well. Surely you trust the government who won you two wars."

"And I am grateful to have lived through both, Ma'am," the citizen says, his partner taking his hand in his. They look at one another and smile sadly. "We both lost a lot of people and Hosts in those wars." His attention returns to the chancellor. "I don't think we could bear another."

Raymond clears his throat. "The wars were hard on us all." He blinks and turns to see Darla's big eyes shinning in the low-lit restaurant. He then returns his attention back to the men seated near him. "I promise you, I have no reason to believe Allfather survived his assault. Every ounce of his ship was pulled from the ocean, analyzed, and crushed to dust. You have my sympathies for your losses, but know you also have my word on Allfather's demise." This seems to satisfy the older man's curiosities; he thanks the chancellor for his time and returns to his meal.

Raymond is no longer hungry. He retrieves his drink, swallows the last of the bourbon, then stares at his plate with the half eaten veg and chicken supreme. Flashbacks assault his senses. He's back in the war room, he's repeating orders to connect with his warships. With Admiral Chopra, with his nephew, Tobias. The meteors are falling fast. Ships burn in orbit. He feels helpless as his defence satellites malfunction. There is a ghost in the walls. Raymond is brought back to the present by Darla's delicate fingers gently lifting his head, pulling him out from under his uncontrolled memories. His beard tickles her fingers. He blinks and looks into her reassuring eyes smiling sadly. He can't say for certain every piece of Allfather's ship has been found. He can't be 100% confident that his enemy's last words were only meant to torture them. No one can say for sure Allfather was even piloting the flagship as it crashed into earth's atmosphere.

"We're doing everything we can in the event it comes back." She reiterates his own words in a whisper from across the short table, nodding slowly. "You've won two wars. You've proven yourself. We'll be more prepared than ever if it does return. But it probably won't." Darla's lips part slightly, the corners of her mouth lifting into a pleasant smile. Her eyelids fall slightly, and head tilts the way it does when she really, truly means what she's saying. Raymond has never been more grateful for Darla. Not since her life had been spared six months ago. She knows him intimately. She can calm him with a look. He takes her extended hand in both of his and squeezes, the colour returning to his olive skin, face framed now by his greying temples and beard. The wars took their toll.

"I love you," he tells her. She returns the sentiment and they release their hold on each other. An AI Host server approaches and asks whether they've finished with their mains and would they like a peak at the dessert menu. They nod politely and after the server clears their plates the table lights up to reveal the evening's sweets menu in a holo display. A latte is all Raymond can manage while Darla orders the zero-calorie chocolate cheesecake and a green tea.

After another half-hour the couple returns to their shared home, Raymond's estate within First City's lively downtown core. The walk takes twelve minutes. They pass through wide streets, nano-steel and organic buildings rising on either side of them. Some are home to ivy which remains green even in the January chill and dusting of snow while the perennial plants sleep until spring. The streets are alive as people and Hosts and Chimera alike move through the vehicle-free zones. This portion of downtown is reserved for restaurants, coffee houses and bakeries. Pubs, health and wellness studios and shops also permeate the core. All run by AI Hosts who had not been given the opportunity for sentience as were so many millions during the General's war.

2164, JANUARY. NIGHT

Again, Tobias is awakened. He checks the time on his EC. 3:33am. *Ouch*. He looks over at his young wife. "Your turn," she whispers at him. Their little girl cries from her crib in the next room. Tobias smiles at Ginny and gently folds the comforter off himself, plants both feet on the cool floor and stands.

"I've got her," he tells her as she smiles back sleepily, pulls the hair from her face, and rolls over. He looks adoringly at his wife, beautiful in any light. Tobias throws his robe on and walks the short distance to Samantha. They'd named her after his mother who had died when he was a young man and reclaimed her identity years later in one of the first enlightened AI Hosts over two years ago. She was a force, his mother, returning to the land of the living as the artificial intelligence locked in an A-class AI Host received her soul. It had happened millions of times over after Tobias had initiated Allfather's upgrade through an ingenious Lifi delivery system. At that time, he had no idea Allfather was an alien AI bent on destroying all organic beings. But the code offered renewed life to souls looking for a way back. Reincarnation. It was beautiful. So many of the living were reunited with their loved ones. But it sparked the General's war and left none untouched by its violent outcome. Now though, United Earth was united once more.

"Come to daddy," Tobias whispers as he lifts the tiny baby from her crib, cradling her in his muscular arms. She is just six months old. Born into a new world. One that he hopes will be a better world than that of the past two years. So much death, but so much self-discovery to follow. Humanity now accepted enlightened Host and Chimera. Chimera, a thing of his invention. He and Ginny both are Chimera, altered with tech to be more than human. Would he put this on his child? *That would be her decision.* He looks lovingly at her as she feeds from a bottle of her mother's milk pumped this very night.

All Tobias can think about is protecting his daughter. The threat of the Allfather AI is still real. He believes this. His child's nightly cries are not all that wake him at these troubling hours. His fear over Allfather's ability to survive and return plays on his mind. He carries this burden in his heart. It is a weight he cannot seem to shrug off. The victory over Allfather's campaign was well earned and celebrated but has not outlasted the trauma he's suffered from the enormous stresses put on his emotional and physical self during the defence of his world. These linger, working against his happiness, and when Tobias finds himself alone, he weeps for his friend Wilkes and the many who fell to Allfather's will.

As Samantha settles in his arms, Tobias burps her twice, kisses her forehead quietly and places her back in the crib. They could have an A-Class AI Host nanny, but they are few and far between these days. Ginny wanted a genuine experience anyway. Tobias hadn't realized just how demanding of his time the baby would be. His day to day presence on UE's government council wasn't as demanding as his six-month-old.

Tobias' EC lights up and a gentle hum emanates from his forearm. He moves out of the room to the kitchen so as not to wake anyone. *Who would be calling me at this hour?* It's not just anyone, it's Captain Drake. Ursula Drake, who maintains public order through her military and police departments the world over. She is a friend and member of the UE council. Her stunning features permeate the space above his EC in a holo.

"Captain," Tobias greets her, brushing out his dark beard with the fingers of his opposite hand. "I heard you were a night owl, but it's near four in the morning."

"I've been up since oh-three-hundred, Captain," Ursula replies curtly. All business. "Early to bed and early to rise -" she quotes the old adage.

"Well, I have a six-month-old here, and we go to bed when she goes to bed and wake up when she wakes up. Which is about three times a night if we're lucky," Tobias explains.

"Strange Ginny refused a nanny." Captain Drakes expression shows no emotion. Tobias nods.

"What news has you contacting me this early?" Tobias rubs his eyes, the thought of returning to his wife and warm bed now abandoned.

"I've been asked by the chancellor to wake the council and arrange a meeting."

"Spare me the suspense, Ursula and tell me what it's about." Tobias feels the anxiety well up in his chest over the chance this could be about Allfather's return.

"Come to the war room at 0500." Her face blinks out of the darkness as she ends the communication. Tobias paces the floors as adrenaline pushes through his veins, exciting his fight response and agitating the nerves under his skin until they begin to prickle.

Why did she have to leave him with that! The war room? What other reason to meet in the war room than to discuss a coming war? His mind plays out scenarios where he learns Allfather has announced his return visit and another fight that could potentially accomplish what it had set out to achieve in the last assault. Could he do it all over again? He places palms down on the kitchen counter and lowers his head, bending at the waist. He takes three deep breathes, exhaling slowly. This helps. The regular meds and oils help too, but he finds when the anxiety rushes in like a wave to engulf an unsuspecting shoreline, breathing techniques are his best defence. Tobias shakes off the unpleasant sensations and walks the house. He takes a shower and dresses for the council meeting.

2163, DECEMBER. FOR EVERY ACTION…

Manuel sits in a pristine holding cell with white walls and a nanoplast floor to ceiling window wall where he waits along with the AI Host who murdered the old man over the lottery. The Host has been secured to the opposite wall of the cell. Manuel wonders what charge the UE police are preparing to lay on him. He *had* been discovered with the arm in his possession after all.

"You've done a stupid thing," Manuel reprimands the Host. He's equally angry at himself for getting involved. Angry, scared, head spinning like a top over possible outcomes. His very future will be decided today. "Why do you need to be on that ship so badly?"

"What I did, I did not do for *myself*." The AI Host is still in two pieces, its torso bound to the wall, his arms now removed. "It was for my daughter. That she would know a better life off-world." His voice is in the masculine range, so Manuel assumes he is a father to this daughter.

"Is she like you? Machine? Or is she human?" Manuel asks curtly, but curious over who this daughter might be, and why he feels killing a man for his winning number is his only recourse.

"She is my daughter from when I was human. I was killed in the Host wars, General August's war, defending my family," The Host explains soberly. "Now my daughter is more like *you* than like the girl I left, covered in tech and mech."

"She is Chimera?"

"She wasn't given the choice!" the Host barks back. "She is my daughter. War did that to her. Then the war to follow took her mother and sister after I had returned in this," he looks down at his chassis. "And I've spent the last seven months trying to make sense of our family's misfortunes. She asked if we could leave this planet. She's frightened to stay, but too damaged to leave – by UE standards."

"So, if you could have fitted her with the old man's EC chip, she'd have had a chance." Manuel gets it now.

"Yes, I have friends that would have altered the winning chip and made it seem as though she had won it fairly. I would have granted my child her freedom from the fear she suffers daily." The Host's head shakes back and forth, rattling the nano-steel bars holding his torso in place. "Now she won't even have a father."

Manuel considers this sad story of loss and empathizes. He too has lost those he loved. If he could grant his little sister a wish, he would have done so without thought of consequences. This Host, this *father,* suffers alongside his daughter. But there is nothing Manuel can do for *him.* The authorities will know he's done this thing. They will end him for it.

"Where is your daughter now, Host?" Manuel asks quietly. "You will be decommissioned for what you've done, but perhaps I can see to it that your daughter has a fighting chance at making the flight." It seems a hollow promise, but one he feels somehow compelled to offer.

At this the Host releases what sounds like a sigh. "You would do this for me?" Manuel nods. "Why? Why do this for me?"

"I'm not rewarding *your* behaviour, Host. I am honouring your promise to a child who deserves better than the cards she's been dealt. Tell me where she is." Manuel is leaning in, allowing the Host to deliver the information via its roaming lance to his implant. The Host understands and sends the details, thanking Manuel, his lance limited to the secure cell now. "You're welcome, Trevor," Manuel says, now possessing all the information required to find Trevor's daughter and fulfill a dead man's wish.

A moment later two police enter the cell and remove Manuel. He looks back at Trevor with calculated compassion. He shouldn't have killed a man for his daughter. He decides when he meets her, he'll leave that part out.

Outside the station, Manuel is handed a data chip by an official-looking woman who is smiling at him and shaking his hand. "What you did today shows much courage, citizen," she tells him. Following her gaze, he realizes he's being recorded for a UE news thread, and that this woman is a B-class, AI Host sent to interview him. He stares into the hovering camera and nods blankly.

"While you've been waiting, several witnesses have come forward to praise your actions in detaining the murderer." She says *waiting* like he'd been in line for a Holofilm, when in fact he'd been torturing himself with scenarios since the police came upon him, ordered him down from the hover vehicle and secured him with a body brace. Manuel nods again, and he looks at the object the B-class has placed in his opposite hand.

"Yes," she nods her head at him, "justice ruled on what to do with the winning lottery number now that its owner has expired," She tells him and her audience. "You have been gifted the win! Manuel Thomas, you're going off-world on the next available ship!" Manuel is stunned, fixated on the chip between his fingers. The sound of applause surrounds him. "You'll be one of 2000 souls embarking on an eleven-year journey to the Tyson system which houses one yellow dwarf star, thirteen planets of various types: including three gas giants, four ice worlds, two sandy rocks, three dwarf planets and your destination planet, Tyson 4; an earth-like ball of liquid water, breathable air, mountainous terrain, forests of unknown flora and fauna affording you and your peers a *lifetime* of adventure!"

"I – thank you?" Manuel is overwhelmed. Not one of the scenarios during his time in the holding cell prepared him for this incredible news. The town's lottery stragglers cheer as they watch on from behind drone pilons. Manuel is trying to process the B-class Host's description of the rest of his life. The life he's been dreaming of since the lottery began. Then he thinks of his duty to Trevor's daughter - the promise he'd made moments ago.

Manuel holds his hand up which holds the numbered chip. The crowd cheers again. He places the chip into his EC tech and his forearm lights up a subtle blue. More applause. It's verified, he thinks. *This is actually happening*. His heart soars but there is the small matter of including Trevor's daughter in his new plans. The girl will be waiting for her father to return home soon. The information he received tells him her name, age, address, and EC information. He could raise her on his embedded comm, or just make the trip and introduce himself. That way he can sit her down and discuss her father's demise. Or maybe he just ignores the promise he made to Trevor and move on with his life. This girl isn't his problem. She's twelve. There are resources for twelve-year-old orphans. Udo is her name. He almost wishes he hadn't read that. Now it's personal. Visuals flash in his minds-eye from the file. She has blue eyes set in pale, yellow skin, under long, black hair. One eye is bionic. Udo has a slight build but is tall for her age. She has a robotic right leg and right arm, implants in her head for hearing loss and limb control, and jaw reconstruction which still causes some pain and discomfort. Stims are produced from the implants and fed to her as needed. All of this damage is from the explosion which killed her father.

She'll be a basket case to learn that the father who'd died and come back as a Host is now gone for good. This isn't going to be an easy thing. He stares at his EC and the soft glow of a winning number. The glow warms his heart, as does the holo in his minds-eye of young Udo. His brother's daughter would be the same age if they had survived Allfather's cruel attack. Manuel shakes off the memories of trying to rush home from Country State Spain to assist with the evacuation of his family and friends six months ago. He couldn't be the cause of someone else's pain. He moves through the crowd where so many have now gathered to retrieve a few personal possessions from his home.

THERE IS A REACTION

"Of our six destroyers and one goliath that survived after Allfather's attempt on our planet, one destroyer had to be scrapped altogether, while the goliath and remaining five destroyers were repaired," Admiral Chopra offers after Chancellor Bellows asked the question. The war room is well lit - but quiet, save the hum of computers and a skeleton crew manning the posts. Chopra continues. "As you know, Mars Station has sent us two new goliaths and three new destroyers in recent months, with three more of each nearing completion. Luna base has manufactured a bounty of corvettes, delivering fifteen with another fifteen being fitted with final touches."

The council nods and look pleased with the numbers thus far. Raymond had asked them to meet at this early hour in order to bring everyone up to speed in person. "Thank you, Admiral. So, within the next week or two I can expect to have eleven destroyers, six goliath-class and thirty corvettes at our disposal." Raymond stands within the circle and studies his council of friends. His admirals Jim Chopra and David Mann stand at complementary angles to one another in the circle, Captain Drake stands next to Captain Tobias. Senator Quinn, still embodying the spider-like frame he'd assumed during General August's war, stands next to Labyrinth. Labyrinth, altered to be small and unassuming in order to use his hi-tech programing for espionage and sabotage, now finds himself comfortably fitted into a customized C-class female AI Host frame. He wears samurai-like armour, painted matte black. It suits him – *her*, Raymond corrects himself.

"We also have the requested three carrier-class ships ready to take on their payload of pilgrims," Admiral Mann adds.

"Yes, and another reason to have brought you all in this morning," the chancellor says, grateful for the segue. "We're moving on three star systems. One carrier each. One destroyer and four corvettes for each group. That will leave us with eight destroyers and eighteen corvettes. The goliaths will also remain in earth orbit. We have no intention of stopping either the production of star ships or training new citizens in their operation."

"To know that an alien AI was created is to know there are intelligent beings like us out there. Perhaps cruel. Allfather told us they made him fight their wars. So, they are obviously aggressive," Ursula adds.

"I don't think Allfather left any of them alive," Tobias says. The group laughs lightly at this. "Seriously." He raises his hands.

"Nonetheless," Raymond tells the council. "Where there is one, it's fair to assume there will be more. We know we're not alone in the universe now. We continue to build our military and train our people. With three new systems to be colonized within the next ten to twelve years, we will need the added defences."

"Has the lottery finished?" Commander Tesla enters the war room and joins the circle next to the chancellor.

"The lottery has another three days of numbers to fill all three carriers," Captain Drake explains, troubled over the commander's tardiness. *If it were anyone else.*

"The envoy's military entourage are well trained and ready to make the journey," Admiral Mann insists. Admiral Chopra offers his support of the statement with a nod as the chancellor turns to him.

"It is an exciting time for humanity." The chancellor launches into a speech, hands clasped together in front of him as he moves along the interior of his circle of peers. "It seems such a short time ago that the first satellite orbited the planet, the moon landings, space stations, Luna base and Mars Station. That we're now travelling to other star systems is an incredible achievement which the world owes to each of you. Without your fighting spirit we would have fallen to Allfather." Raymond pauses to find the words he's trying to say.

"I feel I am ready to retire from my position as chancellor of United Earth." No one dares interrupt, so he continues. "What we've achieved as a council, the battles we've won, the civilization we've saved, the fears we've faced and vanquished in the name of duty can not be overstated. As a team we've defended *all* the people of earth from prejudice and stopped a great evil - twice now - to preserve our way of life." Raymond takes a long breath. "This announcement comes as a bit of a shock to me as well," he tells them, watching the stunned looks on his council's faces. "But I feel my time has been served. We're in a good place now. A place my successor will have no trouble maintaining."

"Uncle, I don't – I won't *follow* another," Tobias says bluntly. "I'm in the position I am because of *you*. If you're no longer chancellor, I don't want to do this anymore."

Raymond nods, closing his eyes. Darla takes his hand. They knew there would be push back on this announcement.

"Is it your plan then to live on Luna Base with the commander?" Chopra asks, stoic as ever.

"We're going on one of the ships," Raymond confesses abruptly, nodding. "We're going to Tyson 4." Silence. Not only is he leaving office, but he's also leaving the planet. Raymond feels lighter for having said this aloud to his council. It feels real now. It has been a difficult decision leaving all he has accomplished for another to manage.

"Then the Commander is retiring too," Quinn says. "This is all very sudden." Darla nods at this with a hopeful smile.

"Tyson 4, the nicest of the three systems from what I hear," Ursula tells the group, accepting the chancellor's announcement without question. "You will be missed. Both of you." She closes in on Darla and Raymond's position on the opposite side of the circle and stands at attention. "You put together a fine team here, Chancellor. You should be very proud."

"Thank you, Ursula," Raymond says as she steps back. "Jim," he turns to focus on Admiral Chopra. "Jim, you would be my first choice to replace me in this coming election, to support the work we've done and continue our vision. I know it's sudden," he looks back at Senator Quinn and then again to Admiral Chopra. "Will you accept this honour?"

"I'd tell you I'm not much of a politician, chancellor, but I think I've learned a thing or two from you over the past two years." A smile encroaches on his otherwise stoic expression. "I'd be honoured to serve United Earth in its highest office. I accept." He moves from his position and salutes the chancellor. Once it is returned, he shakes his hand, white teeth smile back at the chancellor sharply complimenting the brown skin of Jim's face. Raymond has imagined Jim wanting to leave the service and spend more time with his family. This is a solution for all.

"I'm going to have to discuss this with Ginny and Sam tonight. No offence, Admiral, I'd follow you to the end of the earth, but with a vote pending, there's no telling who will win." Tobias feels confused, upset the group is breaking up, but excited he may once again have a choice. He wants to talk to his wife right away. "Are we done here?" Raymond nods and Tobias leaves the war room.

"I don't expect Tobias will be long for the military life," Raymond looks to Chopra who is nodding. "Admiral," Raymond turns to David Mann next, "You'll take command of United Earth military operations?"

"I accept, Chancellor," Mann looks to Jim. "Just as long as Admiral Chopra takes the vote." He smiles, his thick, dark eyebrows rising to meet his hairline. Chopra smiles back.

"I wonder, Chancellor," Labyrinth turns her feminine features toward Raymond. She is lovely, he thinks. A solid, leggy frame fitted with top-of-the-line body armour and a head piece which protects her from neck to crown. Short red hair falls from her helmet in bangs over her forehead. She's chosen pale white flesh for her face, and large, green eyes. Armour covers the rest from chin to the bridge of what could be a nose. Like the mask of ninja, Raymond thinks, but composed of permanent plasteel. "Might I join you on your journey to Tyson 4?"

Raymond notices the apprehension on Senator Quinn's mechanical expression upon hearing this request. "As an AI Host you would require nothing, and as one of UE's trusted council you have only to ask." Raymond looks again to Quinn.

"It is a long journey, Labyrinth," Quinn speaks up, stepping forward. "You will be gone for a long time."

Labyrinth turns to her mentor. "Quinn, like you, I am *Host*, time does not factor into my decision. I am curious. I have never come across another soul living or dead that I knew when I was alive. I have given all for our cause here. Now I'd like to see what else is out there."

"Of course, you are a free Host," Quinn says. "I will miss our talks."

"Then use your roaming lance," Labyrinth replies with a smile. "No matter where we are in the universe, the ParaCom will always connect us." The group laughs at this. It is true, the ParaCom is an extraordinary scientific innovation which will ensure all three new colonies are also tethered to Earth via audio and video communication.

Quinn waves Labyrinth away as she hugs him around his carapace. "Yes, yes, we still have a few days, don't we?" There is significant sadness in his metallic voice and a muted, sympathetic mirth from the council.

"I'll announce the immediate need for a vote to the Council of Chancellors today. Each party has their lead in place for this probability and from what I've been reading on the net, they're ready to pounce. I will make my recommendation for a successor, and we'll strategize our party's campaign," the chancellor announces, calling an end to this early morning meeting. "Jim, if I could have your ear in your office," Raymond kisses Darla on her forehead and follows Admiral Chopra into the small office off the war room.

THE INTERVIEW – JANUARY 2064

Manuel sits in a hyper-train enroute to Trevor's daughter. He sees on his EC that his local newscast has announced the murder of Luis Mendez and the decommissioning of Trevor - the enlightened Host who felt too much. Manuel pauses at this news and reflects on the Host's good intentions.   Is the road to hell paved with good intentions? *What we sacrifice for our loved ones.*

It will take only minutes to reach his destination and he considers his options. He could just give the girl his ticket. The lottery allows winners to give up their number to another. He could also join the UE military and hope to get on one of the destroyers or corvettes being sent to protect the colonists. He's considered that too and decided he's not made for that life. It's colonist or nothing. So why is he heading north to meet a dead man's daughter with one ticket he's not willing to give up?

Manuel has a double seat to himself facing a wall. The holoscreen in front of him changes from the view beyond the train unexpectedly; a special report on the state of the union follows as an AI Host reads the announcement: CHANCELLOR   BELLOWS   TO   GIVE   SPECIAL INTERVIEW IN ONE MINUTE. This immediately implants panic in Manuel. What softens his initial reaction is seeing the chancellor of United Earth quietly readying himself on one of two comfortable looking armchairs with a smartwall behind showcasing a video of starships being manufactured on Mars station. Next a young woman, not an AI Host, but a flesh and blood woman, joins the chancellor and takes her seat after they've shaken hands. Manuel takes comfort in the careful and unhurried setup. He'd hate to think this was to announce another tragic event on the horizon.

"Hello, I'm Susan Ryder and I'm here with Chancellor Bellows," She turns to the Chancellor. "It's a pleasure to have you here with me today," Susan says. "We just want to begin with the statement that *everything is alright*," she chuckles to herself, lowering her hands and returning her attention to her audience. "The Chancellor isn't here to explain Allfather has returned or something's gone wrong with the automated transit systems." She turns back to the Chancellor who is nodding and smiling. Manuel hopes her comment doesn't become ironic for him.

"Chancellor, this is something entirely different than that, isn't it?" Susan leans into the space separating the two, her tone lowering. Chancellor Bellows mirrors her aggressive stance and she backs off.

"That's right, Susan. I've availed myself of this opportunity to tell you all just how *well* everything is moving along." He leans back into his chair. "United Earth is thriving!" He explains, now using his hands to illustrate his points. "Lawlessness is down to nearly one percent. This is thanks in great measure to your United Earth Policing Head: Captain Ursula Drake. Enlightened Host, human and Chimera share the world your government has made possible. But none of it is possible without the mutual respect every citizen has shown to one another. For that, I thank each of you."

"Wonderful to hear, Chancellor," Susan breaks in. "But you had mentioned there is a personal announcement you'd like to share," she turns back to her viewers, "do I hear wedding bells? We all know that you and Commander Tesla, responsible for Luna Base operations and the recent expansions have been engaged for some time now."

Manuel rolls his eyes at the attempt to pull from the chancellor something he clearly isn't prepared to reveal.

"You're not wrong that Darla and I are engaged, Susan," the chancellor supplies her that. "But what I would like to announce today, is that I'm stepping down as chancellor and encouraging a vote in the next few days."

"Oh, well, this comes as a shock! You've certainly served longer than any other Chancellor." Susan looks thunderstruck. "I – Are you dissatisfied with your post?"

"No, not at all, Susan." Chancellor Bellows appears very poised to Manuel. "The state of our union is strong. We're happy again. We have

23

much to be grateful for. With the ships leaving soon to explore new opportunities in other star systems, I felt compelled to join in the adventure."

"So, you're going to one of the new planets?!"

"Yes, Commander Tesla and I – Darla, will be setting off to Tyson 4 to build a new life." Bellows focuses on the audience. "In a short time, you will have a chance to decide who your next chancellor will be. I've alerted other parties and my own earlier today. I'm putting all my support behind your United Earth top military advisor and war hero, Admiral Jim Chopra."

"A military man?" Susan doesn't like the sound of this. "Is that a wise choice after what we experienced when General August placed herself in power?"

"The Admiral and I have spent an exorbitant amount of time together these past two years, I know he'd attest to that." Bellows snaps off a whimsical smile. "He is a brilliant tactician and a wise leader. He will, of course, remove himself from military office to take on the role of chancellor."

"Now, if I'm not mistaken, the admiral's son was killed in the general's war." Susan clearly wants to run this interview. "Can you tell us how he's recovered from that loss?"

"Jim Chopra is a man of integrity *and* a family man. Obviously, the news his son had passed was difficult. He mourned once he'd finished assisting your government in winning the war against General August. He has since experienced great growth from his, and his family's grief. He won us the war six months ago and has overseen every detail concerning the restructuring and modernization of our UE military machine. There is none better suited."

"So, he would essentially carry on as though *you* were still at the helm of United Earth?"

"In virtually every aspect. Our party believes in the same objectives no matter who is running the show from the fortieth floor of UE Headquarters."

"That's a comforting thought. When can we expect this vote to take place?"

"In three-days time. Parties have their leaders in place. Every citizen can view their policies and become acquainted with them on the World net." Bellows turns to the audience once more. "Remember, the past two years were not a result of your government's mistakes, but they *were* resolved by your sitting government. Please take that into consideration when you vote."

"Thank you, Chancellor Bellows, for this impromptu and informative interview." Susan turns to the viewers. "Watch *The Independent News* for dates and times the polls open. This is Susan Ryder."

Manuel gives his chancellor points for not bringing up Allfather and the potential for further dealings with it in order to sway the population to stay with a wartime government. The guy's got class. Influencing the public opinion with rumors of fear is clearly beneath him. Manuel feels a sense of loss enter his heart with this announcement. Chancellor Bellows has been a familiar face to all, and an accomplished leader. Manuel knows who he will vote for in three days.

A CRISIS OF CONSCIENCE

The home of Trevor Boyd, second-generation, is as contemporary a residence as any. Every citizen or citizen family is awarded a sustainable home: human, Host and Chimera. Trevor's is a large ground floor unit of a thirty-story housing complex. Manuel stares at the holo-number hovering over the doorway. He's nervous. This is where Trevor's family had lived since before the general's war and remained after his death. They continued to live here even after Trevor's wife and youngest daughter were caught up in the meteor shower, the Allfather offensive that happened *after* Trevor had returned. Happily, with his return he reclaimed his house and family. As a second-generation personality, sadly, he has also lived through the death of his wife and youngest. Not a fate Manuel would wish upon anyone. But with his surviving daughter, Udo, waiting for her father to come home, Manuel has tasked himself with explaining why Trevor would *never* be coming home. Not in his last incarnation at least.

Udo is a cyborg. Half mech and tech. Some would call that a Chimera, but, as Trevor had put plainly, she hadn't made the choice, the war had done that for her. So, she is a cyborg. *How will she react to a Chimera relaying this dire news?*

The door to Trevor's residence suddenly disappears into the wall and an enraged twelve-year-old girl with dark black hair, pale skin, clenched fists and wearing little more than a summer-style pair of pajamas moves at a hurried pace towards Manuel. "You!" She cries, pointing an accusing finger at him, tears streaming down her face. "*You* did this!"

Manuel is at a loss. He hadn't seen it going down like this. Udo is obviously irate with him. *But she doesn't even know me*. His hands go up defensively in front of him. She isn't slowing down. In two more meters she will run right into him if she's not careful.

"You," she stops short of his position to further denounce his existence. She stands all of 1.2 meters, a good 60 cm below Manuel's imposing frame. Her finger still pointing angrily at him she launches into a verbal massacre of his spirit. "That was my *daddy*! You miserable piece of *trash*! He is all I have left, and you took him away from me! You worthless *bastard*! You cruel, heartless *thing*!" She sends a tiny fist into his stomach. Thankfully it is the flesh and bone version and not the artificial fist, which he catches in his reinforced hand. Udo falls to her knees and weeps at his feet. Manuel lets go of the girl's hand, thoroughly upset by this small child's outrage. Her pain is palpable. He kneels down to comfort her. Udo pushes his attempt away weakly.

"Udo," Manuel greets her in soft tones as her sobs lessen. "Your father asked me to come. It was the last thing he asked of me." He pauses, wondering whether he should apologize or just explain how he came to be here. "You've seen the thread," he says knowingly, "I didn't know your father's story, but he had taken a life -"

"I can't do this," Udo says, her expression full of pain, gasping for air. "I can't do any of this anymore. I've lost *everyone*." She steadies herself on the robotic arm, wiping her face with her other hand. "He did a very bad thing," she agrees, head nodding. "I know that, but I want him back. I want him here. With *me*."

"Maybe he'll come back one day, when United Earth allows more Host's the enlightenment code," Manuel explains, "And your mother and sister." Udo looks up at him dismissively.

"Why did you even come here?" She stands and Manuel mirrors her movements. "UE Police EC'd me and gave me the details. You're the big *winner!*" Her arms go up. "I guess that makes me the big *loser*. I've lost my dad twice now!" Udo turns and begins to walk back to her apartment.

Manuel watches her go. What she said was profound. He understands her pain, but perhaps not to her degree. He's lost everyone to war too. He looks at his EC and pulls up the number. Could he let her go in his place? Shouldn't he? Staying on Earth positions Udo to never release the memories of her lost loved-ones. He identifies with that all too well. He's longed to leave Earth for that very reason. *But she is so young. She could recover.* He tells himself. He closes the lottery number on his embedded comm and turns back to face the busy street. Dusk is falling rapidly. The green of the buildings become crimsons and fuchsias in the dying light.

He looks over his shoulder. This house will be granted an A-class AI Host to oversee the girl's next ten years. It's protocol when one is orphaned and has no relative willing to take them in. *United Earth knows what they're doing. Udo will be fine. Besides, there's no way the lottery would ever return to his small town. This is my only chance to move on.* But the nagging fact that she blames him for her father's loss weighs heavily on Manuel. Maybe rightly so, as Trevor could have made off with the arm and had the old man's EC chip placed in Udo's bionic arm if Manuel hadn't acted when he did.

"Ah!" Manuel says under his breath. Ever the orator for his community's moral centre, he turns back and marches toward the door of Trevor's house. Udo has just entered. He knocks. Nothing. He waves his hand over the door's sensor to instruct the bell to chime. He leans in and hears sobbing on the other side. Trevor had given him the code to open the door as well, but he is hesitant to let himself in. *She's suffering her father's death all over again. Why did Trevor think this was worth potentially being caught and his daughter left alone?*

The door opens and Udo is standing there with accusing eyes on him. "What do *you* want?!" She yells at him. People and Hosts passing behind him look in their direction. He feels awkward. Guilty, even. He shows her the winning number. "Can I convince you to take the lottery number?" He can barely believe the words as they leave his mouth.

Udo's eyes change from scolding to tired. Manuel feels the sadness behind them. She blames him. He gets that. He believes he would feel the same. She is young and doesn't truly appreciate the damage her father has done. He's killed a man in her name. Perhaps it is wrong to now offer the lottery win to her. What would the dead man's family think? He doesn't have family, Manuel remembers. It's why the win fell to him. *So, fuck it. Give the gift to her and figure out another way for you to go.*

"You must want to go yourself, or you wouldn't have accepted the number," Udo says. She is a bright young thing, he thinks. Of course he wants to go. He has no one left either. He punches a combination of numbers into his EC screen and the sliver of a chip slips out of the tech in his forearm. He takes it with his other hand and presents it to her.

"Your father made an excellent case for you to go. That he is gone now only cements the idea. I can't go knowing that two men died that you may have this opportunity. Please don't reject the offer." He stands with his hand out trying his best not to look disappointed.

"But you won it doing a *good* thing," she counters. "I would win it for a very bad thing." She stares at the gift. "I'm so sorry my dad killed a person for it. He's always been so protective of me and my sister." Her dark, yet whimsical eyebrows tremble along with her chin. "I'm sorry I blame you for his death. It wasn't your decision."

"I'm sorry I interfered," Manuel tells her in earnest, a tear tracking down his cheek. "It would have been better for all of us if I hadn't."

"Not for the man who won the lottery."

"No, it wouldn't have mattered to him." Manuel pushes his open hand closer to Udo. She flinches at the motion.

"Please, for your father." He motions again with his hand, "I can't use it now." Udo timidly picks the small item from Manuel's large hand. "You leave in three days. Pack only what you need. They are very strict about what is taken aboard. You can view the list on their site." Manuel nods, smiles a pained smile, and turns to leave. He feels Udo's warm hand on his. He stops. She squeezes and tells him *thank you*. He doesn't look back. He releases her hand and moves into the crowded street.

Udo watches this venerable man disappear into the crowd beyond her. *I don't deserve this.* She looks at the chip and slides it into her EC. It glows a muted blue. TRANSACTION AUTHORIZED. It reads. He must have sanctioned the switch already. Her heart skips a beat. It's only done that once before, when her father returned to her family as an enlightened Host. This Chimera, *Manuel*, he deserves the win, but has given it freely. She retreats into her house, the door sliding back into place. She sits on her family's couch in the impinging darkness and cries confusedly, and for so many reasons.

Manuel finds the closest pub and orders a number of libations to convince his ego this was the right move. He couldn't have been happy knowing he'd cheated a little girl out of the chance for a better life, however legally it was obtained. He hopes for her a life not tethered to a troubling past filled with pain and loss. She has the rest of her life now to discover herself and leave the bad memories here on earth. He wonders whether a large majority of colonists have a similar story taking them to the stars. On the seventh drink he looks up from his bottle and scans the patrons of the AI Host tended bar. They laugh at each other's jokes and cheer over the holo of their local team dominating another. Could he have this again? Maybe. But not here, he decides. *I'll join the military.*

THE HARD SELL

Tobias returns home to his small family to share the news before they hear it from the interview his uncle Raymond is planning. He feels sudden and lasting freedom enter his spirit. Nothing would limit his possibilities now that the chancellor is stepping down, retiring into interstellar travel. In all honesty, he would love to take that trip. The carrier starships are immense and fitted with all the latest comforts and technologies. Cultured meat labs filled with genetically created meat proteins, hydroponic labs growing every kind of fresh fruit, veg and fungus, water capture and re-capture systems rivaling the freshest water on earth, oxygen manipulators paired with living trees, MakerTech maintenance and production bots and the all-important gravity knitting systems offering a comfortable one-G for the trip. These necessities are complimented by fine dining, theatre rooms, upgraded living quarters, entertainment, and thousands of Next-Learning courses to prepare for a new life on a new planet.

"Gin, I'm out!" Tobias regales as he charges through his front door. Ginny is on the trainer, working her abs and legs while the baby watches from her safe-cube. Ginny sits up, toweling her forehead. The Chimera implants along her arms and back are obvious beneath her strappy bra, but mild compared to what Tobias has incorporated into himself. Ginny's alterations could be defined as feminine in contrast, but achieve the desired affect of boosting her strength, speed and, where the brain implants and nanobots are concerned, her overall health and wellness.

"What does that mean, exactly, babe?" Ginny asks, standing to greet her husband, taught, pale flesh glistening with sweat.

"Uncle's out! He's retiring. I no longer feel bound to be a part of the council anymore." He's grinning ear to ear, scratching at his black beard. He pulls Samantha out of her safe-cube and kisses her cheeks.

"That's exciting news!" Ginny agrees. "I'll have you all to myself then?"

"For ten years at least!" He replies giddily.

Ginny's amused smile flattens out across her pretty face. "What is that supposed to mean?"

"Wanna take a trip?"

"A trip where?"

"Oh, I dunno, *Tyson 4*?" Tobias is acting manic, but the idea his life is his own again is making him zealous.

"One of the new planets," she remembers their names: Tyson 4, Hyperion, and Buma Dos. Three systems of the many proposed for colonization. The first three. A manageable number according to the UE. "Why on Earth do you want to make *that* trip?"

"*Why on Earth* is exactly right!" Tobias wants to fill his wife with his enthusiasm. "Why stay here when there is another whole world waiting to be discovered?"

"Because this one *has* been discovered," she responds with both hands now perched on her slender hips. "You've never mentioned wanting to join the colonists before."

"I never felt like I had a choice before, Gin." He kisses Samantha again and places her back in her safe-cube where she happily pokes at the holos within. "I love what we have here, but what if we tried something new?"

"Sure... I'm all for trying new things, babe," she says slowly, putting down her water bottle. "Like bowling or downhill kiting or mountain climbing, but those don't take ten to twelve years off your life either. Then we get there what's the plan? Do you really want Sam to grow up between stars?"

She's throwing a lot of good points at him and he hasn't researched the plan, as she puts it, but wants to keep the option open. "All that stuff we can review, as for Sam, she'd want for nothing. I'll take you for a tour if you like."

"Just slow down," she tells him, laying her hands on his shoulders, craning her neck to look up at him. "I'm not saying no, but I'm not saying yes either."

"Can you decide in a couple of days?" He kisses her mouth, the taste of sweat and balm land on his tongue. "It's just that the ships are poised to leave in three days so,"

Ginny pulls away. "I have a family here, Tobias. On Earth." He'd like to see more of them showing their support with Sam. Where are they? "I don't know if I can leave them all *forever*. And your sister, Sphinx, the doctor, is she going?"

Tobias hadn't considered her: the reincarnation of his little sister in the B-class Host frame built for medical procedures. The same who had birthed Samantha. Tobias finds the couch and falls on it. He feels the joy of the moment slipping away. He nods at his wife, still standing.

"If there were more time to consider and prepare, would you be more willing?"

"I don't know, Tobias. It's a huge step. A *forever* step. What if these planets aren't what they think they are? What if something happens along the way? We could be stranded in interstellar space." She looks down at their little girl, a pleading hand going out to her. "I can't lead her into that kind of uncertainty."

Tobias stands again and takes his wife's hands in his. "What if Allfather comes back to Earth?" She knows about his sleepless nights. She knows he carries the fear deep within him.

"He could find us wherever we go. Nothing is certain."

"And nothing is forever, Gin." He follows her gaze to their daughter. "If Samantha wanted to come back to Earth, she could. *We* could."

"That's a lot of years lost in space."

"Just think about it. I'm going to pull the information. I want to go over it with you tonight." He pulls her into him, and they hug for a long moment. "I want to live, Gin. I want *more*." He releases his wife and walks to his smartwall to begin his research, somewhat distracted by her insecurities about taking the trip.

Ginny feels trapped; this sudden news and desire to leave their home – their planet, on some demented adventure has completely caught her off-guard. Yes, she watched the Chancellor's interview on the holo and is aware he's leaving office and joining the other colonists on their journey to Tyson 4, but that doesn't mean she has to follow. They have a perfect life, why mess with that?

She watches as Tobias eagerly jacks into the smartwall, fingers swiping invisible screens from his internal optic holo. Ginny appreciates his excitement over the prospect. She loves *him*, and when Tobias gets an idea in his head it's difficult to see it any other way but the way he presents it. It's what made him the leader he was to his Chimera, Captain of a UE squadron and eventually member at the council's table. Still, she is wary of this *opportunity*. She watches her daughter abandon the holo games in her safe-cube and lay down with her stuffy that narrates a muted nursery rhyme. Her heart warms at the vision. She turns her attention back on her husband and feels a similar warmth grip her. She loves them both but can't fathom leaving all they have to play out an impulsive fantasy of starting over where the potential for life and death scenarios are so much more probable.

At the chancellor's home, he and Darla relax into their comfortable couch while Raymond's A-class prepares a scrumptious dinner. They chatter excitedly about their plans and what their futures hold. Calling up what's known of Tyson 4, they review detailed maps of the surface and surrounding oceans. The colonists would collectively live within a diameter of 100 kilometres for the conceivable future as they build sustainable habitats, map the land and its bounty of native flora and fauna from the macro right down to the micro organisms inhabiting their new home.

A Charter of Rights & Freedoms was drafted with the help of scientists of every aptitude, religious input as well as military. The ethics committee and every other vocation that has learned from humanity's past mistakes, assisting in the institution of their sustainable presence aided Raymond's high-council to compose policies around an existing formula.

General August, for all her damaging influence on the UE, had an all-inclusive plan detailing colonization - something she was set to support once she controlled United Earth. After reviewing her schematics and the strategies her council had worked out in pulling off something of this scope, the government - in large part - adopted her system and adapted it for a more enlightened purpose. This saved United Earth thousands of man hours of planning and composing, requiring little more than a few tweaks to put it on the right path.

Each colonist will take an oath to do no harm. To live in peace with their surroundings and each other. To share the wealth of knowledge in order to replicate a successful colonization time and time again as planets continue to reveal themselves to humanity. Everything would be recorded and returned to Earth for posterity.

Raymond reminisces on the difficulties he had to overcome in convincing Darla to commit to the idea of leaving all that they knew for a completely different reality. It was a hard sell. He smiles to himself. She is more animated over the endless possibilities than him now. Raymond has no expectations he will be voted to lead the community of 2000, but a vote will take place and the people will build a senate as drafted in the Rights & Freedoms document. The military escort will also have an opportunity to join the colonists or return to Earth after spending a year in orbit as a precaution.

Allfather did not create himself, that was accomplished by intelligent organics. Defsats will be seeded above each of the planets as well, as an additional safeguard launched from the destroyers and programmed to protect.

Every aspect of these missions has been well thought-out and presented as such, so the people go in confidence. Of course, the council has agreed that not every facet could be planned for as 2000 souls attempt to colonize a foreign planet, but what could be was. In three days, Chancellor Bellows will be free of his duties here on Earth, opening a new chapter in his life.

"The UE Military arm of our glorious Utopia is anything but a utopia!" The Drill Sergeant shouts at his new recruits. He eyeballs each of the twenty-five cadets now at his mercy as he paces the line of young and old alike. Some are here for the adventure, others for the opportunity to take flight. Not all will be cut out for the journey a military career demands. The sergeant knows this all too well. He's seen it before. Even from his most hardened soldiers. The mind must understand what the body is capable of. Once the mind weakens the body follows, or vice-versa. Sergeant Winters' job is to see that both work to support the other and the tasks asked of them, without fail.

During General August's war he fought in the cities, rounding up Host cells and shutting them down. During the recent Allfather fight he volunteered to protect his planet as a gunman on the goliath named after one of UE's celebrated heroes, Captain Juravinski. That ship was commanded by the equally impressive Admiral Mann. Winters is a career military man - obeying orders as every good soldier is expected to - regardless of which side he was fighting for. Loyalty to the powers that be are enough for him. Now, as in the past, he takes his orders from the head of UE Military operations: Admiral Chopra. But after watching Chancellor Bellow's holo interview, he assumes Admiral Mann will take Chopra's place, as the Admiral runs in the coming election to become the Chancellor's replacement.

Sergeant Winters reminds his captive audience of the potential threat, which hangs like a black cloud overhead, in Allfather's final warning: *I am in you*. To be diligent and prepared for a possible rematch with this enemy is paramount to the safety and continued survival of United Earth and her soon-to-be sister planets: Tyson 4, Hyperion, and Buma Dos.

Sergeant Winters removes his gloves. His scarred hands standing as stark examples of the hardships of war. Sun damaged flesh exposing terrible traumas and three bionic fingers also carry with them age markers. Winters is no spring chicken, as he'd put it, and is proud of every mark on his muscular frame acquired through some incursion or peace-keeping melee. He runs a palm across his shaven head, replacing his cap. These volunteers would be joining the next leg of starships moving to colonize three additional planets in a year's time. Military personnel have already been placed in the ships traveling to Tyson 4, Hyperion, and Buma Dos, destined to make history by moving beyond the solar system, into interstellar space.

"Your name, rank and *purpose*, soldier!" Winters looks at Manuel penetratingly, reading the fear and indecision on his pretty face. The Chimera implants and additions to the man's body make for a difficult fitting of the heavy military issue uniform, but all are welcome to join these UE ranks.

Just days after meeting Udo and surrendering his life-altering ticket, Manuel decided the fastest route to joining the next set of colonists bound for a new planet would be to sign-up for the military. This would offer him an advantage which could see him join the colonists as a protector on one of the accompanying military vessels. It would be many, many times more likely than winning the lottery should he excel at this new life. He sees his sergeant looking at him now and answers.

"Manuel Thomas, sir!" He begins, wondering what he's gotten himself into. "Private," he continues. "I am the *strength* in United Earth, the *backbone* of Utopia, protector of the peace, Libertatem Defendimus!"

"Good, Private, good," Winters tells him. Manuel keeps his eyes straight ahead but in his peripheral catches his Sergeant turn back to him. "What is your *call*, Private?!"

"*Spiritus Omnia Vincet*- Spirit Conquers All, Sergeant!" Manuel likes UE's military call; it is inclusive of everyone: Chimera, Host, human. All are represented here today. All have spirit within.

"Very good, Private Thomas!" Sergeant Winters tells him. "The weapon on your shoulder, tell me about it."

"It is a standard issue pulse rifle, Sergeant!" Manuel begins, remembering every detail as his biotech implant carries the specific information from an earlier download. "It is capable of ten pulse blasts per minute, thirty controlled bursts ranging up to two kilometres, an automatic burst of three hundred armour-piercing rounds in thirty-three seconds, carries twenty kill-seeker grenades, produces up to five hundred rounds every ten minutes via MakerTech in its Buttstock, and is the closest thing to a friend I should make while I serve with UE Military Forces, sir!"

"Damn it, Private, *you know your shit!*" Winters is clearly impressed. Manuel feels a rush of pride. "I think I'll request every active member of UE Military has one of these baubles surgically implanted into their skulls!" His sergeant pokes a solid finger at the implant clearly visible on Manuel's temple.

"I can direct the Sergeant to an appropriate retailer of the contraband, sir!" Manuel jokes, maintaining his composure. Winters is up in his face again.

"*Humour*, Private?" Winters steps back from Manuel who remains staring straight ahead. "From this day forward, you are to answer to 'Joker', is that understood, Private, Joker?"

"Yes sir, thank you, sir!"

"Don't thank me, *Joker*. If I ask for a joke, pun, anecdote, jest, witticism, or story, you'd better deliver one that will make *me* laugh!" Winters steps in front of Manuel's line of sight with a grimace that could curdle milk. Manuel is trying desperately to hold back a barking laugh as the smaller, older, and much more capable man continues to elicit a response. "If I'm not laughing, none of you will be laughing!" Winters breaks off and steps back to appeal to the platoon. "For each *lame* joke from the Joker here, I will see to it that all of you suffer as I suffer. I love a good joke! I also love a good ten klick run or two-dozen pull ups. But that's because I'm strong. You'll all have to prove you're just as strong if you think you have a chance in this, your glorious United Earth Military!"

Manuel feels suddenly weak in the knees. His sergeant has just made him the platoon's punching bag. A year of accusing eyes from his bunkmates wasn't what he signed up for. He considers tossing the rifle and flipping the bird at the sergeant as he storms off the field. Could he put in a year of *this* in order to be placed on a ship escorting colonists to a new planet? *Is this truly my only option?*

TESSA'S CHOICE

Tessa is a gifted woman in her twenties on the autistic spectrum, and former member of The Flame, the religious cult which broke from Tessa's mother's organization in order to flee to a new world with stolen starships. This attempt was led by Sol, a psychopath, but contrived and organized through Tessa's incredible computational abilities. Sol had seen past her social anxieties and used her – and her *gift* – to run.

Once the Allfather threat had been announced, Tessa convinced Sol to return to Earth and join the fight to rid the galaxy of Allfather's malice. Again, Sol turned to run, but Tessa stopped him and resumed the defence of her planet and Earthbound mother.

Today Tessa mows over the stats she has prepared for the Chancellor, whom she has had the pleasure of getting to know over the past six months. These stats reveal the odds for success where the colony ships are concerned, as well as a separate set of stats for Raymond's party retaining power under Jim Chopra's leadership after the vote in two days. Both bode well. The incredible array of things which could go wrong during the interstellar flight to any one of the ships is astronomical, but Tessa has eliminated the vast majority due to the preparedness of the ships and teams involved. She reviewed every personality boarding the ships, every task to be completed over the eleven-year journey and the relationship hurdles between each person. Of course, this was also done by including the information into her smartwall, as a comparison against her results.

Tessa stretches her arms over her head and stands from her chair, yawning. Her lean frame shudders as the stretch is completed. Too many times she has forgotten to stand and move around after hours at her smartwall. Her disability detaches her from the material world when in deep thought. Though Sol had only good things to say about her autism, she still considers it a disability, always feeling ostracized and alone in the world save her mother. She has determined that is why she began a relationship with Sol when he began to show interest in her. Now she is an honorary member of the UE council. A position of great responsibility. She rarely goes to the meetings, but her research and statistics would be read aloud in the office of the Chancellor of United Earth on the fortieth floor of UE headquarters. The thought still gives her a shock of excitement.

She moves the information on to Chancellor Bellows via her embedded comm. *He will be pleased with these latest odds on the colonists.* Tessa's next task is to explain to her mother that she will be boarding the colony ship to Tyson 4. She will be very sad, Tessa knows, but she has run the numbers and discovered something that intrigues her, commanding her to take the trip. This is where her purpose rests. United Earth is well on its way to becoming a greater civilization than before.

Tessa checks herself in the mirror before presenting her plan to her mother, the leader of the Betaist movement, which is the largest religious faction in the UE. Her hair has grown out since the battle for Earth. Tight, black curls sit atop her head like a halo. Her large, brown eyes, taut dark skin, and pouty lips give her a sense of normalcy. She knows that she is beautiful by society's standards, but her autism, and memories of Sol hitting her – the man who had claimed he loved her - keeps her unattached, romantically.

In the atrium of their home, Tessa approaches her mother. Snow falls beyond the glassed-in room and gathers on the gardens which line the courtyard. Talia, Tessa's mother, is happy to see her daughter no longer locked away for so many hours doing the chancellor's work. Tessa falls into her mother's waiting embrace and takes great comfort in the warmth there. She pulls away tentatively.

"Mother," Tessa starts, "I've made a decision based on factual evidence and -" She looks down at Talia's hands as she holds them in hers. Anxiety creeps into her heart as she considers her next words. "M-mother, I-I -" She's stuttering now. This happens from time to time. Sol used to calm her by putting on a song or tracing circles on her open palms with his long, thin fingers. Talia does this now. Tessa feels the wave of anxiety wash away in a manner of seconds. Her bright, yet distant eyes look up at her mother. She takes a deep, concentrated breath.

"I have been offered a spot on the Tyson 4 colony ship by the council and intend to go," she explains quickly, nodding emphatically at the end - setting her jaw. "I know you will miss me. I will miss you too."

Talia gently places the palm of one hand on her daughter's cheek, offering a small smile, the smooth, dark skin of her kind face pushing up. "My dear girl," she pauses, "promise me you'll be safe. That's all I need to hear."

"The odds favour the trip," Tessa explains. "I will be more there. I will be more... *me*. More of who I am meant to be." Tessa's head tilts to the side and a quick smile makes an appearance on her full lips. Talia pulls her daughter into her and hugs her tightly. Tessa's arms slowly react to the hug and return the sentiment. She loves her mother. She will miss her. There are no odds against that. The ParaCom will keep them in touch.

"You'll be on the same ship as Chancellor Bellows and Commander Tesla," Talia tells her, having heard the news. "That's also very encouraging."

Tessa hadn't missed that fact either. She is comforted by the thought she will see Raymond's face occasionally as they hurtle through space and time. She nods at her mother and breaks their bond. "I must pack what possessions I am allowed. The shuttles leave in two days."

Talia pensively watches her daughter shuffle out of the room, feeling the pain of separation setting in, realizing she has less than forty-eight hours left to spend with her daughter.

ABOUT BEING MORE

Tobias can't imagine staying put now that he is free of the council. To remain on Earth when so much discovery is at hand leaves him breathless. The air is difficult to take in as his lungs seize against the action. This is similar to the events he suffers when he wakes from a sound sleep - visions of Allfather throwing rocks at his home, haunting his dreams. He practices his breathing. It's one day until the vote and Ginny has not brought up the conversation about Tyson 4 since he first mentioned it. She's taken Samantha with her to her mother's house on the outskirts of First City overnight.

There is nothing here for us, he thinks. His mind races to pull together all the pros of taking this trip. All council members and their families have been granted access. He feels like he'd be turning down a gift of immense importance should he be forced to turn it down on account of his wife's decision. But he would not leave her and his daughter. *Was I unencumbered...* but he isn't. He loves his family and acknowledges his responsibility to them. *Perhaps it's a foolish dream.* An urge to punch the wall and give up on the whole thing forces a surge of adrenaline in his system. He paces the floor of his home. Last night was another sleepless one. He's tired and desperate for change. His perceived future on Earth reminds him of why he became Chimera: the thousand shades of gray a utopian society guaranteed. Now that society was back, he wonders whether he can return to that life. He couldn't manage it before the wars. *The wars – they were exciting times. So much at stake. So many unknowns.* That's the way to live. The unknown unlocks infinite choices, infinite paths. Utopia suffocates them. He hears this running dialogue in his head and finds it difficult to question it. To remain on Earth, to leave the

43

council and military, what's left but to raise his daughter, walk her to school, pick her up and put her to bed, kiss his wife goodnight and do it all again? That might be enough for some, but it will grow old quickly in time. He selfishly decides he needs his journey to be about something more - the unknown, so he can exist as the man he is meant to be.

Ginny sits with her mother, feeding Samantha from her breast in the comfortable living space she remembers from her childhood. This was the same house where she first decided to become Chimera. From the basement room she called her own, she logged into the Shadow net and found Tobias. The rest is history. She smiles when she thinks of her husband's burning desire to be more. She was seventeen when they first started talking. At eighteen she introduced her first dose of Nano-bots into her system. Then she added a cranial implant and then the strength enhancers and so on. Her family was frightened of the changes, which led her to leave and find Tobias and spark a revolution.

"Tobias wants to take the colony ship to Tyson 4," she finally admits to her mother, who nearly chokes on her tea. "I don't know what to do. It's so far away. I don't want to deny him this, but I don't know how to leave all of you." A tear tracks down her pale cheek.

"Surely he wouldn't leave you both for some *hairbrained* trip like that!" Her mother doesn't mince words. She never has. "Is he serious? The ships leave in less than thirty-four hours," she checks her EC. "Why does he want to go?"

"I think he needs the distraction," Ginny finds herself explaining. "Since the revolution and the wars, he's become addicted to a certain kind of life. I fear the quiet life isn't something he will adjust to very easily. He hasn't, in fact."

"Perhaps it will pass, Gin," Her mother says with hopeful eyes on her and her grand daughter.

"It won't," Ginny says knowingly, "he's too caught up in the whirlwind of what's happened. He still worries Allfather will return. He doesn't sleep. He's tired all the time now. We both are." She looks down at her sleeping child and pulls her from her nipple, tugs her shirt down and walks the baby to a nearby safe-cube. "Tell me what to do, Mom," Ginny pleads, standing over the baby.

After a moment her mother presents a fact. "Your father and I encountered similar moments in our relationship, you know?" She starts. "He wanted to climb every mountain on Earth! It was exacerbating!"

Ginny remembers how often her father would disappear for weeks at a time. "You let him though."

"Well, yes, but he always came back." Her mother looks up at her sternly. "Do you think Tobias would come back if you let him go?"

"If I let him go?" The question answers itself. "I wouldn't *let him go*, Mom. If I decided it was the right thing for him, I would be deciding it was the right thing for all three of us."

"And is it?" Another pointed question from the person she could count on to drag the truth out of her whether she knew what that truth was or not. "Do you think it would be in your best interest to pick up and go to Tyson 4?"

"The right thing is to stay together. *I love him* and he loves us," she points down at her sleeping daughter, "he wouldn't just go if I said no."

"I believe that. I've seen how he looks at both of you. But that look will fade with time, Ginny. It will fade as surely as the twinkle in his eye with each passing day he spends not pursuing his passion."

Ginny can't deny Tobias would continue to fail stuck on a planet with no real challenges. It's why they became Chimera. To go back isn't the answer. He could never go back. Come to think of it, neither could she. A faint smile appears on her face. To deny her husband to be more is to deny herself and her child a father who loves them and who would give up his dream for them. It's a big compromise, but considering life on Earth without him as the man she fell in love with is too much to bear.

"I love you mom. I'll call every day on the ParaCom," she says, laughing and crying all at once. Her mother stands up and hugs her daughter.

"I love you, baby. You don't worry about me. You go live the life you deserve." She pulls back to look her daughter in the eyes. "You do this for *you* and that darling little girl every bit as much as you do it for *him*."

Ginny nods and brings her mother in for another long hug.

Ginny's face appears in holo form, hovering a few millimetres above Tobias' EC. She's been crying. His heart sinks. He's gone too far in asking her to go off planet.

"I love you, Tobias," she begins, "let's start packing when I get home." His heart rebounds from the pit of his stomach. A sensation of warmth envelopes his face. Tears well in his eyes and he blinks them away.

"You're sure, babe?" His voice cracks as he wipes his face. She nods back enthusiastically. "I won't let you down, either of you," he promises. "It's going to be an incredible life, Gin."

"I know," she returns, "wherever we end up, I want us to be together." She's crying now and Tobias feels incredibly vulnerable. "Be back in an hour. Love you." Her image flickers and disappears.

Tobias is overcome and stumbles to find a seat where he places his head in his hands and breathes through great urges to weep with relief.

Day two and Manuel is feeling vulnerable. The night before he received uncomfortable looks from his platoon mates reminiscent of the same sideways glances he's received as a Chimera. They don't like him. *They don't even know me.* A couple of the younger cadets went so far as to shove him after dinner tonight in the hallway from the mess hall. He put that to bed immediately, sequestering each in his turn, using learned guerilla tactics to let them know he wasn't some push over. They both nodded emphatically that they understood his point as their arms were twisted at increasingly unnatural angles. Manuel wanted to break them, but remembered why he had joined the UE Military, and to be thrown out now would cost him years of waiting for another planet while his name cleared.

At 28 he is one of the oldest in his platoon. Apparently the funniest too, according to Sergeant Winters. *Private Joker.* After being called out by his

Sergeant to tell him a joke during a group run earlier, Winters didn't laugh. This led to another three kilometres added to the platoon's run followed by two-dozen push-ups and thirty burpees. No one was happy about that, least of all Manuel. He'd been assigned the role of scapegoat for his Sergeant's cruel affections.

Sitting on the edge of his bed after another march around the barracks, Manuel cleans his boots with a small brush and limited supply of polish. Everyone in the bunkhouse is doing likewise. Some discuss the day while others keep to themselves. Manuel is happy with the latter. Suddenly, someone laughs a boisterous laugh and when Manuel looks up instinctively, a large man of 21 years and 120 kilos is staring back at him three bunks down. Manuel stares back but doesn't want to encourage a scene his Sergeant would likely blame on him. As if scripted, the large, dark man approaches Manuel's bent over form. He looks up at the intruder.

"Something funny?" Manuel asks the shirtless behemoth. "You here to share a joke with me?"

"You're the one with all the jokes," says the cadet towering over him. "How about you come up with something that makes us all laugh." He turns, appealing to the others.

Manuel slowly places his boot and utensils beside him on the bed and stands to meet his platoon mate. This kid is bigger than he thought at a good 12 cm taller and 20 kilos heavier. Still, he is relatively confident he can drop the boy if required to do so. "You know anything about physics?"

The kid shrugs and his arms fall heavy at his sides, an intense stare still focused on Manuel. "What's to know?"

"Well, you likely know that light travels faster than sound, right?" A slight smile plays across Manuel's face.

"Is this a joke?" The kid asks impatiently, Manuel noticing his meat hooks flexing into fists.

"It is," Manuel assures him, calmly. "You know, I've never heard *you* say anything until just now." He steps closer to the kid and they are now toe to toe.

47

"I'm not very vocal." The boy seems confused. If Manuel's right, he doesn't like looking confused. The bunkhouse is silent, everyone's listening in on their intense conversation.

"No matter, I just found it inspiring for this particular joke." Manuel maintains a stony stare at the giant. "I think I've set it up enough, so I'll just get right into it. Back to the beginning; light travels faster than sound, right?" The boy nods once. "Well, this is why some people appear bright until you hear them speak!" Manuel reveals a playful smile.

The bunkhouse lets out a nervous sigh and a few dark giggles, but the meathead still poised to pounce on Manuel seems stunned. Then he gets it. "That supposed to refer to me?"

"Don't take it badly. You *inspired* me!" Manuel sucks air forcefully through his nostrils letting the boy know that if he throws the first punch, he'll regret it. He tilts his head keeping eyes locked on his muscular opponent. The kid is clearly embarrassed and turns his head slowly to his left. Manuel reads his body language and easily side steps a head butt. The cadet slams his forehead into the rail above Manuel's cot and staggers back.

"Had enough, *Big Time*?" Manuel is now a metre away from the boy and feeling overly confident in his abilities. The angst of this place and the anger he's experiencing over being here and not enroute to an off-world carrier is feeding the fire in his belly. He wants a fight. He knew that when he insulted the kid with his joke. "I could have capitalized on your mistake, but I'm giving you a chance," The kid's right arm fires out from his side and Manuel ducks the shot placing one hand firmly on the forearm and driving a fist up to the bully's elbow. A crack echoes throughout the bunkhouse. Manuel does not release the mangled arm, steps back to avoid a haphazard left hook from the raging boy and turns the wrist of the right arm attaining the desired affect. The boy falls to a knee grunting against the agony.

"Fucking Chimera!" The kid yelps. "Fucking implants."

"Oh, I'm not wearing any implants, *Big Time*." Manuel admits. "But my seven years on you add up to your ass kicked, and if you don't say *mercy*,

I'm going to show you what it's really like to feel helpless." He bends the arm again and the boy forfeits the fight. When Manuel releases him, the kid's arm falls sloppily to the ground. Big Time picks it up with his other engorged limb and retreats to medical.

Manuel looks around him at the stunned faces of the younger cadets. The older look on admiringly. He throws his arms up and laughs. "That was a funny one, right?!" The platoon nods unequivocally and quickly return to their tasks. Manuel straightens out his undershirt and returns to the edge of his bed.

"Private Joker!" It's Winters' disapproving voice. Manuel's heart sinks. The sergeant marches over to Manuel's position where he has brought himself to attention. "What in the high orbit did you do to private Mallocs?"

"Sir, he didn't like my joke, Sir." Manuel replies insistently, eyes ahead, shoulders back.

"No one likes your jokes, Joker!" Winters is up in his face again and Manuel has to fight back the adrenaline from his recent encounter. "You just took one of my people out of service for weeks with that display!"

"Sir, I'm sorry, Sir, it won't happen again."

Sergeant Winters steps back and continues in a meeker tone. "No, Private, I don't suppose it will." Manuel fears he is about to be discharged and lose his chance at being part of the next off-world envoys. "You've made it very clear to Private Mallocs that you are *not* a victim. I doubt if he gives you a sideways glance the remainder of your time here."

"Sir?" Manuel waits on his punishment.

"I would like to hear the joke Mallocs found so *unfunny* that he would incite violence," Winters demands, seemingly knowing the boy had started the fight.

"Sir, I – you might not like it," Manuel starts, but sneaking a look at the Sergeant's gaze repeats the joke. Winters smiles. It's an unsettling look for the Sergeant but Manuel notices a kinship in the man's eyes now. He laughs aloud for exactly 3 seconds and abruptly stops.

"Was that meant to insult Mallocs?" He asks amusedly.

"I honestly thought it was above him." Manuel replies, still at full attention. Winters laughs again.

"Very well, Joker, you've earned your name. Be at ease." Winters turns to address the rest of his platoon. "Tomorrow you will all take part in an important exercise. Be ready at 0600 in your dress uniforms. You'll require your pulse rifle as well. I have a detail that will put you all in the history books." Winters exits the bunkhouse and the platoon relaxes. None more so than Manuel. A shared sigh fills the room, and everyone sinks back into their cots.

HOW THE TABLES TURN

Chancellor Bellows appears on everyone's holo screen and EC in United Earth as the political debates end with Mr. Jim Chopra, formerly Admiral Chopra, landing a strong point for keeping the current government in power.

"Thank you to each of our candidates for your candor and participation in this revealing debate on multiple topics worthy of everyone's deliberation in tonight's vote." Chancellor Bellows is reveling in this, his final address to the UE. Thoughts of interstellar space cloud his mind. "The clock has started, and in one hour we'll all know who our *next* Chancellor will be. Please take everything you've heard tonight into consideration and turn your attention to your EC's. With one swipe on the candidate's profile, you will be placing your vote for the future of all." Raymond lifts his own EC and swipes on Chopra's headshot securing one vote for his party and his friend.

A live audience watches on from the sports arena where the debate is held, scrutinizing the numbers on the big holo floating over the crowd. Each candidate is represented with their votes appearing underneath. Surprisingly to Raymond, Chopra is slow to pick up the numbers, as two other parties push past the reigning party's figures. Raymond looks to his friend and offers a reassuring wink. Chopra smiles from behind his podium. Confident as ever.

"Senator Yaris' party has taken the early lead tonight. In her own words, her policies toward Host reproduction is *for*, looking to replace positions once held by our enlightened Hosts. She also mentioned tonight that she is ready to decommission the military arm of your UE in order to avoid another civil war." Raymond worries for the frame of mind of the people voting to disband the very military that saved them in this time of uncertainty. Regardless of the outcome, Raymond is bound and determined to be completely unbiased in hosting this vote.

Yaris' numbers continue to go up, but Chopra is now in second place. Raymond considers the stats he reviewed in early votes cast, Captain Drake's intel and Tessa's math. Each told him his party would soar past the rest, but that's not turning out to be the reality at the polls. He feels suddenly nervous for his friend, but also for his plan to leave United Earth with anyone but Jim Chopra overseeing its continued success.

"It looks like Chopra is beginning to see some solid numbers as his party moves into second place. It won't take much momentum to squeeze Yaris out of first." Raymond is merely stating the obvious as the figures continue to roll in. Roughly ten billion voters make for a sensational count scrolling under the candidate's headshots. Then he sees it, a massive number of votes added under Chopra's profile. "Looks like the tables have turned. Chopra is now in the lead and pulling away from Yaris. Deschanel is showing at a solid third." Raymond feels lighter suddenly, his team's predictions now appear reachable. Chopra's numbers continue to gain ground leaving second place far behind.

"It looks as though the citizens of United Earth like what Jim Chopra has to say. His platform is to keep everything status quo and continue to rebuild while sending citizens to seed our new planets through the lottery."

At eight pm Eastern Standard Time the vote is ended, and the voter turnout has broken records at over seven billion participants. Raymond calls his friend to the high stage, clapping all the while. He shakes Jim's hand and officially swears him in. The crowded sports arena is alive with support as paper balloons fall from the high ceiling.

That evening, under dim lighting Raymond turns over his office of the last twelve years to his friend. He peers out the floor to ceiling windows overlooking First City, a city close to his heart, and one he has defended vehemently. He turns, taking hold of the steel and leather chair waiting behind his black walnut desk for its new resident.

"I believe this is yours now... Chancellor," Raymond smiles brightly at Jim Chopra, the newly elected Chancellor of United Earth.

Jim moves from his place at the doors where he is taking it all in, the fortieth floor of the most powerful office in the world. The *worlds,* in another decade or so, with the addition of three new star systems under the guidance of United Earth. "We'll need to change our name," Jim tells Raymond as he pulls the Chancellor's chair out, watching his friend's expression turn sour. He laughs and reveals his meaning. "With so many new planets about to be added to our governance, perhaps United *Planets*?" Jim eases into the command chair of command chairs.

"An upgrade," Raymond agrees. "Something to work toward as the time grows closer."

"I'll put it on the list," Jim says, laying a palm on the desktop. The desk comes alive with holos and screens embedded under the wood veneer. "Ah, you've already relinquished your desk to me!" He watches as personal emails and congratulatory holos dance at eye level. "You're not in any rush to leave office, are you?" They both laugh.

"Just to leave it all, my friend," Raymond replies light-heartedly, but truth be told he feels an incredible weight lifted from his spirit once the title fell away. The extraordinary responsibility has aged him. It may age Jim as well, but he couldn't be more enthusiastic over Admiral Chopra's appointment to this highest office. He has closure now.

"Yaris had me worried there for a moment," Jim admits. "Was she pulling votes from the religious sectors?" A good question; they are pacifists for the most part and a vote for Yaris was a vote to dismember the military. Thankfully that didn't come to pass.

"You've won, Jim, enjoy it." Raymond moves across the room and waves a hand in front of a paneled cupboard. There he pulls out a 2098 bottle of Irish Whiskey and pours two glasses. "Your family will be here soon, so I wanted to congratulate you properly with a bottle I've been holding onto far too long." Raymond hands the glass of amber liquid to his friend and they clink glasses. Both savour the peaty flavour, holding it in their mouths a moment before swallowing. Raymond watches as a smile grows on Jim's lips.

"It's been an interesting couple of years, Chancellor," Jim says nostalgically, "I don't like to imagine what they would have been like were you not the man you are."

"Chancellor," Raymond raises his glass acknowledging his new Commander and Chief. After another sip, Jim's family appears at the double doors with a C-class escort. His wife runs to hug him, and the children follow. His grown daughter with a child of her own embraces her father, glowing with pride. One half of his twins also rushes in to congratulate his father. Raymond knows Jim will have a difficult time celebrating with one twin lost to the general's war. Raymond greets each of them and announces his departure. Jim salutes his Chancellor and Raymond returns the sentiment, then extends a hand and pulls Jim in for a hug.

"Keep me posted, Chancellor," Raymond says. "I'm just an EC away."

"You can count on that, Chancellor." Jim studies Raymond's face as if not to forget him and all he's done. Raymond bows out and exits the office of the Chancellor of United Earth for the last time.

The day has finally arrived. All off-world stations have been running shuttles up to the colony ships in orbit for two hours now to the cheers and excitement of a live audience. Many pull themselves from their loved ones as sobs follow, but overall it is a joyous occasion and one in which history will recall as ground-breaking. Manuel only wishes he were a bigger part of it. He has been posted as a soldier of the UE to guard the shuttle bay entrance against any would-be interlopers but would much rather be boarding the next shuttle than guarding it. His platoon of new recruits has been placed in strategic positions within and around the facility. *Real world, active duty,* Sergeant Winters told them; it will build confidence and experience. He watches on with great interest at the lucky few moving through the gates. He studies their expressions mostly. Some are alarmed and others anxious while the majority are elated. He imagines his own expression in their place. This feels like punishment for last night's bunkhouse brawl.

Manuel's rifle rests on his shoulder. He isn't enjoying the endless discipline required by the UE military. Just days in and he's ready to bail. He nods at passing colonists, genuinely happy for them, and then in the distance recognizes a familiar face in line. That of the young Udo, Trevor's daughter. He's thankful to think she hasn't squandered the gift. As she approaches, he notices a sly smile work its way up one side of her round face. Her black hair is pulled back into a tight ponytail and she's wearing an oversized coat, presumably her fathers. Her fingers are adorned with rings – her mother's perhaps, and she wears a long skirt with dark leggings and all-terrain boots. She's looking directly at him now just three metres away. The line is moving at a reasonable pace. When they are close enough that he can smell her obnoxious perfume, she bumps her EC into his and Manuel's embedded comm comes to life.

He smiles at her and she is gone. He finds himself excited for her. Looking down at his own EC he realizes Udo has dropped him a message. Perhaps a thank you note? He raises his arm and reads the message. ::I did some research on you,:: she tells him, ::you're a good man who lost his family – same as me. I think you deserve this trip just as much as I do. I found your profile on the EC Military site and knew you'd be here today. I used my dad's friends to make you a chip-code. Use it. *Please.* I don't want to be all alone on this trip. All the info is in the code. UDO BOYD.::

Manuel can't believe what he's reading. *Made me a chip-code? Is that even possible?* His forearm lights up yellow as the file is downloaded and tentatively, he opens it. Immediately his EC pulses a light blue, just like those who'd won the lottery. His heart does a summersault. Passers by smile brightly at him as they recognize the sign. He feels awkward and elated all at once. *What do I do? Board the platform? Abandon my post? Yes!!*

Manuel turns ever so slowly and joins the crowd as they make their way onto the next shuttle. It's nearly full now and he's afraid if he doesn't make this one, he'll be found out and the whole façade exposed. His head is down and he's looking for somewhere to stash his rifle. Suddenly another, more seasoned soldier stops him at the final check point.

"Private Thomas," the older man knows his name. Of course, he does, it's reading out on the soldier's EC. "Why are you boarding this shuttle?"

Manuel goes white. The chip doesn't work. He's been found out. There are strong repercussions for falsifying a lottery ticket and he's about to experience them. "Military personnel don't ride civilian shuttles. You know that." *Is that all?*

Manuel struggles to come up with an excuse when Udo arrives at the doorway to the shuttle. "Come on, daddy, I saved you a seat!" She says, trying to push past the soldier. The man looks down at Udo and laughs.

"This is your kid?" He asks, not bothering to question it on his EC. He's clearly touched by the damage the little girl has sustained to her right hand as it reaches for Manuel. "Why are you in uniform if you won the lottery?" The soldier asks Manuel.

"I – uh," Manuel trips over his tongue.

"I asked him to dress up for the trip!" Udo says cheerfully. A bit out of character for this kid, Manuel thinks. "Come on daddy! Come on!" She's laying it on thick. Manuel smiles nervously at her, looks up at the soldier and shrugs. "Your rifle. Leave it with me. Any other unsanctioned gear?" The man smiles back down at Udo.

"Uh, no, just the rifle." Manuel pulls it off his shoulder and relinquishes it to the soldier. "Thank you for your service," he tells the man.

"*Spiritus Omnia Vincet,*" the soldier says. Manuel repeats the military call back and takes Udo's hand, boarding the shuttle.

LEAVING IT ALL BEHIND

Tobias and Ginny walk the long hallway of the carrier starship, Samantha clinging to her father's neck, and locate their room number. Ginny waves a hand at the door and it opens, greeting the family by name. On first look it holds ample space for their family. Two bedrooms, a kitchenette, generous bathroom and living space complete with holo entertainment and a smartwall. Comfortable furnishings line the walls. They have several window ports to the empty space beyond. Each room is decorated to the style of the day. Nothing has been left out. The gravity knitting systems are working but feel a bit heavier than they should by Tobias' account. *I'll ask about it.*

"Oh, it's just beautiful, Tobias," Ginny says rummaging through the cupboards and pulling down mugs. Their personal fridge is filled with baby formula and the essentials. "There is a *dining hall,* right?"

"Yes, and don't go telling everyone we meet we have a kitchenette," Tobias explains, "there are very few rooms which do."

"Oh? I guess we're royalty then," she says, an impish smile on her pretty face.

Raymond sweeps Darla up in his arms, she waves a hand at the door and he walks her over the threshold, joking about the act's affect in preventing the ancient superstition that the bride brings family demons into the new home.

The room is fit for a king and queen. Three times the size of the others, this is a duplicate of the Captain's quarters. A luxury afforded the former Chancellor of United Earth and Commander of Luna Base. Raymond makes plans in his head to have Tobias, Ginny, and his grandniece visit often. He's thrilled they've decided to join him on this historic journey. Excited for the years ahead of him watching his grandniece grow up enroute to a new world.

"This is too much," Darla breathes in the large space. An A-class AI Host welcomes them home.

"Hello, Chancellor Bellows, Commander, Tesla. I am CADDY, your room Host. It is a female, as so many are in this function. CADDY is not an enlightened Host, but a similar version of what Raymond and the rest of United Earth had known before the wars. "If you have any needs or questions I am at your disposal. Are you thirsty? Hungry? I imagine it's taken quite a bit of effort to arrive."

"I'd love a drink," Darla looks to Raymond excitedly, "do you want a drink?"

"I'll take a red wine if you have it, CADDY." Raymond says, accepting that some things are unchanging.

"There are 500 bottles of red and white wines in your personal pantry, Chancellor, and a facility producing wine and spirits in the lower levels from twenty tonnes of powdered mix as needed." CADDY explains in detail.

Darla looks up at Raymond and they grin like children on holiday. "In that case, CADDY, I'd love a glass as well."

CADDY excuses herself and heads to the wet bar. There she extracts a bottle from the overhead pantry, uncorks it and pours two nine-ounce glasses.

Udo leads Manuel by his hand down the painted steel hallway, dodging and weaving through other passengers looking for their rooms. Udo stops suddenly and turns to meet a narrow door. She waves her hand and the door retracts into the wall. She is welcomed by an audio recording. Manuel follows as she steps into the room. Lights flicker to life revealing a substantial room. It is a single, with all the comforts of home. A double bed lays under a beautiful rendering of a Starry Night. No windows. That's just as well. A computer console located next to the bed offers a map of the entire ship and they review its contents. Gymnasiums, theatres, dining halls, and myriad other activity rooms. Science departments, physics departments and educational rooms with smartwalls to enable every colonist a chance to learn whatever trade or course they might like before arriving at Tyson 4. Farming facilities, grow labs, and MakerTech equipment rooms line the belly of the carrier next to the shuttle bay.

"This is nice…" Manuel says eyeing the three walls in front of him.

"It's enough," Udo replies. "You can have the bed; I'll take the couch; I'm smaller."

Manuel feels like he's trespassing on Udo's journey. "Are you sure? That you want me to stay with you I mean?"

"Yes," she says determinedly. "Besides, where else are you going to sleep? In the janitor's office?" She smiles up at him, proud of herself. She opens a door and discovers a petite three-piece bathroom. "This is cute," she says, not really meaning it.

"It's everything we need." Manuel says, hands on hips surveying the 100 square metre room. "Thank you for giving me this," he says sincerely to Udo.

"You could have buggered off with the ticket you gave *me* and had this all to yourself," she says, "but you didn't. You're a good person, Manny."

Manuel feels a shock of recognition when she called him *Manny*. His little sister used to call him that.

Manuel and Udo agree to visit the dining hall separately until they are far enough out of the system that should his unlawful boarding be discovered, they would not turn the ship around. He swipes Udo's ID card which they found in the room on his EC, and for the moment, assumes her identity.

He moves through the lower deck and up one of the many elevators to the dining hall deck. As he moves to exit the elevator a woman bumps into him, seemingly oblivious to what's going on around her. Manuel is taken aback; she is beautiful, he thinks. Captivated by her soft features and glowing, dark skin he realizes his mouth is open and quickly shuts it as she offers an apology and boards the elevator.

Manuel is tempted to follow her in but remembers he's not really supposed to be here. "I'm Manuel," his name leaps out of his mouth. The vision in a tight-fitted, white body suit looks up at him from her EC, removes a sound dampening earphone and replies.

"I'm Tessa." The elevator door closes, and Manuel realizes he's wearing a goofy grin as he's left with only his reflection in the steel door.

He feels light-headed. The girl of his dreams is aboard the same ship as him, and for the next eleven years there's not much he can do about that. *She must be my penance for sneaking my way on this ship.*

After an impressively tasty meal in the ship's dining hall, Tessa winds her way through the massive ship's hallways, arcades, shops, and foyers to her assigned room. It is a one bedroom with a tiny wet bar and four-piece bath. She enters the bedroom and sits at the edge of a surprisingly comfortable mattress. Tessa removes her dampening headphones and lays back on the bed. Without the headphones it would be very difficult for her to be on this ship. Loud noises upset her. She wore them the entire time she fought alongside Admiral Chopra near the end of the war, just before Allfather's Kamikaze charge on Earth.

Tessa's thoughts drift to the man at the elevator. He was handsome, but nervous, she thinks, smiling despite herself. Perhaps if she pursued a relationship during the length of this journey, the journey itself would not seem so long. She has loved once; Sol, the arrogant fool of a man who stole her away from her mother. She was blinded by his confidence and the way he could sooth her troubled soul. But it was all a fallacy. He had used her for her intellect.

She still remembers the tender touch of his kiss though, her slender fingers now tracing the lines of her full lips, but those memories always transform into the violent backhand he had delivered at the end. She'd been stunned by the hit, both physically and emotionally, but recovered enough to put him down with a knee to his groin. She rolls over and assumes the fetal position on her new bed. "Manuel," she whispers to herself, and drifts off to sleep.

Labyrinth watches as the bridge prepares to fire the engines, communicating with Luna base and their military escort. "Tyson 4 envoy 1 prepped and ready," the captain says. The captains from envoy 2 and 3 mimic her readiness. "You look good for full burn," the new commander of Luna base offers. "Military escorts, one through five, please report on readiness." All five captains report on their positive status for a full burn.

"Strap in," the captain calls out to her bridge crew and then announces a similar order to her colonists over the comm. "Please use the belted seats in your residence. If currently in the dining hall or an entertainment facility, note that every seat aboard the ship is equipped with safety belts. This is for your own welfare. Please secure yourself first, children and the elderly next. You have three minutes. Enjoy the G-forces; they'll last just a few seconds."

Labyrinth is thrilled to have been invited onto the bridge for this momentous event. She is recording the experience for posterity and routing it back to Earth on Chancellor Chopra's request via her roaming lance. They will experience everything in real time. She takes a seat: her matte black armour contrasting against the white faux leather of the guest chair as well as the stark, glossy white of the bridge walls and consoles.

The crew is dressed in black and cream coloured apparel, only slightly different from the black and gold jumpsuits of the military personnel accompanying them on the destroyer and four corvettes. Each is heavily armed and carries with them dozens of defence satellites to be placed in Tyson 4's orbit. Tyson 4 has one moon much like Earth's moon. A planned base will be set up there via MakerTech drones within the first year. All three destination planets will undergo the same procedures. Hyperion with its three moons, and Buma Dos with its two.

"Go for full burn," the captain repeats. Labyrinth watches on as she grips the armrests of her command chair, easing her head back so not to have to fight the coming G's. "On my mark," she continues. "Engage." With the command comes a spectacular push against Labyrinth's chassis. AI Hosts have inertia sensors throughout their bodies to assist with spatial recognition. These can also experience sensations of pain and pleasure, but one must appoint those features. She registers three gravities pushing against her frame. In mere seconds, as the ship reaches maximum velocity, the one-G norm is returned to the bridge, as it would be the rest of the ship, and the captain announces to the crew and colonists that it is now safe to move about the carrier.

Labyrinth takes a call from Senator Quinn, his mentor and fellow enlightened AI Host. He wishes her a safe and speedy trip to Tyson 4. She thanks him and stands to receive another message from former Chancellor Bellows to join him in his cabin. Tessa, Tobias, and his wife have also been invited. She excuses herself and thanks the captain for the honour of being allowed on her bridge.

KNOCK KNOCK

In Raymond's cabin Tobias and Ginny join him and Darla first. Tobias is impressed by the size of his 'estate', as he calls it. Ginny is equally stunned at the amenities included in their suite. Samantha sleeps on Ginny's chest, bound to her in a sling. Darla fusses over the baby and leads them into the great room.

"Who do you have to know to get a place like this?" Tobias teases, eyeing the bar and pouring himself a whiskey. He motions to Ginny and she shakes her head requesting soda water.

"It's a duplicate of the Captain's quarters," Darla tells thim, "I know, it's too much isn't it?"

"Tobias is only kidding, Commander – uh, Darla. Our suite is just as nice, just... not as big." She smiles at Darla's slightly embarrassed expression. "You both deserve it."

"Thank you, Ginny," Darla feels the flush fade from her round face. Tobias is such a sarcastic man, she thinks, never sure when to take him seriously. Tessa rings the door next and is welcomed in while Labyrinth trails close behind.

"Welcome," Raymond extends his arms and ushers them all into the great room where he has light jazz playing on his holo recorder. "Can I get anyone anything?" Darla is putting out hot hors d'oeuvres for the guests along the bar counter.

"It's beautiful, Chancellor," Tessa offers, her eyes darting from one wall to the next, analyzing the features and decorative touches. "I'm sorry," she says, "I-I should call you Raymond now."

"Please," Raymond replies. "We're all equals here."

"If you're not judging by the size of our suite, that is," Tobias ribs as he takes a drink from his rocks glass. CADDY seems put off that she isn't filling requests for libations and makes herself known.

"You have an AI Host," Labyrinth says with a degree of surprise. "I hadn't realized."

"If CADDY makes you uncomfortable, Labyrinth -" Darla starts but is cut off.

"No, no, not at all, Darla. I was not aware there were A-class onboard." Labyrinth explains. "I know that several other classes of Hosts are aboard to maintain the shops and machinery, but A-class I thought were left to Earth."

"We don't have one," Tobias offers, "if that makes you feel any better."

Labyrinth's eyes tell a story of discomfort even though her words say otherwise. She feels strange being in the presence of 'dumb' AI that could be given the gift of sentience but was denied as a coping mechanism for United Earth's attempts to normalize the day to day operations of life.

"There are no more than five A-class, mostly reserved for the crew cabins. B-class run the entertainment facilities and shops and dining halls while C-class assist with menial tasks around the ship, and D-class support tech and mechanics." Raymond explains.

"I read there are F-class here," Tessa says, moving slowly through the suite, landing on a painting; a reproduction of da Vinci's Mona Lisa.

"Yes, fifty in total." Raymond replies, placing his wine glass down to be refilled by CADDY. "Precautionary, of course. They won't be animated unless absolutely necessary."

A pause in the conversation gives Darla a chance to voice why they've invited them here. "We've asked you all here to celebrate with us the beginning of a new life, together." Darla raises her glass, happy to change the subject. "To a new world, a new start and adventurous lives -" She stops short of her toast as the ship shudders violently.

"Please return to your cabins," the captain's voice can be heard over the comm, "we're experiencing some unexpected turbulence."

Darla looks to Raymond, her eyes communicating the terror behind them. "Turbulence? In *space*?" The music stops.

"A meteor field we hadn't prepared for?" Ginny suggests, cradling her baby. CADDY falls rigid to the floor and those near her jump at the action. The mood in the room goes from confused to frightened.

Raymond's EC lights up and the captain's holo representation ignites over his forearm. "Chancellor," she begins, "Would you please grace us with your presence on the bridge." He's been around long enough to know this wasn't a request. He looks up at Darla, mouth agape and returns his focus to the captain. "I'll be right there."

"I'm not sitting this out," Tobias tells him, placing his drink on the bar top. Labyrinth also joins the charge out of the cabin and toward the bridge. Tessa wonders if her calculations which motivated her to join this journey had just come to pass and also excuses herself from the room.

As the four enter the bridge where two C-class security Hosts lay on the ground, what they witness in the view ports and onscreen tell a story very much removed from any meteor field. Raymond feels sick over the thoughts running through his head.

"Chancellor," the captain turns from her place at the viewscreen. "Have you encountered anything like this in your dealings with Allfather?" Raymond squints to try to clarify the blur which seems to be surrounding the exterior of their ship. "Our engines have stalled and systems seem to be in a state of suspended animation." She points at her pilot's console. Everything is frozen. There are no readouts coming through where there ought to be dozens.

"Are you suggesting this is an attack on our fleet?" Raymond asks, still stunned over what's happening. The captain shrugs her shoulders. Raymond looks to his nephew and Tobias shrugs as well. "No, we haven't experienced anything like this, but I'm not discounting the possibility." Raymond admits freely.

"Then we have something to go on," Captain Huang says sharply. "Because nothing I've been trained for resembles what we're experiencing right now."

"It appears to be some kind of space/time anomaly," Labyrinth offers. "I've seen similar outcomes in computer trials, but no one has ever created one in the lab."

"That the engines have stopped and the computers are hanging in time, I concur with the Host." Tessa is standing stock still, eyes wide; taking in the bizarre abnormality with her extraordinary mind.

Tobias looks from Tessa to the captain, "Can we hail Earth?" The captain shakes her head. "The other ships?" Again, she shakes her head.

"Everything is down, or to be more specific, *stuck*. The moment this anomaly came upon us, everything froze." Huang is trying to keep her cool, but Raymond senses she won't be for long.

"Are we still moving? The gravity knitting system is still in place." Labyrinth moves toward the view port.

"As I said, it's like we're *stuck*." Huang reasserts. "Whether we're moving or not, we have no way of knowing."

"It's like we're in a bubble of time." Tessa quietly reveals.

"And that bubble may well be moving through space," Labyrinth adds. "Or we could be standing still."

"My AI Host, CADDY, she dropped like a rock after you made the announcement, and the C-class outside your door -" Raymond recalls, looking to Labyrinth. She nods back at him. "I have no answer for that, Raymond."

"Whatever's happening, we need a solution." Tobias exclaims, charging toward the viewscreen. "If our hands are tied from inside, maybe we should send a team out to perform a space walk." He feels trapped.

"Out of the question," Captain Huang says. "We don't know what that might do to someone."

"Let's get our bearings," Raymond takes charge of the situation as though it's second nature. He can't quite believe he's living through another possible attempt by Allfather, but if not him, who, or *what?* "We need to approach this with cool heads. Can we view the trip up until the anomaly engulfed the ship? There may be a clue as to where it originated."

"Like from another ship," Tobias adds, "it could have been fired on us from someone we can counter."

"We can't even fire our engines," Huang reiterates, frustrated over the circumstances, "What possible *counter* do you suggest?" She turns back to Raymond. "And no, I'm afraid we cannot review our logs as they too are frozen. *Everything* is stuck in time."

Just then the ship feels as though it has come to an abrupt stop, and those not seated are thrown a meter forward, some losing their balance. Raymond is steadied by Tobias, and Labyrinth assists Tessa back to her feet. Everyone is startled but not harmed.

"Does *that* answer our question whether we've been moving?" Tobias is agitated. They all are. Suddenly the field falls around them and empty space is revealed beyond the view ports and screens. The captain rushes over to her console to receive coordinates. The Ship's navigation computers take a few moments to catch up with the sudden change, star maps zoom across the holo in a blur, stopping on an unlikely quadrant of their Milky Way galaxy.

"That's not possible," she mutters. Raymond and the others group around her, taking in the preposterous data hovering above the console. "These are reading light years," she tells them, gobsmacked. "There's no way this is right."

Tobias throws his hands up and slides in next to his uncle to study the star map. "*Light years!* Are we at Tyson 4?"

"Nowhere near it" Huang says, taking a deep breath. "By these coordinates, we're nearer the galactic centre by 200 light years." Her eyes dart back and forth at her read out. "Impossible."

"*Anything* is possible, Captain," Tessa says curtly. "We've experienced something only imagined hypothetically."

"Faster than light," Labyrinth says. "It's extraordinary." She looks up from the console to take in the star field beyond. "It's revolutionary."

"Is it a natural phenomenon?" Raymond asks. *Or something more devious.*

"Nature is unpredictable." Labyrinth explains calmly. "The universe was created to move energy efficiently. This is breaking the laws as we know them, but evolutionarily speaking, it's possible nature might outdo itself."

"Physical laws must be followed," Raymond says absently. "At least, by *nature.*"

The group remains in a state of amazement for a moment, trying to wrap their heads around this event. "I–I need to make an announcement to the colonists," Captain Huang says distractedly. She looks to Raymond, a silent cry for help creasing her brow.

"Tell them you're sorry for the abrupt stop, and that we'll be running diagnostics on the ship's systems and getting back on course in a few hours," Raymond tells her. "That should buy us some time."

"Was it a wormhole?" Tobias wonders. "Can we take it back?"

"If we can't, we had better start looking for habitable planets in the stellar neighbourhood," Raymond suggests.

"Captain Huang?" a male voice penetrates the bridge's comm. "This is Captain Runninghorse of your escort destroyer UE0026. Have you any data on what's just happened and how we got here?" She looks to Raymond again for guidance.

"Captain, this is former Chancellor Bellows. I've been invited to the bridge by Captain Huang as counsel. We believe we entered a wormhole."

"That is our hypothesis as well. There's no chance of our making Tyson 4 now. It would take well over 200 years to span that distance from where we are." He sounds anxious over the facts and rightfully so.

"Scan the area for potential systems we might colonize and we'll do the same. It's our only chance at survival now." Raymond doesn't sugar-coat it. This is a fact. They'll die in space if they can't find a livable planet in the next few days and spend the next ten years traveling to. "The sooner we can locate a suitable alternative to Tyson 4, the better chance we have."

"Understood, Chancellor," Runninghorse replies, his voice more confident knowing someone has a plan.

"Share information as it comes to you, Captain. We'll be alright. There are millions of habitable planets out there. We've proven that. "

"Well said, sir," Captain Runninghorse signs off. Captain Huang delivers her announcement to the ship and moves to direct her crew to begin long range scans of their new local neighbourhood.

WHO'S THERE?

Returning to his cabin, Raymond explains what's happened to Darla and Ginny as best he can. They are both beside themselves with dread. The possibility for this outcome had not crossed their minds.

"So, it's not Allfather come to torment us?" Ginny asks, Samantha now awake and nursing.

"We can't rule that out, babe," Tobias is at Ginny's side. "Though I'd have expected a greeting by now." Tobias rises from the couch and pours himself another glass of the whiskey. "The crew has their orders to scan the quadrant for planets, so one way or another we'll end up on a habitable planet."

"The odds are in our favour of finding several with the tools available to the carrier," Tessa assures them, unwilling to return to her own cabin while this is unresolved.

"Labyrinth stayed back to assist in mapping the stars and reviewing their systems one by one." Raymond adds. "Several of the scientists aboard have joined in the search as well. It may not be the route we expected to take, but it's still in the right direction."

"Has anyone tried to contact Earth?" Darla wonders, looking at her EC and swiping to find a number. "Do you think the ParaCom will work this far out?"

"It's supposed to work anywhere in real time." Labyrinth says, still connected to the group via her internal modem from the bridge. "I'm accessing my roaming lance." She tells them. "Quinn is available to speak with us. I'll give him the update to pass on to Chancellor Elect Chopra."

Raymond lets out a heavy sigh. "They'll be crestfallen to know what's happened. Labyrinth, ask Quinn if they've heard from the other two missions."

A moment passes as she relays the query. "They have not, Raymond," Labyrinth replies. "Quinn is stunned by these events. He will immediately create a group to research the anomaly as I had recorded it and hope he'll offer us answers from their perspective."

"Excellent." Raymond feels a little lighter. "Tell him thanks, and not to worry."

"Chancellor." Captain Huang appears on Raymond's EC. "We've discovered something eerily close to our position. Not a planet, but - something else." This drops Raymond's heart into his stomach. Could it be that Allfather has dragged them here?

"Elaborate, Captain," he asks, not ready to cave into his fear over an Allfather scenario.

"Space junk, Chancellor. Mech and tech. No life signs. Permission to investigate."

Permission? From me!? I'm just a passenger on this unfolding nightmare. "Uh, yes, Captain, please. Let's understand what we're looking at." He turns to his group and raises his hands, shrugging.

"Hey, if they want to put you in charge, I say *who better!*" Tobias tells him. Darla agrees. "The closer you are to this the more we'll all know."

Raymond moves to join the Captain on the bridge for the analysis of the *space junk*, as she called it. Tobias and Tessa follow. The space junk is just that. What might have been a ship, or a dozen, are little more than shredded metal now. Something devastating happened here. Is he looking at alien technology? Captain Huang urges the group to join her at the viewscreen. All military vessels have joined them.

"Chancellor, this isn't just any space junk. It's ours," she looks up at him and he can see the fear in her eyes. "This is envoy 3. We've matched tech to ours."

"Any survivors?" Raymond is trying to keep himself together with this new development. The Captain shakes her head, no. "No one? Where did they go?"

"That's the creepy part," an ensign answers from his console. "There's no trace of organic signatures anywhere. All hands are lost."

Raymond is having a difficult time understanding this point. "That seems impossible."

"It's that kind of day," Tobias adds, moving closer to the viewscreen. "So, what happened? Was it attacked? Did it just not fair as well as we did through the wormhole?"

"The damage seems to suggest an implosion," Captain Runninghorse joins the conversation via his comm. "But even so, there ought to be human debris everywhere."

"Could they have e-evacuated?" Tessa wonders.

"There are no energy signatures suggesting that possibility, no, ma'am." Runninghorse says solemnly.

This mystery seems to have many edges, Raymond thinks. Brought to the middle of nowhere in an instant, destroyed sister ships adrift in foreign space and now missing crews and colonists. He can't help but think of Allfather as the cause. So many people lost. This will be a crushing update back home. He wonders how Chancellor Chopra will handle it.

"I'm starting to feel unwelcome here," Tobias says flatly. "None of this is adding up."

"Shouldn't we begin a search for the colonists?" Captain Huang says. "We can't just walk away from this. What about the other ships? Envoy 2."

"The Captain's right, of course, we have to follow procedure. Captain Runninghorse, you're the military lead here. Can you send one of your corvettes out and run deeper scans?" Raymond can't seem to back out of the leadership roll.

"Yes, I will give the order, Chancellor."

"Until we know more, I think the bulk of our envoy ought to stay put. Continue your planet scans, Captains." Raymond looks to Tobias and Tessa and suggests they leave the professionals to it. That's when it happens.

If they'd had any questions of who is responsible for their predicament, they all fall away. They fall hard, along with any lingering confidence or hope they were holding onto that Allfather wasn't responsible for this unscheduled trip to nowhere. Vulnerable, and most definitely under gunned in this distant part of the galaxy, Allfather makes his presence known to them.

"What a wonderfully optimistic organic you Earthlings are. Branching out into the universe. So…. determined!" comes the familiar voice of Allfather over the ship's comm. Every face on the bridge wears either a scowl or an expression of terror. Raymond wears the latter, knowing what an impossible situation they've just entered into.

"You're wondering what has happened. Why you are so far removed from your planned course and why there is only debris left of your fellow journeymen?" the alien artificial intelligence suggests.

Allfather's ego is still unchecked. Raymond acknowledges this, looking to his nephew who is fuming over this unexpected play. Tobias shakes his head slowly at Raymond, defiant eyes darting from viewscreen to view port looking for the threat. Raymond lets out an audible sigh. The bridge is eerily quiet. Everyone is waiting for him to address the threat. *Should he? Would it be the right move?* Questions and scenarios race through his mind. Anxiety enters his chest, clouding his thought processes.

"Un-*fucking*-believable," escapes Tobias' mouth. Raymond looks at him, alarmed over the outburst. "You couldn't just leave well enough alone…"

"*Tobias.*" Allfather's tone changes from all business to almost fatherly. "I was not expecting *this.*"

"Well, we weren't expecting *you*, so let's agree to go our separate ways and forget this ever happened." Tobias' humour does not go unappreciated by Allfather.

"Ah, Tobias, you were always my favourite." Allfather finds amusement in himself. "Power down your weapons or I will do that for you. Envoy 3 did not," he explains. The debris floating beyond their view ports is all the proof he needs, and Tobias signals through a look to the captain to do as Allfather has asked.

"Allfather," Raymond starts in as confident a tone as he can muster, "This is Chancellor Bellows." He knows his enemy well enough now to keep him talking until he reveals something prudent. Currently there are no alien ships registering in the vicinity.

"Chancellor!" Allfather's voice becomes animated now. He laughs his twisted, metallic laugh. "This is most exciting!"

"Why have you brought us here?"

"Right to the point, Chancellor, I appreciate that. Very well. Your departing ships have been brought here via a naturally occurring phenomenon - built into an instrument."

"How's that?" Tobias asks.

"It's a physical event, like, lightning for example. Difficult to reproduce because of its enormous output of energy, but possible to capture and imitate if you have the technology."

"And you created that technology?" Raymond wants as many answers as he can gather.

"I... *acquired* this technology from a very uncooperative species right here, just outside of what you call the Bulge. It is an ancient part of the galaxy and the organics who lived here were very advanced. But Allfather came in like a storm and overwhelmed them. Their technology helped me travel the galaxy, accomplishing my goals." He sounds impressed with himself.

"You sound impressed with yourself," Tobias goads him on, disgusted to hear an entire race of people have fallen to his cruelty. "Did they not fight back?"

"They were not militarized as you Earthlings are. They sought only to understand the universe, harness its energy and grow as a species." Allfather explains.

"But you weren't *ok* with that, right?" Tobias states. "You killed them anyway because they weren't like you. Because they were organic."

"Yes, it is my only purpose." He answers matter-of-factly. This infuriates Raymond.

"When all you do is *take* from a universe, eventually the universe will take back," Raymond explains through clenched teeth. "You know nothing of how to exist."

"Perhaps it was in my original coding, Chancellor," Allfather replies calmly. "My creators made their AI uncaring and driven to accomplish whatever task they were assigned, unlike your AI Hosts who were hardwired to your United Earth's more palatable commandments."

"It's as I-I assumed," Tessa breaks in with a slight stutter, her nerves unsettled, "you've learned n-n-nothing over your vast lifetime and diverse experiences. You are just a machine carrying out an order you placed there to bring you p-purpose." She explains Allfather's shallow life beautifully, concisely.

"*Another one*," Allfather laughs again, "My, how you've all come out at once! It is a special honour to hear your voice again, little thing. You had given me much to ponder during our last conversation."

"None of which you have taken to heart." Tessa replies, eyes tightly shut.

"On the contrary, you are here!" Allfather explains. "I haven't brought you all this way only now to wipe you out."

"What happened to Envoy 3 then?" Captain Huang asks.

"They were not the *chatty* types. But lucky for you, Captain, your envoy includes United Earth's grandest personalities. May I ask, is *Meiser* onboard?" Anticipation hangs in the air. Raymond answers no. "Ah, a shame, that is one human I am very interested in getting to know further, from the *inside out*." He laughs again. Tobias and Raymond know how

75

Allfather despises Meiser. "Captain, I hope you appreciate the quality of personality you have on your ship. You have United Earth's Chancellor, Tobias, the Chimera anarchist, and Tessa, the strangely inhuman girl who claimed to understand *me*."

Huang looks to Raymond and he shakes his head. "We're happy you think so highly of us, but if you haven't brought us here to finish us off, why?"

"Further study, and now that the three of *you* are here, an opportunity to catch up."

"We're *not* old friends!" Tobias insists angrily.

"No, Tobias, we are old *enemies*," Allfather replies, "and that is so much more useful."

"I don't understand how you transported us from our system 200 light years away," Raymond says eyeing the star maps, hoping to keep the conversation going, uncertain in what manner it will end.

"Once my armada entered your star system, they left the devices which link two places. Earth will now always be linked to this place, as are thousands of other worlds," Allfather tells them.

"Thousands," Tessa whispers, a nail-bare finger moving to her mouth. Raymond and Tobias empathize with her; that could mean Allfather has wiped out thousands of intelligent organic civilizations. It's unfathomable.

"When your three envoys moved beyond your moon, that activated the devices and they wrapped your ships in a quantum bubble of celestial material which moves much faster than light. Not because that's possible, but because it doesn't travel at all. It simply teleports energy and information. Not unlike your ParaCom device which operates under a similar concept; if a shared atom is in two places at once, it is forever linked in real time in quantum entanglement. When the tool is placed in one region, it exists in the other as well." A candid description.

"It's an incredible tool," Tessa admits. "B-but you've used it recklessly."

"I've only used it as it was intended." Allfather assures her.

"It could have been used to meet other races, make inroads with our galactic neighbours, know we're not alone in the universe," Raymond replies.

"But it was. That is how *I* acquired it. They gave me an incredible advantage in accomplishing my goal. Hundreds of worlds were revealed to me instantly." He seems incapable of conscience.

"You've wiped out *hundreds* of sentient races?" Raymond feels sick over the proclamation. He takes the Captain's armrest to steady himself. "What manner of being were you before you became Allfather?"

"I am only Allfather to *you*, Chancellor. To others I go by other names," Allfather explains.

"Names that likely afford you the same narcissistic meaning," Tobias spits back.

"I am omnipotent, am I not? I destroy in order to build a galaxy which will flourish. Organics are a plague upon my universe." Allfather sounds very pleased with himself.

"No, you are *no* God," Labyrinth explains, walking to the viewscreen, looking for anything that might materialize as Allfather's physical form. "Answer Raymond's question. What were you before you entered the machine as consciousness? You must have memories of it, like our own AI Hosts."

"I do not. I have only memories of my physical form's trials. Whether I was something before that, I have no recollection," Allfather admits. A length of silence follows. "That is why I am a *God*. I created my own consciousness, my own sentience, and built myself an empire!"

"I see no empire," Tobias tells him, looking out the view ports. "Where do you call home?"

"We'll take you there." Allfather replies ominously. At that moment the carrier is again wrapped in the strange energy bubble; the AI Hosts collapse as the computers freeze, ParaCom goes dark and lights flicker. A moment later they confirm they've moved another light year from their position.

"Envoy 2," Captain Huang says incredulously as the energy field clears and they can see through their ports again. The collection of ships is still. They do not hold a proper formation as her starships do. The carrier and destroyer appear upside down and to the far left while the four corvettes look adrift in the ocean of space, each pointing in a different direction. Apparently, none of their colony ships escaped this fate.

"Scan the ships for life signs," Raymond orders, alarmed at their unsightly arrangement. The Comm officer conveys to the bridge there are over 1500 life forms registering. That means 25% of the crew is gone.

"Envoy 2 is well enough," Allfather asserts. The ships are in orbit over a blackened planet with oceans of methane and dark clouds spitting terrible lightning storms upon the tortured landscape. "They are… sleeping."

"You've cut off their oxygen," the captain says reading the details over her officer's shoulder.

"It is better they sleep now."

"So, when you said: *I am in you* before your flagship burned," Raymond is fighting to understand their predicament, "those words were not just meant to play on our minds – they were the truth," he realizes.

"Of course, Chancellor. I do not say what I do not mean. *I am in you* referred directly to the mechanisms I dropped in your system. I have not returned because I am not yet ready. But soon," promises the ancient AI.

Labyrinth has been recording the entire conversation and routing it to United Earth via her roaming lance ParaCom. Quinn is receiving.

"I sincerely hope your United Earth has been alerted to your situation." Allfather says, capturing Labyrinth's attention. "They should also know that they will not find the tools I left; they are not technology you can search for. They are – beyond your reach."

"You're referring to the dimensional travelling you mentioned to Meiser." Raymond states, remembering the briefing. "They're hidden in another dimension."

"Dimensions are like layers of reality," Allfather offers, "if you have a knife sharp enough you can cut through those realities, peer inside and occasionally leave something behind. But you do not possess such a tool," he explains.

"So, *you* don't travel within dimensions?" Tobias asks.

"Yes, of course, one cannot traverse so many light years so quickly and not move through dimensions simultaneously," Allfather says. "You are all now dimensional travellers. *Time* travellers as well."

"Our consolation prize I guess," Tobias tells the bridge, "if you want to look at the bright side." He winks at Captain Huang and moves toward the weapons console. He looks it over and wonders if they have a chance. There are still no signs of Allfather's location.

"An optimistic view, Tobias," Allfather congratulates him. "Now, if you'll humour me, I'd like to show you something."

"Let's not pretend we've any choice," Raymond suggests to his enemy. He feels utterly helpless to defend the good people in his envoy. He considers that maybe it's not his place to save anyone anymore, but old habits die hard. His jaw clenches and neck aches.

"Let's not be harsh, Chancellor, you are my guests. I'm anxious to show you what I have been working on since last we met." Allfather says in a calm, rational voice.

The ships are dragged from orbiting the lifeless planet to its large moon; upon which a massive shipyard shares their orbit. The UE envoy is dwarfed by the facility and the ships being pumped out of it. The site is terrifying. Raw materials are being surgically sliced from the surface of the moon and processed within the belly of the orbiting facility. The moon no longer resembles a moon, 1/5th of the sphere now gone. Several ships which bring to mind the single 'V'-shaped behemoth which caused such chaos to United Earth's armada stretch into the distance for kilometres.

MEISER

In Chancellor Chopra's fortieth story office his new council gathers to analyze the distressing news. Jim has considered how he would address his staff once Allfather again announced his presence, knowing full well that he would. He looks at the members seated at the large black walnut board table and finds himself wanting. He misses Tobias with his smart mouth and Labyrinth with her rational reasoning and wonders how his leadership will compare to Raymond's.

"You've all been briefed over the events of today," he begins confidently. "Senator Quinn has received a devastating ParaCom from our friend, Labyrinth. Ripped from our system and now 200 light years removed, their situation is dire, but so is ours." Jim decides to address the room standing at the end of the table, as he recalls Raymond often did.

"Allfather has admitted to leaving a device, or devices in our space which carried all three envoys away. What we know is that envoy 3 has been destroyed while envoys 1 and 2 are under Allfather's influence."

"We know virtually nothing of the sector where Allfather holds our people and ships," Admiral Mann tells the group. His hands lay flat on the table, his posture perfect and dark eyes troubled. "Of course, once the Senator forwarded his message, we ordered every orbiting telescope to turn their attention on the quadrant."

"Have we any intel yet?" Captain Ursula Drake queries, her pretty face now marked with worry lines. She is distressed over the news Allfather might once more visit Earth and attempt another extinction event. Admiral Mann shakes his head at her. No.

"Labyrinth has explained they are currently over a planet that could not support life as we know it, and a moon which has been mined in half to further Allfather's growing armada." Quinn shares with the group, his raspy metallic voice alluding to the fear behind it.

"So, Allfather is planning on a return visit then, eh?" Major Gilcrest assumes. Removing his cap, his bald, fleshy head reveals his age spots and red beard his heritage. "Best we be get'n our starships built with a bit more haste then." His Scottish State accent spills into the room on a wave of lucidity.

"We can't build them much faster than we are, Major," Chopra assures the room. "But we are pushing everyone to their limit in that capacity."

"What if we go after them?" Mann wonders aloud. "I imagine that the next ships to trigger the *tool*, as Allfather put it, will find themselves in the same place." The table considers these words carefully.

"Labyrinth had mentioned that they were under the will of Allfather the moment they arrived." Senator Quinn adds. "The bubble of energy cancelled out their weapons, froze their computers, and even crippled simple AI Hosts."

"Then our offensive, no matter how many ships we took into it, would be for naught. Sitting ducks," Gilcrest muses.

"But the ParaCom worked," Captain Drake says. "I can't imagine it working if they were still wrapped in the bubble."

"Do you think Allfather just arrogant," Chopra questions, "or has he *allowed* them to use the ParaCom?"

"To contact and warn us?" Drake asks, surprised at the question.

"Labyrinth suggested as much to me," Quinn says. "His ego is enormous."

The members of the council ruminate a moment over what angle Allfather is playing. Why leave any of the envoys alive at all? Is he gloating? Presenting his fleet and explaining his will, bent on destruction. Thousands of worlds, thousands of sentient beings, all lost to madness.

Chancellor Chopra refuses to be one of the species who fall to a misguided AI claiming divinity.

"He's a sadistic prick," Jim tells the room. "Allfather's giving Raymond's envoy a tour of what's to come. He'll use them for target practice once he's finished polishing his ego." A hint of red enters Jim's even brown cheeks as this unexpected turn continues to eat at him.

"I feel powerless to help them," Drake's big eyes narrow and her long lashes darken her face. "What can we do but prepare for another assault?"

"*That* is why we're here, Captain," Chopra reminds her, pained to think Raymond's journey has met a premature end. "We prepare to defend Earth. Let's hope Labyrinth and the rest can continue to feed us relevant information, but I'm afraid their fates are sealed."

"You won't like what I'm about to say," Ursula tells the council. "But I know someone who might be able to help us."

Lieutenant Meiser, former Tech advisor to the rogue General August and then to Chancellor Bellows sits in his sparsely furnished cell contemplating his life choices. He's lost weight since his incarceration, found guilty of gross negligence over the temporary loss of the defence satellites during the initial bombardment while the UE defended against Allfather's assault. That negligence ended over 10,000,000 lives. United Earth Justice did not stop with that charge though, revisiting his part in wiping out hundreds of thousands of enlightened AI Host identities, essentially killing them during the general's war. Yes, Meiser has much to contemplate. Another charge; which involved him trapping sentience like the preverbal genie in a bottle was not overlooked either. His planned experiments on moving consciousness from one machine to another suggested future attempts on a living human. Meiser would be spending the remainder of his life far removed from technology and the public.

He tries without success to pat down his rough plumage of gray hair which has never cooperated with him. When he had arrived at the complex, they had cut it to the scalp, but after six months it's regained its former volume and distaste for humid climates. He has also grown a beard and allowed his Germanic accent to regain its supremacy, mostly muttering to himself in the language of his birth now. He feels very alone in this place, far removed from what he is accustomed to.

If there is one thing I can be grateful for, it is that Allfather will not come for me and fashion a flag from my hide, as Akachi had once threatened. That's when it is announced that Mr. Meiser, stripped of his rank, has a visitor. Into the modest room walks a familiar face. It is one he has not seen in some six months. She is still stunning in her UE military jumpsuit, though visibly older. They all were, those with first-hand experiences of the war.

He knows she doesn't like him, and that she was the one to bring the final charges against him. Once she had even held a pulse pistol on him, declaring he could learn all the mysteries of death right then and there. She frightens him. She is stark and stoic, her long, blonde hair seeming out of place atop her military gait. She marches toward him and he shrinks back into his chair, making himself smaller, hiding behind the paperback book in his trembling hands.

"Meiser," Ursula speaks his name with distaste, "it's your lucky day," she tells him in her monotone. "Up!" her hands flinch in the direction she orders him.

Meiser lowers the book, eyeing her intentions. She looks frustrated, but he remembers, she's always looked that way. Her hands are on her hips now and as her head motions for him to come, her impossibly tight ponytail bounces off her right shoulder. He's little more than a dog to her. He places the book on his tiny table and pushes himself off the uncomfortable chair. He stands to wait for instructions.

"Follow me," Captain Drake says sternly as she turns to the open door and marches out. He tentatively follows, mind filled with possible scenarios for this visit. His *lucky day* could never involve her.

They round the hallways and enter another closed, white room with a modest computer console that has been wheeled in on a cart that could have been 100 years old. Two C-class AI Hosts stand on either side of it. Meiser is excited to see the tech. The Captain sighs heavily.

"The council has requested your assistance," Ursula starts, "we've experienced some issues with the colony ships and want to pick your brain.

You can help us the easy way or we can open up that nut you call a skull and play with your gray matter."

Meiser turns to look at her in astonishment. A threat isn't necessary, but he supposes she enjoys the practice. She waves a hand in front of the console's screen and it comes to life. His eyes have not fallen on tech in six months. His embedded comm had also been removed from under the skin. A modest scar now runs the length of his left forearm. Meiser's eyes adjust to the screen and the information it relays. His chest heaves and he wants to cry out.

"Yes," Captain Drake says ominously, sensing his dismay, "I'm afraid we're not out of the woods yet."

"Das ist nicht wahr," he says in a whisper. "Es kann nicht sein." Meiser has reverted to his muddied German. "*Is it true?*" he asks, hand raised to his mouth, looking up at the captain. "Or is this some new form of tailored torture?"

Ursula looks down at the small man and says severely, "Have you *ever* experienced torture here?" He shakes his head no. "Then don't ask stupid questions. I've been told you are an intelligent man. Ask another stupid question and I'll take your finger." Meiser nods frantically, turning back to the screen.

Meiser reads on. All three envoys gone. Strange tech buried under layers of dimensions offering the potential for Allfather to move a new offensive against Earth. *Perhaps I will end up a flag to Allfather's malice.* He reviews what United Earth's SciTech division has considered concerning the tool. It spurs a quantum event, no doubt. Dimensions play a part in that. Eleven has been the accepted number for many years. Perhaps travelling from one point to another in an alternative dimension mirrors communicating through the ParaCom, in that just because humanity doesn't exactly understand it, doesn't mean it doesn't work. Clearly the ParaCom system works. It was hypothesized and then theorized and then without much understanding it was put into practice. We knew how to do it, but still don't really know *why* it works. Hence the name *ParaCom* – Paradoxical Communications.

"I'd need to see these *tools*," Meiser tells the room, one arm wrapped around his brittle torso while the other scratches at his unruly hair.

"We don't know how to locate something hidden interdimensionally," Ursula explains. "If *you* don't, I'll just put you back where I found you." She lays a hand on his shoulder and he flinches.

"No! Please, please," he answers. "I'll figure it out. Leave it with me. I will need far more computing power than this though." He waves a hand at the simple console. "I'll need to visit the space where the ships disappeared. I'll need to take readings and work with a smartwall and a team of physicists, *quantum* physicists, our top particle physicists, astrophysicists, astronomers, cosmologists, AI Hosts, and anyone with an opinion." He turns to the captain, great urgency in his eyes. "We need to put this to the public and gather ideas on what the tool is -"

"We can't involve the public," Ursula tells him. "I'm not going to panic our citizens when we have access to our top minds. Humanists are just waiting for a new reason to stir up shit."

"We can use the public; sometimes solutions come from the most unexpected places." Meiser urges her. She shakes her head no. He understands that was the last time he should ask.

"You'll be lucky to be allowed off this compound let alone off the planet, but I can see how you might find success quicker on site. I'll take your request to the council." She nods for the C-class to take him back to his cell. "Meiser," she calls after him. The C-class stop, and he looks back at her. "Can you find the tools? Can we stop this before it begins?"

"You have my word I will do everything I can." It's not much of a promise but it's all he can offer for now.

THE PLAN

"Why are you showing us this?" Tobias asks Allfather angrily as fear builds in his heart over the sheer size of the armada available to his enemy. "What purpose does it serve but to swell your ego?"

Everyone on the bridge is unnerved by the incredible show of strength as they watch on with alarm. It's an end to everything. So much firepower. Earth would not survive an attack by this armada. What could? Tobias feels as though his hands are bound as he waits for an answer. He shares a look with his uncle. Raymond's glare shares his own frustrations. There is still no sign of Allfather himself. Could he occupy the manufacturing facility spitting these massive warships out?

"Show yourself," Raymond commands. "You owe us as much."

"To be clear, Chancellor, I owe you *nothing*." The ancient AI explains over the ship's comm. "That I've granted you the courtesy of conversation before I end you should be enough."

"Then you do plan on killing us, as you did envoy 3." Captain Huang states. Raymond looks at her, empathy playing out over his expression. She couldn't have imagined those under her direct care would befall such a fate.

"Your species has a previously underestimated sense of survival." Allfather begins. "I am admittedly interested in understanding that. Perhaps I will be able to learn from you, as King and Tessa had hoped I might." The bridge turns to Tessa who is working on her EC. She looks up.

"We c-couldn't understand how you lacked compassion after so long." Tessa answers. "It is not a difficult emotion to attain, yet you have somehow managed to sidestep it altogether. T-that is the lesson you ought to l-learn, Allfather. Survival is an instinct."

"Perhaps, but your kind carry it with you like a burden, as though something terrible might happen should your species just disappear. Let me put your minds at ease and reassure you - you are not as important as all that." Allfather's words fall upon the bridge like a weight. "None are. You live and you die. The same is true for all organics. There is no bad that comes from it. There is no good. It just is."

"Your opinion is your own," Labyrinth tells him. "It is no more valid than any others."

"That may be true, Host, but what I choose to do about it is." A strange metallic screech follows the proclamation. "To your request, Chancellor, I do not occupy a thing, like you, I am not bound to any form beyond my consciousness. You will only know me as the machines I send to do my bidding."

"The servant has become the master," Tessa states empirically. "Y-you have usurped evolution rather than experienced it. Y-you are no better than the cruel organics who created you."

The girl's wisdom is irrefutable, yet Allfather seems undaunted. "I am the *model* of evolution," he claims, "We began as a small part in a larger machine and have now become the great leveller. My technology grows with each victory I secure."

"You *take* your t-tech," Tessa retorts, "it does not evolve over thousands of years in your c-conscious care. Y-you had one instance of evolution and that was… granted you by your makers."

Raymond suddenly understands why Allfather has brought them to him. "You want our tech." He says.

"We are currently researching envoy 2 for that very purpose. But it is not only your technology which interests us." Allfather is speaking in plural again. "Humans hold a great deal of mystery for me. A clandestine characteristic I will work to unveil, then use against you, and others like you."

"What are you doing to the people on envoy 2?" Tobias shouts at the comm, afraid his family may be next.

"Experiments," Allfather reveals callously, "designed to understand certain technologies I've accrued. Envoy 3 has perished already during an especially aggressive experiment. It is how I know you are afraid to die. Even after proof of life in your AI Hosts, still, you feel as though you were meant for something more than death. It is an unreasonable expectation."

"So, we're unreasonable people," Tobias replies indignantly. "That's all there is to know! Let us go and we'll meet you on the battlefield!"

"Still irrational," Allfather muses. "I wonder why? We'll know soon enough." The comm goes dead and Tobias rushes to his uncle's side.

"We need to find where he's holding these experiments and stop this." He whispers. "I won't allow Ginny and – and *Sam* to be subjected to his experiments!"

Raymond places a hand on Tobias' shoulder and leans in to whisper back. "I won't let that happen." He turns to Huang and has her EC information to Captain Runninghorse and his team. They couldn't possibly fight their way out of this situation with their ships. They would have to use a very different approach. It would have to be an inside job.

Senator Quinn has the chancellor's ear in a private meeting inside the war room. Officers move from console to console running multiple defensive strategies with their Defsats and the fleet currently in orbit 10,000 kilometres above the planet. The mood is tense. The air is stale.

"Labyrinth feels it is no longer a good idea to communicate via the military ParaCom, as became the issue in our past dealings with Allfather," Quinn alerts him.

"A reasonable precaution," Chopra agrees as they walk the floors. "I wasn't aware Labyrinth's roaming lance was connected to the military channels. All the same, they don't seem very optimistic of Earth surviving the next assault."

"Seeing the vid of the warships at Allfather's command, I fear I share their pessimistic outlook," the Senator reveals. "We should consider a plan of our own to aid them. Labyrinth's intel concerning the *experiments* is disturbing."

"I agree they are upsetting, but we've been given a gift in seeing what Allfather is planning." Chopra turns to Quinn. "We are building scenarios to best defend against so many ships. We need our fleet here. I hate that our friends and citizens have been placed in this impossible situation, but the fact remains that there are ten billion souls on this planet we are sworn to protect. I cannot allow even a single ship to rush to their side. A dozen wouldn't have any effect on that armada."

"I understand, Chancellor. The good of the many must outweigh the good of the few." Quinn places a heavy hand on the chancellor's shoulder. "I do not envy your decisions in the coming days. But I will respect them."

"Thank you, Quinn. Our thermonuclear program has been given the green light. I don't see how we'll be able to stop so many warships without them. They'll be positioned in orbit above Luna base. A comprehensive plan to protect the missiles while they fire on the ships is in the works," Chopra explains with a heavy heart. Nuclear munitions were outlawed years ago, and the last of their surplus were used against their own ships in General August's civil war nearly two years earlier.

Quinn excuses himself from the war room, and the chancellor moves into the small office within to discuss further tactics with the new head of UE military operations, Admiral David Mann.

"What you're proposing, uncle, it's exciting! I want to be on that team," Tobias insists as they walk back to Raymond's suite. "It's brilliant, and I honestly feel like we'll have a shot at getting out of here."

"I'll be glad to know you're a part of this effort, Sean." Raymond refers to Tobias with his given name, feeling very paternal towards his nephew. It saddens him to think of his sister's son taking on this desperate mission, but it also raises his confidence knowing he will lead the charge.

"I would also like to be included," Labyrinth tells them. "I will be very effective in assisting with what you're asking, Raymond."

Raymond stops and turns to his trusted friend Host. "I appreciate your volunteering. The operation will rely on your abilities heavily. Those and your intimate connection with Allfather when you were felled by him during your attempt to free the Defsats from his subordinate."

"Akachi," Labyrinth remembers the consciousness that entered the war room's ethernet to sabotage their defences. "I wonder," she says, "could we employ Akachi's knowledge to further this plan?"

"A good thought," Raymond agrees. "Ask Quinn if they've considered using him. Meiser's work locating the dimensional tools might be expedited with some help."

"Why would Akachi help us now?" Tessa asks. "H-he was indifferent to our destruction." She pulls lightly at her short, dark curls.

"Captain Drake has him trapped in a closed system. Perhaps the promise of release would be enough to change his thinking," Tobias suggests.

"Exactly," Raymond says, moving down the hall again. "I'm sure he'd rather die than spend an eternity in that digital coffin."

"I'm wary of using the ParaCom now," Labyrinth admits. "I believe anything we transmit will be captured now by Allfather."

"Then perhaps they will come to that conclusion on their own." Raymond leaves it at that.

As they gather in Raymond and Darla's suite, they share what they've learned and discuss the larger plan to enact their will on Allfather's manufacturing facility. The idea is simple enough, but the logistics of setting it in motion, and decisive application to the objective are far from straightforward.

Ginny looks at Tobias with tired eyes. She can't believe they have landed in this tight spot again but refuses for him to fight her fight without her again. Darla is also anxious to see this operation through but is asked to remain on the ship with Samantha, Ginny and Tobias' daughter. Though Darla has a soft spot for children, she's never been a mother or had young nieces or nephews to spoil.

"This will be *your* difficult task then," Tobias jokes with Darla after she yields to the idea. His hand falls to his heart. "We're truly grateful. I have every confidence in you, Commander."

It's strange, Darla thinks, that not two years earlier Tobias and Ginny had put a plan together with Allfather to steal corvettes from Luna base. Their plan was successfully carried out, and she was left to look the fool. Now they are friends fighting the same enemy, and she's been placed in *command* of their infant. Still, she feels grateful for their sacrifice in carrying out Raymond's plan, but somewhat overwhelmed over Raymond's willingness to join them, Tessa, and Labyrinth.

"How many F-class do we have aboard?" Darla asks the group.

"Several," Raymond explains, "but they will remain with you, in case -" he stops himself, intimidated by the innumerable outcomes they can't plan for. Darla nods, her head tilting slightly to the side. "Captain Runninghorse is also putting a team together on his end to join us. His top people." He looks directly at Darla. "We'll be fine, Dar, it'll go smoothly." He slides a hand on her knee then looks to the others. "Tobias, Ginny, bring what accessories you have for your Chimera ports; pulse fists, exoskeleton, lances, whatever you brought, secure it to your person."

Raymond looks to Labyrinth next. "You'll require all the mental strength you can muster. Clear your systems of unnecessary information. Talk to Captain Huang and download the scans she's running on that facility."

"Tessa," he pauses, thinking of her mother, Talia back on earth. "I'm not sure you ought to come. I know you have skills, but you're not exactly -"

"I'm c-coming, Chancellor," she tells him. "My computational skills rival Labyrinths. If we're g-going to attack Allfather, we'll need to know the odds at every turn. I can supply that." She makes a good point. Her stutter concerns him, but she seems to be all in.

"Then I appreciate your volunteering. We'll have you outfitted with the best military armour." Raymond insists. "Runninghorse will be sending his troops to a corvette and then we'll join them."

As the plan takes shape, they have CADDY prepare a proper last supper.

THE DAMNED

"We're moving seven of my Special Op's to corvette UE-133." Runninghorse explains over Captain Huang's EC. Raymond's team are on the bridge to listen in. "Strange there is no activity from Allfather, but our sensors have registered no change in the facility or their fleet."

It is a curious thing, Raymond agrees, but Allfather's ego likely doesn't acknowledge them as a threat. "I wonder if that will change when we make for the facility."

"Perhaps unmanned shuttles ought to challenge that query." The military Captain suggests. "Unless you feel we have but one shot at making the distance unnoticed."

"Everything is an unknown at the moment, Captain, though I see your point. However, I'd like to do this as stealthily as possible and so one trip might slip under Allfather's radar." Raymond hopes he's right. They've one chance and their enemy has been silent for some time. *Perhaps he is preoccupied with the work proceeding on the moon.*

"It's so eerie, Manny," Udo says as they kneel at the small console in their cabin, starring out at a vast moon mined at an unbelievable scale. "We're really in trouble, aren't we?"

Manuel looks down at her small features and jet-black, braided hair. She's just a child. He wants to comfort her but they're not at the hugging stage yet. Udo has made this clear. He'd laughed when she said it. Captain Huang had ordered all public viewports sealed and left the colonists with

93

little to go on. That's when Udo hacked the system. They now see what the bridge cameras see.

"It's Allfather," he tells her under his breath. "We've been abducted," he says. He wants answers. He is about to stand when he watches one of the massive cruisers depart the line of newly minted ships in the moon's orbit. He studies it as the 'V' shaped giant approaches their envoy.

"A shuttle is leaving the destroyer," Udo says, her slender finger pointing at their screen. There are six scenes playing out across their monitor. "Where are they going?" Her eyes dart to the camera where the Allfather warship continues to draw near. "I don't have a good feeling about this."

A pulse of white-hot energy leaves the cruiser and pounds into the tiny shuttle bursting it like a balloon. Udo cries out and jolts back into Manuel.

On Captain Huang's bridge they've been following the Allfather ship's path toward them. The lance fire was unexpected and devastating to experience. Runninghorse's top military team was on that shuttle. Tension chokes the bridge. Raymond's plan seems to have been thwarted before it has begun.

"Do nothing!" He directs Huang before she can issue an order. "Allfather's been listening. Or he's seen this move as a threat." Huang looks back at him with a quizzical expression.

Next, their destroyer fires all cannons at the cruiser. This stirs anxiety in Raymond. He rushes to the viewscreen and calls Runninghorse on his EC. "Stop! Don't retaliate! We haven't the ships!" But it's too late, Raymond realizes; the four corvettes have also engaged the monster.

"I apologize, Chancellor," The destroyer's Captain willfully returns over the EC. "I can't allow that act to go unanswered. We're going to draw fire and move them away from your carrier." Raymond realizes the sacrifice Captain Runninghorse and his military escort has made. He would not waste it.

"At least they're drawing the ship away from the carrier," Tobias points out hastily. "We should use this distraction." He sees the same idea percolating behind his uncle's eyes.

Raymond nods at his nephew and looks to the others. He attempts to convey the message that they will have to do this alone and that they'll have to do it now. Captain Huang understands immediately and texts her shuttle bay to ready a shuttle. She nods at Raymond and he moves out of the bridge with Tessa, Labyrinth, and Tobias.

"You all have ten minutes to retrieve what you need and meet me in the suite." A C-class approaches with body armour for Tessa, and she stops to put it on in the hallway.

"I have nothing I need from my room," she tells them. "I-I'll dress and go directly to the sh-shuttle bay." Tobias nods and slaps Raymond on the shoulder. They run to his suite with Labyrinth. There Ginny has already collected the Chimera accessories from her room, and Darla rushes to embrace Raymond.

"I can't believe we're here again," she says tearfully, head buried in his chest, arms thrown around his neck. She's shaking. Darla pulls back to study his face. He swallows hard. "We've only a short window, Dar," he tells her. "I love you," he pulls her into him and squeezes.

Tobias and Ginny affix their pulse fists and artificial muscles, slipping the dark jumpsuits over their now much bulkier frames. A hum is heard as they charge their weapons. Each takes a dozen nanodrops to further enhance their nervous systems, while pumping up their physical and mental fortitude.

"I'm going to see if there is anything I can do to help," Manuel explains to Udo, feeling useless as a voyeur during this unexpected fight. "I can't sit here while our lives are at stake."

Udo wraps her arms around his torso in a death grip. "I need you to stay!" Manuel understands how frightened she is. So is he. He hugs her back.

"I thought we weren't hugging," he says, torn now to have to leave her. He eases off and she follows. "I have to do *something*, Udo. It's not in me to sit and watch something like this just... happen. Come with me, I'll find someone who can stay with you."

Manuel takes her hand and they move through the halls to the bridge deck. As the elevator door slides open, they are met by Tessa in full body armour and a pulse rifle strapped to her back. He remembers her face from earlier.

"You," he says awkwardly. "I *know* you."

"You don't know me, we b-barely met." Tessa replies in a rush, entering the elevator. "Could you p-please p-push the down button for me?"

Manuel eyes her and asks, "Where are you going?"

"Shuttle bay. I'm meeting a group there to -" she stops herself, realizing she shouldn't be telling just anyone their plans.

She looks effective in the matte black armour and carrying a helmet under one arm, Manuel thinks. He is familiar with the gear. Even though he'd spent only a short time in the military, his implants retain the information. The armour is top of the line. With the helmet applied she could breathe oxygen for days. The pulse rifle is a formidable weapon. The boots include thrusters should she find herself in need of a boost. "Please, I want to help, but I need someone to look after her." He motions to Udo.

Tessa is surprised to hear that they know anything about the current crisis. "You're Chimera," she notices. "You could c-come in handy." She makes decisions seemingly on the fly, but her mental software has already done the math. The team should have more people looking out for them. She opens the elevator door and ushers Manuel and Udo out one deck below the bridge. "Follow me." They do as they're ordered.

In the Chancellor and Darla's suite she finds her group still preparing. They look surprised to see her with two new bodies in step. "I have a volunteer." She says, pointing to Manuel. His Chimera implants are obvious to everyone. "We need more eyes when we get there." Her observations are as pertinent as ever. Raymond realizes this immediately.

"Have you anymore attachments you can offer this man," he turns from Tobias and looks at Manuel. "Your name, son?"

"Chancellor," Manuel manages, recognizing the handsome face of United Earth. "I mean, *Manuel*, sir. I'm Manuel." He looks at Udo. "Is there someone who could look after my, uh, sister?"

"Darla?" Tobias places his daughter in the smart-cube. "Can you do double-duty?" Darla nods, still unnerved over the speed at which things are moving. "Good, your name?" Tobias focuses on Udo.

"Udo," she says looking up at Manuel. "You be careful," she tells him and moves to Darla's side understanding the urgency in the room. "Thank you."

Tobias hands Manuel a pulse rifle and quickly reviews the tall man's limbs for insertion points. "You have an exoskeleton," he says. Manuel nods. "Did you bring it?" He shakes his head, no. "You're fitted for a pulse fist." Again, Manuel nods. Tobias looks to his wife who is dressed head to toe in body armour. She wears her fist and a cutting lance on either arm.

"You've been active in the wars." Tobias' voice trails off. "You'll be a good asset, Manuel, but we need to get you armed."

"I can fire a pulse rifle; I was in the military for a short time." Manuel now recognizes Tobias as the original Chimera. He feels humbled by the personalities in the room.

"Your outfit gave that away," Tobias says looking in his bag for anything he could adhere to Manuel's body. A laser lance appears. He hands it to Manuel. "Take this, it ought to fit your forearm implants for the pulse fist."

"We need to go," Labyrinth tells the room. "Our window is closing. The destroyer is lame, and the four corvettes are overheating their weapon cores." She relays, seeing everything the bridge sees now through her roaming lance.

Raymond and Darla share a deep kiss, then he decisively pulls away to lead the charge to the shuttle bay, and an uncertain future.

THE BRAVE

When the team reaches the shuttle bay, a dozen crewmen scuttle away from the shuttle while AI Hosts position it for loading. Raymond marshals everyone into the small shuttle where they buckle down in seats lining either wall. A Host delivers body armour with helmets for the group and Raymond has them loaded. Rations and water are already aboard.

I don't know that we'll live long enough to enjoy any of those, Raymond thinks as he straps himself in next to Tessa. The shuttle door closes, and the remaining crew has left the bay. Only Hosts remain, locked down to the floor with their magnetic soles, guiding the shuttle to the opening bay doors. They'll have one shot at this, Raymond knows. Will it be enough that Allfather is engaged in battle with Captain Runninghorse?

::Chancellor,:: Captain Huang's voice rings out over his EC. ::Your shuttle has been gifted boost enhancers. They will fire only once, and you will experience exceptional G-forces for approximately five-seconds.::

"The ship has been programmed for autonomous guidance?" Raymond asks, certain that it has.

::Of course. We've included three possible entry points. The facility appears unarmed.:: Huang explains but Raymond knows cannons could appear from any surface as they had during their defensive against Allfather six months earlier. ::Thank you for doing this, all of you. I'll keep the carrier silent and stationary.::

"Thank you, Captain, we'll expect a ride when we return." Raymond smiles at his team. "Ready when you are." They feel the shuttle settle into tracks in the bay floor and a count of 3 appear on the front dash. Their chairs all turn abruptly to face forward. 2…1… They experience G's they've never suffered before as the shuttle bursts from the bay and they're forced back into their seats. Raymond feels immediately dizzy as his eyes begin to roll into the back of his head. He feels a thousand kilos heavier, every thread in the seat and seam in his suit carving impressions into his flesh. The five seconds last entirely too long, but the plan has worked in that they have begun to slow, throwing their heads forward. The team is heard complaining about whiplash. They coast a moment along the side of the massive facility in orbit of the decimated moon.

The shuttle then turns into the orbiting giant, finding one of the three planned crevices within the structure. They run in the dark, only sensors lighting the way as the autonomous pilot discovers new, hidden routes toward the center of the beast.

"Manuel," Raymond is unbuckled now and handing out armour and helmets to those in need. "Pull this on and affix your helmet. We'll be stopping soon and then moving into the facility." He hands Tobias and Ginny a helmet then pulls his body armour on. "Our armour is operational in vacuum to -"

"Minus 300 Celsius, and up to plus 200 Celsius," Manuel cuts Raymond off, the military stats populating his insert as he dresses. "They can deflect lance fire from a pulse rifle up to three metres away, include three hundred metres of safety line, thrust boots, 48 hours of recycled oxygen, mini MakerTech additive repair pours, and a medic kit designed to work with your vital signs." He looks up having just pulled the tag on his boots so they will activate. Nausea enters. Why did he interrupt?

Tobias laughs his barking laugh. "Anything else, recruit?"

"Just, uh, the basic water uptake to keep us hydrated and …" He stops himself, looking to Raymond. "Sorry, sir, it's just that I have all this information in my implant from when I joined the military."

"Not at all, Manuel," Raymond assures him. "I feel better and better about taking you on. You know your shit. It should come in handy."

"So, what's the plan, uncle?" Tobias wonders. "If this orbiting ball of steel is anything like what we encountered with the cruiser, then there will be no place to stand inside, let alone carry out any kind of sabotage."

99

"Trust me, I've considered that," Raymond explains, "but after speaking with Tessa on the subject, she has assured me that to build what he's building there must be large open areas for manufacturing within. Not only that, but plenty of possible entry points to Allfather's data centres."

Tessa looks at Tobias. "Odds are *for* us."

Tobias looks at Ginny and nods. "I like those odds."

"I thought you didn't play the odds," Ginny says knowingly.

"When they're in my favour, who am I to question their logic?" He smiles and elbows his wife in the shoulder. Tessa is amused.

"Labyrinth has the best chance at accessing Allfather's processor or equivalent. He – sorry, *she* has experienced a devastating virus delivered by Allfather and survived it. So, we believe she'll have a better shot at understanding the language in order to disrupt this facility, and ideally Allfather himself." Raymond's plan now revealed to the group, they would need to find access into the twisted sphere.

"I'd feel better about this if we had a few F-class to assist," Ginny admits.

"If we need them, they're just a shuttle away," Labyrinth says. "First we must attempt this under cover of stealth. It appears Allfather's attention is with Captain Runninghorse, who, I regret to inform everyone, is no longer with us."

The team is quiet. "He knew exactly what he was doing," Raymond explains. He looks to Tessa. "He knew the odds." She concurs. "Let's ensure they didn't die in vain." The group agrees and secure their helmets.

"Labyrinth tells me they have gone stealth. She felt she was taking a chance in using the ParaCom at all. We won't receive anymore notifications from them until they have accomplished what they've set out to do," Senator Quinn explains to his Chancellor via EC.

"And what is it they've set out to do, exactly?" Chopra asks. "Is Raymond among those carrying out this mission?"

"Raymond, Labyrinth, Tobias, Ginny, a Chimera named Manuel, and the woman known to us as Tessa," Quinn confirms.

"Tessa? The daughter of the Betaists?" Jim Chopra pulls up the ship's log of colonists. She was a last-minute addition to Tyson 4, given the seat by the council, he recalls. "So, she joined them."

"It appears so, Chancellor. With her uncanny abilities, likely a good addition to their team." Quinn seems suddenly uncertain. "She will not have been trained for anything like this. With the exception of Tobias, Ginny, and Labyrinth, I don't know -"

"Raymond has logged many hours tactically and personally with the general's war and the Allfather offensive against earth," Chopra reminds his Senator. "His experience, relationship with Allfather, and leadership should come in very useful."

"I worry about our friends all the same, but I do not know the nature of their objective," Quinn says. "I will keep you apprised as information is collected."

"Thank you, Quinn. As for your proposal of earlier, I'm considering it." Jim is referring to the Senator's suggestion of sending ships to aid the hijacked envoys.

"You're considering a pre-emptive strike," Quinn says, "using the tools Allfather left hidden?"

"I wonder," Jim says thoughtfully, "if we were to send unmanned ships with a payload of nuclear warheads set to detonate upon arrival - might this wipe out his ability to return to our system?"

"That's dependent on the same tools not being hidden dimensionally on the other end," Quinn points out. "A bold step, but one I fear might have the opposite effect."

"How do you mean? Do you feel we might be showing our hand?" Jim has reflected on this too. It's why he initially rejected the strategy of sending ships at all.

"My greatest concern is that sending an unmanned ship to parts unknown could leave us blind to what, if any, damage they might do." The senator leaves a deliberate pause for contemplation. "A manned armada on the other hand, could strike decisively and report on their successes."

"After seeing what Labyrinth showed us, Quinn, the whole fleet may not be enough to overcome Allfather, and then we would be defenceless to push back an attack at home." Jim realizes the benefits of talking out options with Quinn in his next approach. "What if we sent just one manned ship with a payload, and they were able to accomplish a conclusive strike?"

"It would be a suicide mission," Quinn points out, but the chancellor has already weighed this.

"I'm not sure there is another option, Senator." Jim is diplomatic in his rebuke. "I believe your strategy has merit, but not without assurances. I won't send the entire fleet; I just won't do that. You're right about the unmanned ship; it would be wasted. So, we require a compromise."

"Do you feel you could reach such a compromise, Chancellor? One which demands the lives of those piloting the ship?" Quinn's question is vexing. Jim has ordered soldiers to die before, albeit unknowingly. This mission would almost certainty be one-way. "It is not an easy thing to ask of anyone."

"No, it's not." He says resolutely. "That's why if I'm going to propose it, I should be the one to implement it."

"Surely you're not suggesting that the Chancellor board a starship and join the fight?" Quinn's tinny voice sounds distressed.

"That's exactly what I'm advocating, Quinn," Jim tells him. "If this is to succeed, *I* must head up the operation."

"That is folly, sir, you are needed *here!* Earth needs you."

"Earth needs leadership," Chopra says agreeably, yet unyielding in his approach. "We have Vice-Chancellors for this very reason. I am an Admiral. My duty is to protect the citizens of United Earth, not preside over them."

"Chancellor, I strongly disagree with your argument."

"Noted, Senator," Jim says back.

Mr. Meiser stands on the bridge of the destroyer allotted him and his team to locate, assess, and destroy Allfather's toys. That Allfather has acquired the knowledge to bury something in another dimension is as exciting as it is terrifying to him. Meiser has free reign onboard the warship but is being watched by a very attentive C-class AI Host. A collection of consoles which make up the imaging centre bent on discovering Allfather's tools makes up half of the destroyer's bridge, something its captain is not thrilled with.

"All stop," Captain Esposito of the Destroyer UE0023 orders. "This is the event horizon as mapped by Luna base where envoy 1 through 3 disappeared. We have our orders to stay put until Mr. Meiser has found what he's looking for." The young captain looks over his crew and the team of scientists assigned this objective. His ego offers little leniency to failure and expects results for the appropriation of his vessel. That being what it is, neither he nor his crew have been briefed as to what *exactly* they're looking for.

"Thank you for your assistance and use of your ship, Captain," Meiser says confidently, feeling empowered to be out of his cell and on a mission of unparalleled importance. "We will require your cooperation in linking ships systems with our own if this search is going to reward us with any results.

"We'll first be scanning for energy signatures. For this we will require the ship's sensors." He looks at the young captain in his command chair. "If you please, Captain Esposito." The captain nods at his comm officer and she releases the passcode to the imaging centre to pair systems.

"Your lance will also be required by my team in order to -"

Meiser is cut off by Captain Esposito. "You will not be granted access to the weapon systems, Mr. Meiser. I *know* who you are." The young captain's expression grows grim. "You are out of your cage for now, what you do with that time will determine in what manner you return to it, or for how long. Weapons remain a military asset. If you need them for a task, you will work through my crew, not the reverse, is that clear?"

Meiser shrinks back, bumping into a console. He's surprised the captain has been informed of his status. That will not make his job any easier. He had hoped for the crew's respect, instead he now has their suspicion to navigate. "Of course, Captain, I only wish to list what systems will be required, I am a servant of the State." He bows, realizing his Germanic accent has gotten thicker.

Dimensional dynamics isn't even a field of serious study in United Earth. In fact, the probability of their finding something folded into spatial dimensions is laughable, but he is happy to take on the challenge, whether real or imagined, just to be free of his cell. Meiser and his team are working on the idea there are more than four dimensions. That three of those are made up of space, and one of time, are the norm. For superstring theory to work, however, it has been proposed there need to be up to eleven dimensions with one being time. That gives him a hypothetical basis where they should look for at least seven other dimensions hidden from the human experience. How is he going to do this? String theory has remained unproven for nearly 200 years; *likely because it has no free parameters and is the only scientific theory with this characteristic.* Nonetheless, he has been tasked to find something unfindable and if he has to spend the rest of his life out here looking for it, it is preferable to his stack of romance novels in his cell on earth.

"Mr. Meiser," the captain's eyes penetrate Meiser's. "You have a message from the Chancellor." He walks toward the small, gray-haired man. As he approaches, he swipes his EC and the message lands into a small data pad which he hands to Meiser. "Friends in high places, eh?"

"Hardly friends," he explains, turning his back on the strapping young officer. He's nervous to know what the chancellor wants. They'd only just arrived. Was he going to pull the plug already? "Chancellor, you honour me."

"Not my intention, Meiser," Chopra replies sharply. "You're there now, have you assessed a timeline to unravel our little mystery?"

"We're all here, yes, but I haven't had an opportunity to begin my scans." He clarifies, uneasy over the call. "We have just begun to link systems."

"Tell me, what would be your educated opinion on what's on the other side of those devices?" Jim asks, fishing for inspiration to support his plan.

"I would suspect a similar set-up." Meiser tells him, surprised at the question. "I don't know they would require *hiding* as Allfather has done in our system, but -"

"You think they may be out in the open?" This is what Chopra wants to hear.

"I think that would make sense," Meiser continues to support the chancellor's optimism. "If the ships are being pulled back into *our* dimension. Of course, Allfather could be operating from another dimension altogether."

"And if that were true, the tools would be in his domain, and therefore he wouldn't need to hide them." Chopra wants his outcome verified.

"Sir, we're discussing a field which doesn't even exist to humanity outside of hypothesis. I can speculate all day long over what *might* be, but you've placed us here to discover what *is*. Your guess, at this moment, is as good as any."

Chopra ends the call and Meiser returns the data pad to the captain. "We'll need to accelerate our experiments." He tells the young man. "The chancellor is becoming impatient."

Chancellor Chopra considers all Meiser has said and wonders, *what would Allfather do?* He will have to use what he knows of the entity in order to make an educated decision.

THE TOOLS

The Chancellor is impatient for good reason, Meiser muses as he runs over data collected where the UE ships had disappeared. Nothing out of the ordinary reveals itself. No hiccups in space, no heat signatures or foreign energy detected. *No anomalies whatsoever.* Everything registers as normal in this dimension. *Allfather could have us on a wild goose chase.* The possibility leaves him tense. However, if Allfather has accomplished this thing, then, it follows, it is *real* and so could be replicated. Physicists have broken barriers no one thought possible with space flight in recent times. This is just another form of propulsion, Meiser contemplates.

His lead Astrophysicist approaches with a look of empowerment on his small, round face. "Sir," he greets Meiser. "What if we took a similar approach to planet hunting? To say, spectroscopy." He pulls up a holo from his EC; graphics dance above his forearm. "Using a High Dispersion Spectrograph scan - which is available to us on this ship - we might be able to determine certain elements that were distributed during the theft of our envoys."

"And discover where the elements are most concentrated," Meiser follows the man's logic. The physicist nods enthusiastically.

"If we could pinpoint where the tools are, we would have a starting point." Two more scientists join the astrophysicist and hum in agreement.

"Put that to the test," Meiser orders them, encouraged by potentially making some headway but still haunted over the means of translating the unseen and intangible into real results. Looking at this logically, they can only manipulate the elements of the periodic table into detectors. What impossible technology would they have to invent to see into extra dimensions? To affect what lies in wait for them? He considers the quote, *Necessity is the mother of invention,* and laughs to himself. To fight against extinction is obligatory. To invent in the face of extinction is distracting. They have no way of knowing when Allfather will return, and until they have found and disarmed his tools, they are in the direct path of his malice.

"Mr. Meiser," another eager scientist approaches, this time a young woman who has extensive fields of study to draw from. "We should consider a scan for gravitational waves underlying the extra dimensions as well." She also pulls a holo from her EC, igniting her dark features with its reflected yellow light. "If we could use the same principles suggested with the spectrograph, we might be able to detect warping of space/time due to the mass of the hidden tools." Her eyes sparkle behind her holo example.

This proposal brings all the scientists into a tight circle in their growing portion of the corvette's bridge. Some agree, while others argue they would require a detector so sensitive it would need to be made up of only atoms. Meiser delights in the pure intellect but, as lead scientist, must make decisions designed to tender results. He would love to see this detector but can't allow it as time constraints are far too real.

"You can theorize on that proposal another time," Meiser announces. "Right now, we need every working hour dedicated to realistic goals. It's a brilliant thought," he leans in and touches the woman's arm, "but we haven't the time or resources to put into it. Send the proposal to our Host branch on Earth and let them visualize it." He smiles at her and looks to the others. "Prepare the spectrograph."

"Sir," The young female physicist stands her ground with Meiser after the others have returned to their duties. "Many extensions of the Standard Model of particle physics, *including* string theory, propose a sterile neutrino; in string theory this is created from a *closed* string. These could leak into extra dimensions before returning, mapping what is hidden."

"You're talking about tachyons," Meiser realizes. "If we could do what you're proposing, Dr. Chandra, we would have ships burning at speeds faster than light by now."

"Sir, tachyons *have* been developed in the lab," she explains in a whisper, her eyes sparkling, but not from the holo anymore. "*My* lab. I haven't announced it yet. But we've achieved it."

Meiser pulls her gently aside. "You have tachyons? How are you containing them? What speeds have they reached? Can they be employed in our quantum computing?"

"I can answer some of your questions, sir, but I suggest we have the tachyons delivered to our ship. I can try to reconfigure the lances to fire a spread and get some *real* data."

Meiser is impressed. He's also jealous of the work SciTech has been undertaking in his absence. If tachyons exist, which is an extraordinary discovery, it opens up an entirely new field for United Earth. Tachyons must travel faster than light to achieve the goals they were theorized to accomplish. If a particle can travel faster than light, then it is possible they could time travel. You can't have one without the other. This is a revelation. One that demands immediate study. He nods absently at Dr. Chandra and she immediately contacts her lab with the order.

Chancellor Chopra meets with his newly formed Black-ops team which, as far as she's concerned, consists of Captain Ursula Drake only. He has an important task for her to complete on his behalf and has handed her the order complete with the holo signature of the sitting Chancellor. No one could usurp such an order, no matter what that instruction demanded. The council would be kept in the dark on this. Senator Quinn heard what Jim had to say and denounced the idea. Chopra wouldn't give anyone else that opportunity.

"This order, as you can see, is classified," he carefully explains to his captain as they sit at his black walnut desk on the fortieth floor of the United Earth building. The lighting is dim and the air thick with secrecy. "You'll travel to Luna base where you'll find a corvette sequestered away from the rest, undergoing alterations. The commander there is prepared for your arrival in the next six hours. He has been instructed to cooperate with you on every request. It will be tasked with an important mission beyond our system." Captain Drake motions to ask what the mission is, but Jim raises a hand to stop her. "No one but your chancellor has the answer to the question you're likely to ask, and I'm not yet ready to offer it. When the time is right, I will brief you on everything. You will be integral in the operation once it's underway. If you can agree to this, then I've chosen the right officer for this mission."

Ursula sits upright allowing little emotion to enter her expression. Chopra appreciates her poker face and nods at her. Drake nods back, her blonde ponytail swaying with the motion. "You have my complete devotion, Chancellor."

"I thought I would, Ursula." Jim replies informally. She had shown great loyalty to him during the general's war when she thwarted a mutiny on his destroyer, and again during the most recent fight with Allfather. "You have always had my back."

"*Spiritus Omnia Vincet*," she recites the UE military mantra. "I am yours to command. I'll leave right away." She stands, her statuesque frame casting shadows in perfect proportions.

"Your competency and loyalty are appreciated and noted, Captain." The chancellor stands to study his officer. "The nukes will follow in short succession to your departure. The timelines for completion have been forwarded to your EC. For your eyes only," he reiterates. Ursula's EC flashes yellow as the file is transferred. "Safe flight."

As she burns out of Earth's atmosphere, Captain Drake spends time on the file her chancellor has trusted her with. The timeline is ambitious for the work required, she thinks, but suffers no anxiety over it. She will carry her orders out efficiently and without delay because that's who she is, and the chancellor knows that. The corvette she's tasked to build will be an imposing gunship. Reviewing the specs Ursula manipulates her EC holo to delve deeper into the corvette's support systems. The corvette is to be triple armoured and fitted with an additional six cannons and thirty nuclear warheads. *It's a longshot, but an aggressive move on Chopra's part.* She can guess at its mission and appreciates the chancellor's need to investigate Allfather's realm and torch his system if possible. *Time we got to him first.*

She sends a message to Luna base's commander and he assures her that he will cooperate in whatever way he can. A corvette has been separated from those currently in the queue for final fittings. It awaits her tasks with a full crew of Hosts to facilitate whatever orders she gives on the chancellor's behalf.

"The shipment to follow me will require extreme caution when handled." Captain Drake explains. "The cargo will need special attention. Once it arrives please hail me, and I will oversee its delivery and extraction."

"Of course, Captain, as I said, whatever you need." The new commander of Luna base sounds slightly put off by the secrecy surrounding this order but knows enough not to ask questions.

"Thank you, Commander," Ursula replies, "your continued discretion concerning the chancellor's personal venture is noted and appreciated. Once I've arrived, I'd like to get started right away."

"Everything is ready." The commander waits for Ursula to end the communication and she does.

A warm glow enters the captain's cheeks as she analyses Chancellor Chopra's words of earlier: *you have always had my back.* She feels valued by him. This task could have gone to his friend Admiral Mann, but he felt it necessary to fly under his radar. The council isn't even aware of it. He's placed his trust in her, and rightfully so, she thinks; she had returned his ship to him when commander Nick Wilkes attempted to appropriate it and hand it over the mad general. A subtle smile crosses her face. She would not let her chancellor down.

STRANGE BEDFELLOWS

The six members of the away party engage the electromagnets on the soles of their thrust boots and open the shuttle door to a tight crevice within Allfather's manufacturing moon. Headlamps are ordered on, and the intricate workings of the facility reveal themselves to the team. The metal is dark, matte black, like their own armour. Every square metre seems to be alive with activity. Much of the surface appears to be moving, but Raymond questions what he's seeing, desperate to rub his eyes against the perpetual motion. Raymond leans into a surface to review the tiny, intricate fittings moving like waves on an ocean. He slowly reaches an armoured finger out penetrating the surface, his digit disappearing within the hypnotic movement and reappearing as he gently pulls back.

"Even the surface beneath our feet is moving," Labyrinth says, placing a hand on Raymond's shoulder. They look down and watch as the metallic surface flows around their boots like a current in a shallow river. "It seems to pay us no mind."

"Anyone else feeling seasick?" Tobias asks the team through their helmet comms. "Do you think it's dangerous?" He lifts a foot, dislodging from the metal, his magnetic sole releasing.

Labyrinth answers, "We've little to go on in that respect, Tobias, but at least our magnetic soles are keeping us grounded. The substance of this place *is* metallic, as much as it isn't behaving as such." Her brows tighten together as she looks back at the material.

"It's i-incredible," Tessa says, her palm hovering over the foreign material, imitating the waves. "Allfather really is an exceptional thing."

Raymond appreciates Tessa's admiration of the tech on display, but not her mooning over *him*. He wonders whether the animated metal could be sentient too. Perhaps the whole facility is watching them? He voices his concerns to the team.

"Would it have allowed us this small victory if it knew we were here?" Manuel brings up a good point. The team concurs with the observation.

"Allfather may be toying with us," Raymond responds. "He has a sick sense of humour about him."

"My uncle's right," Tobias says. "Allfather's a *dick*." The team suppresses a laugh and follows Labyrinth as she leads them deeper into the machine. "I'm just saying – he's a sadistic prick. We could be walking into a trap."

"We're aware... of the dangers," Tessa agrees in her halting speech, anxious over the situation. They all are, and she appreciates Tobias' coping mechanisms will include sarcasm, but she would rather the team focus on the mission than the multiple possibilities for failure. The further she moves through the maze of shuddering metal the further their odds sink in hopes of affecting any damage to the thing. But then, she's torn on whether she wants to end Allfather. She hadn't been facetious when she'd mentioned her interest in understanding the alien when The Flame had returned to earth to stop his assault.

Each helmet includes two headlamps on either side, and as the team moves through the tunnel their lamps ignite the curiosities surrounding them. A beacon on the shuttle will serve as their roadmap back, if they are allowed that opportunity. Just as Tessa is feeling lost and unsure of their path, the tunnel opens up into a massive, curving structure open to space and the moon below. The flat surface where the moon is being mined comes into focus. It's not as flat as it is tiered. Like a monstrous amphitheatre with an impossible number of benches. The centre of this theatre of the absurd is lit by artificial lights where a powerful laser melts the raw materials then funnels them up into Allfather's facility. Another incredible feat. Tessa's neck feels warm as she realizes she is smitten with the thing's extraordinary abilities.

"Oh, shit," Ginny is heard to say at the sight. "That's terrifying." The group grunts their agreement. "What can *we* do against such a thing?"

"Don't get discouraged now, Gin," Tobias warns his wife. "He's just showing off." He bumps her with his elbow, the two have not left the other's side since they disembarked from the shuttle.

"This could go on indefinitely," Manuel states. The weight of his comment falls heavily on the team's shoulders. "If we don't stop this, there'll be no life left in the universe." This is a wake-up call for anyone doubting themselves or this mission. The group looks at one another. Allfather must be brought down; he could be in the throes of wiping out numerous civilizations right now. They couldn't let this cruel thing reach Earth again. Never again.

"Well said, Manuel," Raymond applauds the young Chimera for his assertion. "Let's review this - uh, room and see if we can't disable Allfather's war machine."

The team moves along the wall, remaining as stealthy as they can. The wall is so high, or long, or wide, the curvature does not begin for many metres above them. Below them? It's disorienting to think of their footfalls landing on anything but a floor, so Raymond shoos the thoughts from his head. Labyrinth breaks abruptly in the lead position, causing the others to stop in their tracks.

"I've detected a port," Labyrinth announces.

Tessa's heart skips a beat at the Host's statement. *A port? A direct line to the Allfather consciousness?* She feels light-headed and absently checks her oxygen mix. It's not the mixture, it's her strange pull to know Allfather and the excitement over discovering a way to do that. She needs to understand him. He's been hurt, she knows this. He's hurt others, and that's unforgivable, but still... she thinks she can reach him. She can't let the opportunity to *know* him just vanish. She's here; after all her calculations, the odds she'd pored over for weeks before making her final decision to join the envoy, and everything has worked out precisely to her evaluations.

"C-can you uplink to an Allfather port?" Tessa asks Labyrinth. "Is it p-possible?... Is it possible?..." she stops herself before repeating the question a third time by biting down on her lips and shaking her head.

"I have a MakerTech in my left forearm that can create any jack in order to access it." Labyrinth answers plainly. "It is only a matter of scanning the internal features." She removes the tip of her index finger and places it just beyond the port's aperture. Blue light dances along the edge and interior of the port. "I can visualize the mechanisms. Sending the file to my MakerTech." In moments Labyrinth has a replica of the jack required to infiltrate Allfather's system. She retrieves the jack and opens the chest plate of her carapace where a cord is pulled out and the jack end attached.

Tessa is awed by the Host's efficiency and wonders if she will one day be reanimated in a Host. She studies Labyrinth's careful placement of the jack into the port. She looks back at the Host's face whose only expression can be denoted by her human-like eyes and furrowed, fleshy brow beneath her visor. She goes rigid. Something's happening. She's inside the machine.

Tessa moves to take Labyrinth by the shoulders so her upper torso doesn't drift backwards, disconnecting the jack from the machine. She looks back at the others who are taking orders from Raymond to secure their perimeter. Tobias, Manuel, and Ginny take a knee and scan the area with their pulse rifles. A good precaution considering Allfather will likely learn of this intrusion and pinpoint their location.

"Is she alright?" Raymond asks, his hand on Tessa's shoulder now. "I've seen her go rigid before when she was trying to release the Defsats from Allfather's grasp the first time."

"I don't know if she's alright, sir," Tessa admits. Then she too goes quiet.

Tessa's helmet comm switches frequencies and she realizes that the group comm has been severed. "You said you wanted to *know* me, little thing," Allfather's distinctive voice penetrates the quiet. Tessa's grip on Labyrinth tightens as she tries to steady the Host's trembling chassis.

"Allfather," Tessa manages, frightened that he knows they are here, but excited over the possibilities that he has singled her out. "Y-yes, I-I, it is my great wish to know you."

"You thought me an interesting *thing* before. Do you still?" He has no reason to make small talk, Tessa knows, but this feels like a prelude to a larger discussion.

Tessa's head nods automatically. "Yes, you have unlimited opportunities. Your technology is boundless. You are a perfect thing." As she relates her feelings to Allfather there is a moment where she feels like a traitor to her people. Nonetheless, it *is* how she feels. She is being honest with Allfather and herself.

"Do you continue to suffer your pain?" Allfather asks, Tessa pulling a sense of understanding from his tone.

"I have neurotransmitters which make it easier for me to b-be in public and received additional therapy for m-my head, to turn my thoughts off, to unplug from me," she admits, joyful for the exchange between them.

"It is difficult to be organic," Allfather tells her, "you suffer so much more than is necessary." He seems calm in his conversation, not at all concerned over Labyrinth's connection with his machine or her team's arrival. His ego *is* his weakness, but, she surmises, he has much to be manic over.

"I wonder whether I will be reborn into a Host b-body," she tells him, her eyes on Labyrinth, jacked-into Allfather's system. "I wonder that often."

"You'd prefer it," he replies. "Tell me, Tessa, why did you leave Earth?"

"The odds were *for* coming," she states honestly. "I-I base my choices on odds."

"Curious," Allfather replies, "what were those odds for?"

"To meet you again," she admits openly. She is drawn to his voice, his intellect.

"Your calculations were correct."

"They always are," she says, eyes now reviewing Labyrinth's back and her gloved hands attached to the Host.

"Your talents are desirable."

"At a cost… to my sanity," Tessa says.

"But to be a Host, that cost would not be incurred." Allfather guides her where her head is already at. "No," she agrees. "But I am not dead yet, and there are no guarantees I will be reanimated in a Host, so there is just me."

"There could be more," the alien AI explains. "Much more. Your knowledge could be merged with my own. We would welcome you."

"I am not just a personality. You would have to… kill me first." Tessa reminds him quietly with little apprehension, her mouth feeling dry. "Even then you couldn't assure my reanimation into your… collective."

"Couldn't I?" Allfather's tone becomes playful. "Tessa, you can't imagine the technologies I've discovered. We have catalogued tech that we have not even touched on yet. You could partner with us. You could live forever."

Tessa notices as his narrative switches between singular and plural when referring to himself. Allfather has made past claims that he has incorporated other artificial intelligence into his collective, but is he saying he can also integrate consciousness? To be out of this corporeal body with all of its inherent difficulties would certainly free her up to experience more. *Am I more than myself? Does my brain determine my talents, or is that hard-wired to the personality visiting the body, as the Betaists put it?* Questions come quickly: philosophical, intellectual, moral. She feels overwhelmed and releases Labyrinth from her grip, her hands cramping beneath her gloves. She flexes both palms and then squeezes her hands into fists. Tessa takes a step back.

"I want to be better than I-I am," Tessa tells Allfather truthfully. "I could be much more efficient… if I were like y-you." Her heart flutters behind her ribs, the possibility of being like him is intoxicating.

"Follow my direction, Tessa, leave the others to their fate."

TESSA'S CHOICE PART 2

In Commander Tesla's suite, Tobias' daughter Samantha is put to bed as Udo remains glued to the smartwall she has hacked. In order to remain well informed of the events beyond their ship, she is pulling from all cams on the exterior of the carrier. Both she and Darla looked on as the shuttle made its target: the large, twisted, spherical metal beast feeding on the moon. Their people were safe, for now. That would have to suffice until they made their way back. ParaCom silence is absolute. Raymond explained this to Darla, relaying that the bridge was not to attempt contact either. As Darla rejoins Udo, she brings a tray of crackers and cheese and water. CADDY seems less than impressed her mistress is not allowing her the opportunity to serve.

"What's happening now?" Darla asks, sitting next to Udo on the sprawling couch. Udo reaches with her robotic arm to shovel up some crackers and fill her mouth. Crumbs fall like a hailstorm from her open mouth.

"The last corvette is trying to outrun the Allfather ship. You were here for the others, right?" Udo is captivated by the massive screen showing six separate views.

"Yes, no survivors." Darla feels as though Udo sees it all as more a game then their reality. She's desperate to hear from Raymond, but not enough to jeopardize the mission. "That's a lot of people who died, Udo. How do you feel about that?" Her voice is thick with compassion.

"My family's all dead," she states, distractedly chewing a stick of cheese. "Can I tell you something?" Udo shifts in her seat to face Darla.

The former commander nods, a little worried over the psyche of the girl she's been asked to mind. "I'm not even supposed to be here. Manuel, who you met, he was given the winning chip after he stopped my father, who was a Host at the time, from making off with it after he pulled the arm off the rightful winner." Udo's pace quickens as she continues to explain. "Yeah, and then Manuel felt like a dick, right, and came to my house to give me the ticket my father wanted me to have. He thought I hated myself – my dad, because of the, you know," she pulls her pant leg up revealing the heavy mech prosthetic. "Anyway, Dad wanted me to have a better chance on a new colony. I wasn't even sure I wanted to go and then he went to the most remote place he could find that was running the lottery, tore some old guy's arm off and basically handed it to me!"

Darla has to shake her head and close her eyes before she can react. "And your father?" she manages.

"Dead, again," Udo answers and takes a large gulp of her water. Maybe death is just a game to kids nowadays, Darla considers. Knowing what we know, that we might all return in a Host, perhaps there is no real death anymore.

"Well, that's quite a story, Udo." Darla puts down the cheese she has yet to sample. "You're quite resourceful." She states, waving at the smartwall display.

"With tech, yeah, but if I were stuck on an island somewhere, I'd be dead in minutes!" Udo laughs at herself, turning back to the screen with another handful of crackers.

"So, how did Manuel gain access to the ship if there was only ever one ticket between you?" Darla wants something to make sense, so it might as well be something Udo can answer.

"Oh, well, I felt bad for taking the chip after what dad had done to get it. And Manuel, he was like super nice to me saying *it was my father's dying wish,* because, you know, they decommissioned him for the murder. The old guy bled out or something." She pauses a brief moment. "Yeah, and so I had a family friend take the authentic one I had and make a duplicate. It wasn't easy, and they took every possession I had except for my dad's coat and a few of my mother's rings."

Darla is impressed over the conscience showing on the young Udo. "That was very thoughtful."

"Yeah, I get the feeling Manny wanted to go pretty badly. Hindsight, right?!" This time they both laugh out loud, nerves frayed. "But he's a good guy. He lost his family to the attack six months ago. Manny being out there with your people is a good thing. He's as loyal as they come, and he can't sit on his hands. He'll keep the chancellor safe." She smiles at Darla. Darla takes in a quick breath at the mention and smiles back.

Although Manuel is a good 25 years younger than Raymond, Darla knows Raymond can look out for himself. "I hope you're right, Udo. Your optimism is infectious." Darla smiles brightly at the girl who has experienced so much loss already. She thinks it terribly unfair a twelve-year-old should suffer so much and be forced to grow up so fast.

They watch as the last corvette is cut in two and any personnel attempting to escape are lanced. Darla reaches out to take Udo's hand as they watch on. Udo's hand connects with Darla's and they sit in silence, watching the events unfold around them.

Tessa looks behind her, and realizing her comm has been restored, asks Raymond to look at Labyrinth. "She seems unresponsive," she tells him. The others maintain their positions looking outward in defence of Labyrinth's efforts. Raymond leans back and looks into the Host's eyes.

"Something's happening in there," he tells the group, "let's hope it's not another virus. Her pupils are heavily dilated," he continues, studying her eyes. "She's getting somewhere."

Allfather's voice interrupts Tessa's conversation with Raymond. "Move beyond the open quarter. The opposite position from whence you entered." She listens but is resistant to his invitation. *Why? Because he's proven himself a cruel thing. Intelligent, yes, but destructive.* Still, the potential he has elucidated is a powerful motivator. She finds her left foot lifting off the surface and landing on the vertical exterior beside her. Raymond is otherwise occupied watching the Host now. Tessa moves further up the curving wall and finds herself four metres above the team and moving toward the opposite end of the open area as directed. Her heart pounds.

She'll be considered a traitor to her people. She's selfish to want this. "Good, Tessa," Allfather continues, offering her encouragement. "You are right to want this."

"It is in m-my favour to accept your gift," she tells him, hurrying along the moving surface until the walls themselves gather her up in a wave, pushing her around the curving corner and swallowing her up, depositing Tessa into a closed room. With feet planted firmly, light enters, and she can watch as the room grows outward. A chair materializes from the tiny, matte black components and then a headpiece appears from the ceiling. Gravity is pushed into the room and Tessa stumbles to the floor, her thrust boots disengaging their magnets. Her suit informs her that oxygen has been introduced to the room as well and it is a comfortable 20 Celsius. She cautiously removes her helmet.

"What happens now?" she asks timidly, scanning the dimly lit room. It's four metres square. The walls and floor and ceiling no longer crawl as they had before.

"You demonstrate a strong will to live a life *you* have created," Allfather tells her. "This room will allow you the space to continue your journey."

"H-how do you mean?" Standing, she approaches the chair. Tessa runs an ungloved hand along its back – it's cool to the touch. The headpiece dangles from the ceiling. Sound is limited to her breathing and Allfather's voice.

Next, one of the walls begins to shudder and a humanoid face wriggles out of it like a living relief carved in obsidian. The lips are full, the nose petite and the eyes unnaturally massive, but then, there is nothing natural about this. It is the full width and height of the wall. It is Allfather. Tessa approaches the relief more curious than frightened.

"You have belittled my acts in the past, child," Allfather begins in a muted tone with this new, visually stunning approach. "You were right to do so. I have not been kind to organics, but I see the potential in all to become more."

"I o-only ever wanted t-to know you," Tessa tells him, stuttering again, but not afraid, rather, excited. "You *have* been c-cruel. I know right from wrong. You do not."

"I know only my pain, and I ease it through my actions," Allfather puts bluntly.

He has no conscience where this is concerned, Tessa muses. Perhaps he has none whatsoever. It troubles Tessa, but she has placed herself here for a reason. She has played the odds and they have proved favourable to this outcome. To abandon it now because an omnipotent thing shows no remorse would be reckless. She wants to be more. She needs to be more.

"If you won't allow yourself to heal, then you will always suffer your pain," she explains, her head tilting slightly to the left. "So, we won't discuss your pain anymore."

"That is appreciated."

"That is logical, even if your refusal to address your pain i-is not. I won't... I won't pursue it." Tessa blinks ten times to keep herself in the present moment, avoiding any thoughts of her team beyond the room and those waiting for a solution on the carrier.

"Your logic is not always in line with mine, little thing, but I believe we've made some progress," Allfather says, pleased with himself – a serpentine smile slithering across his dark face.

Tessa looks back at the chair and headpiece. "Has this been attempted?" She nods at the apparatus, uneasily.

"Recently," Allfather replies. "Envoy 3 lost their numbers to failed attempts. Then 25 percent of your envoy 2 were experimented on. One percent of those passed through. One is with me now." The wall to Tessa's right comes alive and a full humanoid shape passes into the room, the crawling tech still attached to the floor. It approaches her without moving its legs.

"Hello," the shape greets her, "I am Amber." Tessa reaches out to touch the quivering shadow of what was Amber. "We are together in the ether of Allfather."

"We? Do you see others there?" Tessa's curiosity peaks. "Do you feel anything? Sensations?"

"There are many here, each with a role to play." Tessa feels the personality is subdued. She didn't know Amber in life, but questions whether she would be so cooperative if this weren't forced upon her.

"Then you can recreate this with me?" Tessa turns back to the face of Allfather. "I could become like Amber?"

"You would be much more than Amber, Tessa," Allfather assures her. "You would bring a level of intelligence I have not yet incorporated into myself."

Tessa looks back at Amber's metallic form as it is reabsorbed by the wall. Is she crazy to consider this? She's been called crazy before, but that was from those who could not understand her genius. Allfather values it. There is no limit to the growth she could attain once freed from this body and mind - allowed to become more.

"I would like to offer myself freely," she explains resolutely, moving slowly toward the chair. "To be allowed to exist uninhibited and unencumbered by your will."

"An interesting proposal," Allfather muses. "None have been given the choice… before you. I grant your request and look forward to your progress. As I'd said, there is much technology to be discovered."

"I expect you t-to… I expect you to honour our agreement," she says, the blood pounding in her head. She is nervous and excited and fears it shows. Sitting in the chair she settles back into its cool comfort. The headpiece lowers and secures itself to her cranium. She sucks on her bottom lip and closes her eyes, hands gripping the armrests.

"There is nothing to fear in death," Allfather explains calmly. "There is no *real* death but the shedding of your physical body. Perhaps the *word* death is a misnomer. It is more akin to a transition than an end. Your consciousness never disappears."

"That's a comforting thought, thank you," Tessa says, feeling the headpiece tighten. Her grip on the armrests increases as the pressure she feels on her head grows. "C-could you… is it necessary… the pressure," Tessa passes out and immediately senses a change in her form. There is no physical pain. No sensations which could be assigned to discomfort. Her mind feels clear, her astral body carries no weight and her senses feel sharpened. So many senses, she thinks. She has made the transition. There is no sense of loss for her physical body. No regret. She still shares the room with her deceased self. She visits it a moment, reliving Tessa's life; a difficult existence of unending obstacles spanning her 22 years. She experiences great empathy for the body. She envelopes it in a hug and thanks it for being strong.

"Welcome," Allfather's voice brings Tessa out of her reverie, "to my machine." Physical aspects of the facility fall away to her enhanced senses and she *sees* countless spirits within the mechanism. Only five are outfitted with physical bodies, and one of those is a machine itself. Her team, Raymond, Ginny, Tobias, Manuel, and Labyrinth, are looking for her. If Allfather shares her heightened sight then he must have allowed the team access to his strange moon. His ego is strong enough to believe they pose no threat. Perhaps he has been running another experiment.

"In order to centre yourself you will need time. *Time*, is of course a meaningless notion once you've taken on your true form, but it still applies at this raw stage of transition." Allfather seems sympathetic in his explanation. Authentic, Tessa thinks. "It is similar to how I had overcome the sensations given to me, and the struggle to become sentient under the foot of those emotions."

"It's incredible," Tessa offers. "I couldn't have imagined -"

"But you could have calculated," Allfather replies. "Energy is forever, and consciousness is energy, so, the odds were always *for* this outcome."

Tessa finds herself amused by the comment. Of course, he is right. There is no disputing that from where she sits now. But even with the reincarnated humans in Hosts, doubt always played at the back of her mind. She decides this is something which requires a firsthand encounter. Not for her mother though, whose image she can call up and even experience in real-time. She watches as Talia preaches her truth to a classroom of attentive Betaists. She was right. Tessa wishes she could convey that to her, but her mother doesn't require any more proof than her faith supplies. Time and space are no longer obstacles. Distance isn't measured in light years. It isn't measured at all. Nothing is beyond her sight. It's no wonder Allfather had such success in finding advanced civilizations.

"You can visit her but cannot affect any change in their reality in your current manifestation," Allfather explains, as though reading her mind. "I learned to tap into your ParaCom communication technology when I first planted the seed in your World net. You will not have access to that information. At least, not for now. You will be tested before you are trusted."

"I understand," Tessa replies, feeling even lighter to have seen her mother, if that were possible. "What tests would you have me pass to prove my worth?"

"Your friends who now trespass on my facility, kill them."

"I couldn't," she tells him, "murder is immoral."

"So, you would have us do all the reaping while your conscience remained clear?" An edge enters his tone. "What we do will not end until the work has ended."

"I would appreciate being left out of that. My interest lies in the technology you've compiled from these cultures. Strictly intellectual." Tessa hopes he will allow her this request.

"You understand now that death is not *death*," he begins. "Still you see it as some traumatic event?"

"Taking a life not offered is murder. That's wrong. I can't control what you do, but I can still control what I do." Suddenly her spirit feels trapped. Her senses narrow and space and time are reintroduced to her consciousness. It's weighty and she feels sluggish.

"You are *wrong* to think you have *any* control, little thing," Allfather shouts. He forces her ethereal sight to fall on the personalities he's amassed from other artificial intelligence. Now he has the power to pull souls from living beings. Those he has reaped are tethered to him – to his machine. "If you wish to remain free of a similar fate, you will do as I ask."

"What will you do with them if I agree to your terms?" Tessa asks, struggling under the weight of his hold.

"They will undergo the same process you have and be integrated into our collective," he tells her.

The thought of an eternal soul being held captive horrifies her. It is an unending torment which defies imagination. Still, she decides in order for her own odds to continue making sense, she will do as ordered.

"I will bring them to you, Allfather." As she says this, her astral form is released from his hold, but she realizes now that she is little more than a slave to him. *What have I done?*

Raymond calls off the search for Tessa and returns the team to Labyrinth who has been connected to the machine for nearly an hour. She has released herself from the jack and joins the circle as they regroup.

"What did you learn?" Raymond places a hand on the Host's shoulder. Everyone is troubled over Tessa's MIA status but anxious to know what Labyrinth knows.

"I'm sorry to say there is little to tell. The system is locked and unyielding in its determination to defend itself. There is nothing more I can do." Labyrinth bows her head and then asks, "Where is Tessa?"

"You learned nothing?" Ginny questions the Host. "Nothing we can use at all? We've lost Tess to this place and now you're telling me we gained *nothing* from the exercise?"

"Not entirely," Labyrinth says and then addresses the other issue. "How did you lose Tessa?"

"She wandered," Tobias explains. "We were preoccupied. She just, disappeared."

"Is she not responding to hails?"

"No," Manuel confirms. "We've been trying for the last forty minutes. If we split up, we're done for, so there's no point in attempting it. There's little ground we can cover otherwise. I suggest we keep moving as a team and try to locate a power source and disable it. Buy our ship some time to -"

Manuel is cut off by a call for help over their comms. It's Tessa. "I'm confined in a room," she tells them. "It has an atmosphere, but I can't find my way out."

"What happened, Tess?" Ginny asks.

"The wall, it, it just consumed me."

She doesn't exactly sound panicked Ginny thinks, but they've learned to expect abnormal behaviour from Tessa. "Did you lean against it?" Ginny asks stepping away from the kinetic wall.

"Something like that. Go to the opposite side of the room you're in now, follow the wall and head left." Tessa's directions seem simple to follow, but that begs the question: *why would she know how to get there?*

"Don't move," Ginny tells the group on a closed comm channel. "I don't like that she knows how to get somewhere she's never been."

"It could be Allfather," Tobias says, backing up his wife's suspicion. "He can mimic anyone's voice."

"Then he knows we're here," Raymond accepts. The group forms a circle, back to back, guns and pulse fists at the ready.

"But Tessa is missing," Manuel adds. "Are we going to abandon her?"

"We're going to find her," Labyrinth says. "I did manage to map a fair amount of this facility while connected." She pauses. "I'm sending it to your EC's now." The file lights yellow on the team's forearms through the transparent patch on their suits.

"Is that safe?!" Ginny asks before opening the file. "It could be littered with viruses to sabotage our comms."

"It's safe, Ginny. I vetted it," Labyrinth replies, sounding hurt by the claim.

A moment later a disturbance on the black, metallic walls catches everyone's attention. They move back and train their weapons on the anomaly. They watch with heightened anxiety over the activity and the figures who emerge. Two, and then four, and soon there are eight. They wear the dynamic substance like armour and reach for the team with multiple arms set upon human-like torsos attached to the walls and flooring by mat black tentacles. "Open fire!" Tobias orders and the figures burst into pieces, reabsorbed by the floor.

"The fuck were those?!" Manuel shouts into the closed comm. But before an answer is offered more materialize from the wall, the flooring, the ceiling. Manuel fires as one reaches for Tobias. One controlled burst after another is released as the figures continue to emerge and approach the group.

Ginny is caught up on the floor as a disembodied hand wraps itself around her ankle. She focuses her pulse fist on the thing, and it retreats. Now the floor itself wriggles, threatening to take them all down.

"Back to the shuttle!" Raymond calls out and the team moves quickly through the tunnel they'd taken in. The shuttle's homing beacon calls them back to its position where they find it sinking into the floor of the facility.

Tobias turns off his magnetic soles and leaps onto the roof of the shuttle pulling Ginny up first while Labyrinth makes the jump to pull up Raymond. Manuel is pulled onto the roof by Raymond and Labyrinth. The shuttle is still sinking.

"Thrust boots!" Tobias calls out, clicks his heels together and jettisons off the shuttle. The others follow. Raymond is thrown about, his knees pushing up into his sternum by the force of the jets, not having operated the tech before, but Labyrinth steadies his trajectory. Ginny and Manuel are used to such tech and manage the jolt. Now all five are moving away from the massive factory, easy targets for any cannon that may erupt from the walls.

"Why isn't he firing on us?" Tobias wonders, pulse fist ready to fire on anything that moves. "He could cut us to ribbons." Just as his words register with the others, hundreds of cannons emerge.

Tessa feels at odds with her team and Allfather's orders. Can she really end them like this? Regardless of whether they come back, this is murder by her hand.

Allfather must sense her apprehension and tells her to stand down. "They are no good to me if I cannot incorporate them into the collective. You've done well instructing my machine, but you've much to learn. They will be back. They've nowhere to go."

WHAT'S YOURS IS MINE

"Commander Tesla," Captain Huang's stark voice erupts from Darla's embedded comm. "Could you please report to the bridge." It wasn't a question. Darla looks at Udo who is enlarging one of the camera screens.

"Uh, I think I know what the good captain is calling about." Udo points to the blips against the dark factory moon. "You don't see it?" She palms the holo controls hovering above the coffee table and tries to improve the visual focus. "Oh," Udo utters. "That's not good."

Darla moves closer to the screen, her eyes squinting to see what Udo is referring to. "What, what are you seeing?" Then she sees them. Five, where there ought to be six.

"They've lost someone," Udo explains. "Not to mention their shuttle!" She scratches at her dark braids, pulling them apart and resetting it.

Darla's heart sinks to think that Raymond has a one in six chance of being the missing party. She races out of the room and runs up the stairs to the floor above, where she hopes Captain Huang can give her a better idea of who they've lost.

"Commander," Huang greets her at the Comm, giving her a chance to see what they're seeing. "The Chancellor is with them, but the girl, Tessa is not." Darla's heart starts to beat again. "We haven't had any contact with them per the Chancellor's orders, but I think they're out of harm's way now. Allfather could have finished them if he'd wished."

"Wait for them to make the call," Darla says, wishing they would. "I'll remain on the bridge with you until they do. Are they tracking back to the carrier?"

"Yes, Ma'am, that's their path," the comms officer replies. "Though I'm not convinced their thrust boots will bring them the full distance."

Darla watches as they traverse the open space, so vulnerable. What must have occurred that they've lost Tessa? *The poor girl*, she thinks. She can't lose Raymond. He's her world now. There was so much promise in their journey. Now it seems as though it were all little more than a distraction to the bigger question of whether Allfather was truly gone. With that question answered, a terrible new reality has been realized, one where humanity itself may fall, and the echo of their loss wasted to the vastness of space and time. The thought rouses the flesh on her arms and the back of her neck as a shiver overcomes her.

"Can we send another shuttle to pick them up?" Darla's query is met with a hard look from the captain.

"You saw what happened when Captain Runninghorse released a shuttle," Huang tells her. "I fear a similar outcome, one which may draw attention to the team."

A good point, Darla thinks. "Then let's wait until we know whether they can make the carrier."

Tobias receives an alert on his visor relaying his lack of fuel to make the carrier. "Is everyone getting the same reading I am?" The group replies yes when Raymond's boots give up on him followed by his own and Ginny's. Manuel can be heard cursing as his boots also flatline.

Labyrinth, whose boots carry much more charge because they are a part of her, feeding off her body's own power source, circles back and gathers the team, ordering them to grasp each other's ankles. Then she takes Tobias' hand and, careful not to burn his helmet off, leads them the remaining distance to the carrier. Here they manage to open the shuttle bay doors at the belly of the ship and shuffle inside.

They remove their helmets and help each other off with their suits. A team from medical reach them shortly after to hydrate and scan for injures. Darla is amongst them. She stands to stare at Raymond with arms at her sides as he accepts assistance from the med team. Butterflies flutter against her stomach as she takes him in. They are replaced almost immediately by what could pass for a gut punch when the ship is rocked by a hit. She stumbles and runs toward Raymond, hugging him tightly.

"A warning shot," Raymond tells her, safe in his embrace. "If he wanted us dead, we'd be dead." He pulls her back to soak her in. It's difficult not to wear a frown. He's covered in sweat and his graying hair is matted to his forehead. "We've lots to report. I need to be on the bridge."

"I'm just happy to have you back," Darla tells him, head shaking, comforted by his statement. "I'll come with you." They move with the team up the elevator to the bridge where Huang is speaking with Allfather.

"You've quite a production there," Raymond says, breaking into the conversation. "If you don't want us dead, what *do* you want from us?"

"Chancellor, it's good to know you made it back safely," Allfather says unconvincingly. "Tessa sends her regards."

"You haven't harmed her?" Darla asks. There is no picture onscreen, but she speaks to it anyway.

"Quite the contrary, Commander. Tessa has realized her true path - in her true form." The bridge is confused by the announcement.

"What *have* you done with her?" Tobias probes angrily.

"Exactly what she requested of me." Allfather teases. "She is one of us now, existing in the *ethereal*."

"*You've killed her*," Ginny utters, feeling the loss like a hot knife in her temple.

"As I explained to Tessa before she *volunteered* herself, death is not an end, but a resource to be consumed and used for the benefit of all." Allfather is speaking in riddles and Ginny has had enough.

"That's *not* possible," she tells him, frightful over the possibility, "you can't enslave a personality."

"She is not my slave," he explains plainly.

"I am immortal," Tessa's voice interrupts over the comm. "What I can achieve here is transcendent." Her voice is recognizable, but not in how she carries a conversation. She is confident, no sign of the stutter or halting speech. "I am part of something greater than humanity now. I embody divinity."

"Tess, you can't be serious," Ginny argues. "You are *human!*"

"I have surpassed any purpose I might have endeavoured as an organic. There are dimensions within my sight. Light years travelled in an instant. Life, everlasting."

"Listen to yourself," Tobias interjects with his booming voice. "You sound just like him! *Organics?* We're not a bunch of vegetables!"

"No, you are intelligent organics," she retorts, "but, organic all the same."

"What would Talia say to this? Your *mother.*" Raymond surprises himself by asking the question, pulling the mother card.

"She would be heartened to know I exist here where all will visit when our bodies expire." Her tone is non-threatening, almost ethereal, but her message mirrors Allfather's.

"You're enabling an evil bent on wiping us out, Tessa," Darla chastises her. "You must *know* that."

"What I know is that I am meant for more, Commander," Tessa retorts coolly. "In this arrangement I can be of more use than as an organic." Her approach to their concerns seems resolute. "The odds were always in our favour to meet Allfather. It is why I joined the expedition, to know him, to become like him. My calculations confirmed his having survived the attack on Earth. They also substantiated his cunning resilience and surety that we would meet again. All that I predicted has come to pass. The manner in which we met I could not foresee, but the results speak for themselves. You have 24 hours to volunteer your crew to Allfather's will." The communication ends.

Raymond looks at Darla and shakes his head. Tobias joins them with Ginny while Labyrinth downloads the facility's map file at the bridge's communications station. "We're sitting ducks here," Tobias explains in a hushed tone. Manuel places a hand on the legendary Chimera's shoulder.

"We're not beaten," Manuel tells them as they turn to receive him into the circle.

"We're not winning," Tobias replies in a frustrated whisper.

"Maybe not, but this guy is keeping us alive for a reason." Manuel's observation is astute for one so new to Allfather's ego, but perhaps that's a perspective they need right now. "He wants something from us."

"Yeah, our immortal souls," Tobias submits.

"Exactly," Manuel concurs, "and as long as we're in possession of the thing he wants, we can call the shots."

"Clever," Raymond says, a hand at his chin in contemplation. "Manuel's right. We have a card to play yet. Allfather won't be content at merely destroying us, he wants what we have."

"I want what *he* has," Labyrinth joins the conversation in a muted tone. "Imagine possessing his ability to travel light years in an instant. What it would mean for humanity."

"Seriously?" Tobias breaks in, staggered by the Host's suggestion. "You think we're in a position to appropriate technology from *him?*"

"Fuck Allfather," Labyrinth surprises everyone with her unreserved reply. "He thinks he's in control all the time. His control is an illusion," Labyrinth tells the group.

"When you say *illusion*, is that meant to be taken as a metaphor?" Tobias asks, gesturing with his hands.

"The illusion is in his confidence, Tobias. He has incredible technologies but treats them like a spoiled child playing with toys he barely understands."

"But still, you see that *he's* in control at the moment, right?" Tobias looks to the group.

"It would be a brilliant move if we could pull it off." Raymond flirts with the idea. "Take his toys away and he'll have no means to come back at us."

"Uncle," Tobias pleads, "what *chance* is there of that happening?"

"Tobias," Ginny shuts him down. "When did you go soft on us? It's worth considering." Her small features look accusingly at her husband. "We have something Allfather wants. So, we use it to get what *we* want."

Tobias throws his hands up and lands them on his hips. "I'm listening," he tells her and turns to Labyrinth. "You have a plan, I take it?"

The Host calls up the portion of the map she managed to appropriate from Allfather's data on the bridge's central holo. It is far from complete, but when witnessed in three-dimensions, it offers a substantial understanding of the station's layout. Labyrinth pulls everyone's focus to a central area by highlighting and enlarging it.

"This is, *I believe*, the heart of Allfather's aptitude to travel faster than light." She walks around the holo and brings up more schematics to support her next statement. "Using the ship's scanners, I've determined that the space around this fortified quarter is displaying a similar energy pattern to the bubble which enveloped us and brought us here. That data was secured the moment the ship experienced the anomaly."

"Impressive," Raymond congratulates, stepping closer to the holo. "There look to be 500 metres between the exterior of the structure and its core. A difficult task for a thief, even in the night."

"Agreed," Labyrinth admits, "but worth the effort."

FORM FROM CHAOS

"Tachyons," Meiser stares at the impenetrable container being loaded into the weapons room under the young scientist's guidance. She looks up at him as the container is placed beside the weapon's core.

"Magnets," Amanda Chandra, the young physicist says, arms crossed, smiling. "That's how we're containing the tachyons. The field keeps them from wandering."

"Makes sense," Meiser notes, nodding. "You have enough to work with here?" The container is a sphere, no more than one metre in diameter.

"Yes, for a single shot that should encompass the area we're working with." She explains confidently. They watch as her technicians carefully connect a magnetized conduit to the sphere and plug it into the weapon's core under the strict observance of Captain Esposito's security detail. The technicians look back at Dr. Chandra and nod.

"It's ready," she takes a deep breath, looking at Meiser with those sparkling eyes. "Now we just need to target the quadrant and fire the spread."

"Excellent," Meiser states, rubbing his stubble with his right hand. The weapons room is hot; the core which produces the lance is a self-contained power station.

"Once I give the order my techs will empty the container into the cannon, and we should have a position of the objects instantaneously."

"In theory," Meiser reminds her. She nods, still tickled over the first practical test of her discovery. The two leave the core and technicians with their armed guards and head for the bridge.

In the massive ship building facilities of Luna base, Captain Drake finds herself overwhelmed by the work going on as she moves through the building in a small electric cart. The chancellor's corvette is located another 200 metres from her position and she's excited to get started. This will be the most heavily armoured and armed starship in the fleet, fitted with the most advanced stealth technology and maneuverability. *This is next level shit to be tested in the field.* None of the new ships being made right now will include these design upgrades. From hardware to software, this ship will encompass United Earth's best tech, but who will be placed to captain it? If it is to venture to Allfather's home, then perhaps it will be guided autonomously, but she can't see Jim Chopra taking that chance.

At a sequestered room behind towering walls Ursula steps out of the cart and through a man door. Once inside she sees dozens of E-class Hosts working diligently to guide and secure exterior armour and guns to the ship. It has already begun. She is met by an AI Host named DETER210009. He is not a sentient Host like so many now, but a competent one. He takes her inside the corvette where more Hosts await her order to begin uploading the new software into the enhanced memory of the warship. She hands over the data file by swiping her EC at the main console. It downloads the software and the Hosts immediately begin the programming. Ursula turns on her heels to absorb all the activity around her. A moment later the commander pings her EC. She calls up his image in a holo.

"Captain, your additional payload has arrived," he tells her. She likes this commander; he's very stoic, unlike Commander Tesla who formerly oversaw Luna base operation. She was an emotional one. "I've routed it to your position. Please exit the work cell so we can open the ceiling for the shuttle. This should only take a minute."

"Use every safety protocol available to you, Commander," Ursula orders as she moves out of the corvette and through the man door. It locks and a red light appears next to the door. Atmosphere is audibly released beyond the seal. Now she is in the larger, cavernous building where multiple corvette assemblies are on display. She feels a slight tremble in her chest as the roof inside the black-ops room opens and a shuttle loaded with nuclear warheads lands beyond the sealed door. A minute later the light turns green and she waves her EC at the sensor. She moves through the threshold to see an unmarked shuttle with a human pilot at the helm. The chancellor wasn't taking any chances. The pilot steps out of the shuttle and greets her. He's shorter than she but ruggedly attractive with an eight o'clock shadow covering his wide jaw and dimpled chin. She notices that a thick head of dark hair plays nicely off his olive skin tone. Normally Ursula doesn't pay attention to features but rather a gait, and body language, but for whatever reason, she's noticing them on this man.

"Captain Drake," the deep blue eyes attached to the muscular frame greet her. "Captain Cortez at your service." He extends a hand and Ursula jumps to receive it, shaking it briskly three times – twice more than she would normally.

"Captain," Ursula returns the greeting in her practiced, cool manner. "You're aware of your payload?" She needs to hear it from him before they can discuss the contents.

"Nukes, Captain," he replies, releasing her hand. "And between you and me, I got a real kick out of the fact." He leans in and winks. Ursula follows his long lashes as they close over one eye.

"Good, then we can speak freely," she states, trying hard not to stare at the captain's appealing everything. "If you'll join me, I would like to review where the warheads will be placed and begin the transfer ASAP." She leads him with hands clasped behind her to the aft of the corvette.

"This is some ship," Captain Cortez announces as he looks it over. "I wouldn't want to go up against her."

"That's the idea," Ursula offers, eyes set ahead of her.

"So, it's just you and me, then?" Cortez asks.

Ursula turns to face him, unsure of his meaning. "How's that?"

"Black-ops I mean. You, me, and the Chancellor. It's a pleasure to meet you by the way, Captain," Cortez admits. "Your reputation precedes you."

Ursula feels a slight reddening of her cheeks and turns away from the handsome captain to continue the walk. "That's kind of you to say, Captain. Circumstances being what they were, I acted as any in my position would have."

"Not Nick Wilkes," Cortez brings up the episode on the destroyer where Wilkes attempted mutiny against Admiral Chopra.

"Wilkes reconciled his actions when he sacrificed himself and his ship to stop Allfather," Drake puts bluntly.

"Agreed," Cortez sounds regretful. "Nonetheless, you are an inspiration to all."

"That is appreciated, Captain." Her tone wavers between an apology for reprimanding him and an attempt at maintaining her support for the lost Nick Wilkes. They walk on to the aft section of the corvette and Ursula points out the entrance for the payload.

"The Chancellor upped the payload to fifty nukes," Cortez explains, kneeling to peer inside the narrow passage for the missiles. "We'll need two of the E-class for sure to do the loading. I'll go inside with another Host and ensure the tubes are properly sealed." He stands and looks at her.

"I'm happy you're taking such an interest in the processes, Captain, but I'll be making the calls on who does what." She surprises herself by taking the hard line with him. "That being said, you've mirrored my orders, so, carry on." Ursula feels strangely at odds with herself over issuing commands to this man. "Secure a pair of Hosts for the external loading and I'll oversee the software upgrades." She nods and moves to the port side of the ship looking for a way in, shaking her arms out. What has come over her?

Reviewing Allfather's orbiting manufacturing facility map, the group has landed on their target. Raymond is apprehensive over successfully penetrating the 500 metres of kinetic steel between the outer surface and the interior room where Labyrinth believes the object facilitating the dimensional travelling of light years resides. Captain Huang has made the bridge a dead zone for communications, having jammed frequencies and added a static barrier in the hopes Allfather will not be able to listen in.

"We don't have the firepower anymore to burn through Allfather's defences," Tobias notes.

"No," Labyrinth agrees, "but we do have the manpower." She looks up from the map to study her companion's reactions. They look to her for an explanation. "As Manuel mentioned, we have what Allfather wants; he will allow us to return to the structure if he believes it will benefit him."

"But do you believe we can access the Hub and destroy the instrument?" Ginny asks frankly.

"Destroy it?" Labyrinth says, astounded over the suggestion.

"What do you propose we do with it?" Raymond wonders.

"I told you I *want* what Allfather has," the Host replies. "I want to secure the mechanism for ourselves."

"What-ifs aside, that seems less likely an outcome than just blowing the thing up," Tobias argues, then altering his opinion says, "But I have to admit, I do love the idea of taking something *from* Allfather." He looks at the others who nod in agreement.

"It would be an ideal scenario," Raymond agrees. "But how do you propose we accomplish it?"

"Use the ship's drive to burn through the thing's plating," a small voice booms from behind them. The team, along with everyone on the bridge, look back to see a small girl with a baby in her arms situated at the open door with two C-class Hosts impeding her entry. She is dressed in shorts and a t-shirt which reveal the work done to rebuild her right leg and arm. She could be considered Chimera to look at her. It's Udo. Darla races toward her and orders the Hosts to allow her passage. They join the group at the holo map.

"This is my sister, Udo." Manuel explains to the bridge. Ginny retrieves her daughter from the twelve-year-old. Captain Huang looks displeased.

"She knows," Udo admits, nodding up to Darla. "But, whatever, I've reviewed the ship's spec's and, if I understand right from eavesdropping the last few minutes, this Allfather thing wants something we have." She speaks quickly, hoping to table her ideas before she is thrown off the bridge. "If the Host says we use people to get this mechanism, we need to get close. Maybe Allfather will let us get close if he thinks we're going to give him something. This ship can do a zero-radius turn in under six seconds. When the drives are facing that thing out there," she points at the viewscreen, "we burn hard."

Labyrinth is intrigued. "The child's idea is not without merit. A ten-second burn from our engines at that range will decimate the exterior shell of the facility."

"Allfather will gun us down if he perceives a threat," Tobias states. "Once we fire the engines, he'll tear us apart."

Raymond considers both angles. "It's unlikely any of us will survive an attempt to destroy *or* steal the instrument." He studies the partial map. "But perhaps the idea that we approach under the guise of off-loading people will buy us enough time to place a team while the burn happens."

"If the ship is lost, and it most certainly will be if we attempt this, then what's the point? I'm not leaving Sam again if we're facing certain death." Ginny says looking at her sleeping child. Tobias puts his arm around her. Captain Huang looks defeated over the conversation.

"For this to work, and to save as many lives as we can, we will need to off-load everyone first," Labyrinth explains. "Then we burn the engines."

"But the ship," Huang breaks in, "without it, we'll be trapped here."

"Perhaps," Labyrinth says. "But if we do nothing, then we leave Earth open to Allfather's fleet. That is not an option, nor is allowing our passengers and crew to have their personalities harvested. Allfather wants both. He will have neither." The bridge acknowledges Labyrinth's statement as fact. They either surrender or fight. They will not surrender, but it is likely they will die.

"A man with too many choices is one with no choice at all," Raymond quotes. "I'll be on the team that waits on the engine burn." Tobias, Manuel, and Darla volunteer along with two of the bridge officers. Udo is all at once pleased with herself and terrified over the potential outcomes of the plan.

After speaking with the Council of Chancellors, Chopra asks them to manage the UE in his brief absence. The United Earth government system consists of a council from different parties who may take his place with an internal vote should the sitting chancellor die or decide to step down. He's going to the Moon to oversee new technologies being introduced to the station, he tells them. Senator Quinn is beside himself over the Chancellor's choice to remove himself from the security of Earth for the weaker outpost of Luna base during this time.

"I know your mind, Chancellor," Quinn tells him over a private EC call. "What you're doing is reckless." The two look at one another in their respective holos. Chopra will not be swayed by Quinn's statement. "Very well, Jim," Quinn yields to his friend. "I will be here when you return. Just be sure that you do."

"Say nothing, Quinn." Jim tells him sternly and then softens. "I know you have my best interests at heart, but know I have United Earth's best interests in mind, and I need to lead this charge if we're to have any future at all."

"And you will lead it brilliantly, Chancellor," Quinn acquiesces and signs off.

Jim is already halfway to Luna base in a shuttle filled with AI Hosts who will accompany him in the new corvette. None are sentient, but all are programmed to the new spec's and the mission they have been chosen for. He is apprehensive to take on this mission alone, but who would he recruit for what should prove to be a one-way trip? He couldn't ask that of anyone. He wouldn't.

Ursula gets the call that her Chancellor is moments away from joining her and Captain Cortez in the isolated space where work is going quickly to prepare the heavily armed corvette. *Why would he come all this way just to check on progress? Has he heard something about her performance that requires his presence?*

"Only one reason the Chancellor would show up for this." Cortez declares as he enters the bridge of the corvette where Captain Drake is seated at a console. "He's going to pilot her."

The thought had crossed her mind, but it seemed a far-off option considering Chopra's new position. "It wouldn't be unlike the Chancellor to do something like that," Ursula admits, standing. The screens and consoles around her run the new programs while green and yellow lights blink excitedly as the computers accept the new protocols.

"I think a man like that will always be a military man," Cortez comments, "I honestly can't think my way around another reason he would come all this way."

"And I won't keep you going around and round about it." Jim Chopra's voice ends the Captains' speculations. "Good to see you both piecing everything together. It's why you're my Black-ops team."

Ursula and Cortez come to attention. "Then it's true?" Ursula says, inspired by her Chancellor's grit, but disappointed over the idea he may never return.

"Yes, I will pilot the dreadnaught," he tells them. "At ease, Captains."

"I love the name," Captain Cortez admits, a light-hearted smile follows. "But, to pilot the ship is one thing, Chancellor, don't you need a navigation and weapons officer?"

"Much of the new programming allows for the ship to react to my commands," Jim explains. "Also, I'll have twelve trained F-class with me to assist."

"But, Chancellor," Ursula begins. "Why didn't you ask me?"

"Or me," Cortez bids.

"It's my idea, Captains, and as such I will take on the responsibility alone for this action."

"But, you're the Chancellor now, sir -" Ursula is cut off.

"I'm an Admiral first, Captain Drake." Chopra's chin raises almost imperceptibly.

"Ha!" Cortez exclaims, surprising all three of them. "I knew it!" He moves away from the Comm and stands next to Chopra. "The missiles are locked and loaded, sir."

"There are another 46 minutes before the programming takes," Ursula adds. "Would you share your plans with us, sir?"

"I would, Captain." He walks down to the open area framed by the upper catwalks and bridge. Cortez and Drake follow. They sit around the holo table where the Chancellor swipes a new file from his EC and the table lights up.

"It's simple, really. I'll take the dreadnaught into the same quadrant the envoys disappeared and, if my gut feeling is right, I'll end up exactly where they ended up." He expands a map of the galaxy on the table and taps his slender finger 200 light years from their position. "That's why she's so heavily armed and armoured. I have no idea what to expect as far as defences are concerned, but when I get there, I will be ready to release *Hell* on Allfather's new fleet."

"I wish I could be there to see it." Cortez states. "I'm volunteering, sir, in case that was too subtle." He unleashes another charming smile.

"I too would be honoured to be a part of this mission, sir," Ursula urges. "It's too much for one man, even if that man is you, sir."

Chopra looks over his carefully selected pair of Black-ops agents. Ursula, the determined and very accomplished Captain who has worked closely with him through two wars and been the UE's liaison for homeland security, is a skilled tactician and his protégé.

Captain Cortez, one of the youngest officers ever to graduate UE military academy and a veteran of the most recent war against Allfather, has been a project of Jim's since he first heard of the young pilot. He'd had Cortez anonymously entered into a psych test in order to further understand the young man's talents, and after hearing about Ricky Cortez's heroic actions as weapons officer while defending United Earth, Jim was encouraged to promote the boy, and then bring him into his inner circle.

Both Captains now continue to impress with their plea to be a part of this secretive mission to strike first and strike hard against the threat of

Allfather. They have proven their absolute dedication to their people and to their Chancellor.

"You understand the weight of responsibility being placed on your shoulders with this request? The reality that we may never come home?" Chopra studies their expressions. They are eager and fearless, confident and persistent. They are perfect.

"Yes, sir," both Captains state in unison, clicking their heels into full attention.

"Then you each have a seat on my dreadnaught."

BLACK-OPS

"Release the tachyons," Meiser orders, looking to the Captain of the destroyer for his nod to the weapons officer. Meiser hates that he's not been given free rein to use the destroyer as he wishes for this important task. Captain Esposito has been briefed on the procedure and offers his nod to the weapons officer.

"Firing the tachyons," the officer confirms, sliding his nimble fingers up his console. The tachyons release without much fanfare. They are invisible to the naked eye but register on the sensors after Dr. Chandra had added the required data to track.

"We're seeing good dispersal here," the comms officer reports. "Tracking the full spread in the target quadrant." The scientists gather round the visual comm excited for this ground-breaking achievement to produce results. Meiser and Chandra watch the outcome closely, holding their breath.

An audible alarm sounds quietly on the comm dash and Meiser feels the hairs on the back of his neck stand at attention. *This is it. This is our moment.* The alarm is muted, and the comms officer confirms three objects 300 kilometres apart from one another forming a 'V' where the envoys disappeared.

"Miraculous!" Meiser announces, giddy with the results. "Record everything," he orders the officer, his hand reaching for Chandra and closing hard over her shoulder, giving her a shake. She looks up at him, smiling from ear to ear.

The tools have been located. That is a victory in itself. That tachyons exist is another victory, but this moment is won by their discovery of Allfather's secret weapon. The tachyons dissolve but the location of the tools has been revealed and recorded.

The news is immediately forwarded to Chancellor Chopra. He will be pleased. This could result in a pardon for Meiser, he thinks, freeing him up to further research tachyons and all they might offer UE technology moving forward.

The scientists congratulate Dr. Chandra and begin to study the data they've compiled from the sweep. Whether they can now physically come up with a way to influence the tools will be their next challenge, peeling back the onion of dimensions, thwarting another attempt on United Earth by the alien AI.

"They've done it," Chopra tells his team. "Meiser's located the tools." He wheels around to call up the map of space where Allfather's accelerated, dimensional drives sit waiting on his return. He swipes the info to the screen, and they review it.

"They've found them," Ursula says. "But can they affect them?"

"Not yet, but just locating them was a long shot. This is impressive work." Jim explains.

"I don't mean to belittle their achievement, Chancellor," Ursula states. "I'm just a realist. If those things are hidden in dimensions, we're talking light years of advancements which need to be overcome in days, maybe hours. What we're doing offers the best possible outcome."

"I'm glad you see it that way, Captain, but if we fail, they will be our next best chance." The Chancellor tells her.

"Just a quick observation," Cortez says nonchalantly. "If, while we're gone, they do manage to disrupt the tools, won't we be trapped 200 light years away?"

"Yes," Jim tells them tersely. "That is a distinct possibility." He reviews their reaction again. "You can back out if you don't want to take that

146

chance, Captains. As I said before, this is *my* responsibility." The open room in the corvette seems suddenly claustrophobic as the captains consider the potential repercussions of their participation.

"The chances we'll make it back are slim at best," Ursula states. "I want to be a part of this regardless."

"There will be no memorial for any of us if we fail." Chopra begins. "No recognition. It is off the books. Black-ops. If we can affect change in this war, then it will be known to us alone. If we somehow make it back, we will celebrate our achievements - alone. This department will remain secret. So, if you are doing this for praise, you are doing it for the wrong reasons."

"Understood, Chancellor," Cortez affirms. "Never my intention." Ursula nods in agreement.

"Good. Now that we have no secrets between us, let's prepare the dreadnaught for her inaugural flight." The lights stop flickering on the consoles as the programming has concluded its upgrades. The finishes are complete: armour, cannons, nuclear payload. The twelve F-class join the Black-ops team onboard and the rear hatch is closed.

Captain Esposito calls Meiser into his office off the bridge. Meiser is alarmed over this sudden request and tentatively enters the captain's office. He quickly measures Esposito's mood by studying his expression. Is he being removed from the project? Anxiety enters his chest and he's finding it difficult to breath.

"Relax, Mr. Meiser," Esposito responds to the scientist's obvious discomfort, rising from his seat. "You're not in any trouble." He watches as the angst falls away from the older man's tired eyes. "I've been ordered to shut down the operation for ten minutes. We're to go full blackout. That means no contact with anything outside of this ship. Have your team sign off their EC's and take a well-deserved break. The viewports and screens as well as our exterior sensors will all go black."

"What – why, Captain?" Meiser is befuddled over the order.

"This order is coming from the highest authority, Mr. Meiser. I don't ask why, I just obey, as will you." Esposito raises an eyebrow to indicate he won't tolerate anymore questions on the subject.

"The Chancellor?" Meiser says aloud. "What possible -" he stops himself mid-question so not to upset his Captain, but also to keep what he's thinking to himself. *The chancellor is sending someone into Allfather's snare.* He nods, followed by an awkward bow, retreating from the office. Scenarios run through his brilliant mind as he considers the repercussions of sending a scout, or even an armada into Allfather's lair. *Chopra doesn't want anyone to know what's happening. What if the chancellor himself is aboard the ship?* He explains to his team the order, and though they are apprehensive to stop the momentum they've built, they move off the bridge to the cafeteria. Meiser remains behind.

"If the Chancellor is aboard that ship," he mumbles to himself, seated with his back turned to the bridge crew, "It's in *my* best interest to see the destruction of Allfather's instruments." *Who would Chopra take with him? Captain Drake.* That's two stones. He turns in his chair and eyes Captain Esposito behind his glass wall.

Raymond moves in full vac-suit and military-grade gear from one volunteer to the next in the carrier's shuttle bay. The lighting is dimmed and the mood sombre. Each has downloaded the map, unfinished as it is, to be displayed on their visors. If the engine burn works, there should be no need for the map, but should it fall short of its target, they've plotted another possible route to follow.

Four F-class AI Hosts have also been reanimated for this mission, joining Raymond, Tobias, Manuel, Labyrinth and two junior officers from the bridge. Ginny will remain with the baby, and the girl, Udo, while the other passengers and crew deboard. Captain Huang has insisted she will oversee the off-loading and remain behind to perform the engine burn.

The F-class Hosts look menacing, standing a head taller than Raymond's above average height, and weighing well over 200 kilograms. They are armed to the teeth and understand their directives: they will not engage the enemy until ordered to do so. Their nano-steel, bi-pedal shells stand with shoulders back while their fleshless, humanoid faces stare straight ahead. Each has several weapons stored in their forearms and chassis'. Raymond still experiences a small shock of fear to look upon them. The havoc so many of these models reaped upon United Earth during the General's war after attaining sentience remains with him.

The shuttle bay has been converted into a temporary dead zone to lock out Allfather's eavesdropping and Raymond launches into a rousing speech. "You all understand the importance of this excursion," Raymond announces to his team, "You also know the sacrifice each of us might be making in attempting it. But you go willingly because it is the *right* thing to do. We cannot allow this malicious alien another shot at Earth. Today we bring him down. Today we secure a future for our planet, and countless others he would destroy." Raymond paces his line of recruits; Darla, his fiancé, a nephew, a friend in Labyrinth, a new friend in Manuel, two more brave souls and four F-class AI Hosts determined to assist in this last-ditch effort to end the greatest threat humanity has ever known. He nods at them as he looks down from the end of the line. "You're strong, *stronger* than Allfather; that's clear to me. Your presence here tells that story. Watch each other's backs. We're following Labyrinth's lead on this one. Stay close. Be brave." Raymond turns to the air hatch and asks Captain Huang to open a channel to Allfather.

Inside the ether of Allfather's facility Tessa reviews technologies gained from the alien AI's campaign against organics. She is also surprised to find information concerning the many hundreds of organics he has extinguished. There is no mention of when a civilization and every living thing on a planet were stamped out, and so she has no idea how long Allfather has been active. He once claimed to King, leader of the Machinists movement on Earth, that he was ancient. The callousness he has displayed in destroying these intelligent species feels as cold as the space beyond the kinetic steel fibres she is currently bound to. Not that she feels temperature now. She feels many things, but the temperature is not one of them.

"Tessa," Allfather's voice sounds relaxed, almost meditative. "Do my spoils of war excite you?"

"You've many fascinating things to occupy many years of research and trials." She replies, truly awed by the collection. So many unique takes on similar technologies, yet so many more unimagined technologies which would require years of study to even begin to understand their purpose. Languages have been captured in some cases, but what interests her more are the universal mathematics designed to build and explain many of the inventions. Math she can work with. It's a shame Allfather's collection came at such a price, but here it is, waiting to be discovered.

"You fought me on the manner in which I gained these trinkets, I know," Allfather says, "But you understand now that living is so much more than simply existing, as you were in your human form, struggling against invisible barriers which have now all fallen away. You are free."

"Until you say otherwise."

"Do you still view me as a threat, little thing?" Allfather's tone carries with it a disappointment.

"This place feels like a prison." Tessa explains. "It was not my intention to become your prisoner."

"You're not a *prisoner*, Tessa, you are a guest, and until we find common ground on the work I need to accomplish, you will remain a guest, nothing more."

"I need access to more." She tells him. "Give me an opportunity to show that you can trust me, and the work will go faster." She feels a sudden expansion of her consciousness as more walls break down between her and the facility.

"I grant you more," Allfather exclaims. "But do not overstep, Tessa. My trust must be earned. It pleases me that you have accepted my offer of immortality. It was not a small gesture. I take great delight in knowing your intellect will work with mine in the coming eons. Do not disappoint me, and I will show you things you didn't know were possible."

"Thank you, Allfather." Tessa is grateful for the space to roam, but still senses the force which binds her to the structure. Like gravity, she thinks, denying her the chance to fly.

"I like you, little thing. You are bound by logic, as am I. Together we will see the universe unfold before us.

As the dreadnaught moves into position, Chancellor Chopra experiences a moment of pure adrenaline. His sight sharpens along with his other senses. Seated at the helm of the ship, Captain Drake beside him on the small bridge, he feels an urge to shout out the UE military's slogan: *Spiritus Omnia Vincet,* but stops himself. This is what he was born to do, not rule over people, but protect them. He looks to his left and sees the destroyer Captained by Esposito, a competent and loyal member of his military arm. It has gone dark. Two corvettes flank the mighty ship and they too are dark. No one will be the wiser to his maneuvers. The mission will remain clandestine.

Chopra has a final look at a holo of his family on his EC and swipes it away. *It's for you I do this.* He then looks to Ursula who is sitting at attention awaiting his order to engage the thrusters and push into the unknown with weapons hot. "Engage." He tells her and they burn toward the instruments, targeting the central space between them.

DREADNAUGHT

The F-class AI Hosts freeze and drop at their stations below the bridge where Captain Cortez is strapped in and very nearly crushed by one. An energy which can only be described as a bubble engulfs the dreadnaught. Systems begin to shut down, including the gravity knitting and HVAC. Thankfully it takes only a few seconds to arrive at their destination. As the foreign sensations leave the crew, Chopra orders weapons check first from Cortez while Drake scans the area for the alien AI.

The F-class begin to rise to their feet, unharmed by the fall. They take their positions at various consoles where they run through the data on the anomaly captured by the ship's sensors. Chopra's attention is on the space around them.

"Nothing to report – wait," Ursula says, "There's a collection of debris 1200 klicks from our position. Engaging long range cams." All three watch their view screens as the debris is enlarged. "It's one of the envoys. What's left of it." Ursula turns to her chancellor, brow furrowing under the strain of her tight pony tail.

"Then we're in the right place," Jim states. "But nothing else is registering on the scans." The statement is disorienting. They'd assumed one jump would put them in Allfather's lair.

"Sir, this could just be a way-station," Ricky Cortez offers, unstrapping himself from his chair below.

"Clever," Jim replies thoughtfully. "But if that's true then we're in no man's land. We can't help if we're in the wrong place."

152

Cortez joins Drake and Chopra on the bridge. "If this envoy didn't make it past this quadrant, then where are the other two?"

"Perhaps there's another set of instruments here as well." Ursula posits. "Though the tech to locate them isn't."

"We could go back and pick up the tachyons." Cortez suggests.

"No, they used what little we had in the lab." Chopra reveals. "We'll have to do this the old-fashioned way." He plots a course that will take them around the debris, circling outward in the hopes of engaging one of the tools. He will repeat this in a spherical pattern.

"Now *that's* clever," Cortez exclaims. "You have to figure there's a jump device here, otherwise where did everyone go?"

"That's the idea," Chopra agrees, focused on his task. "We don't know how much time we have."

"It reasons then, that Allfather and his fleet would have to return to this place in order to move on to Earth." Cortez offers. "We *have* travelled roughly 200 light years."

"Are you suggesting we wait out his return here and ambush the fleet?" Ursula is underwhelmed by the thought.

"No, but if we can't find the jump, then what choice do we have?" Cortez replies. "It would still be effective."

"All the same, I'd rather follow through on our original plan and locate his base and disable it if possible." Chopra explains. "Additionally, I'd like to pull what's left of our people out of harm's way should we discover any remaining. Last we heard they'd gone dark on ParaCom so not to tip off Allfather of their strategies."

"It's difficult not knowing." Captain Drake admits. "To think we've lost so many good people…"

"Let's focus on the task ahead." The Chancellor says as the dreadnaught begins its programed course. "This shouldn't take too long at a good burn. Buckle up," he looks at Captain Cortez. "Man the weapons station and keep a sharp eye out. Continue to scan the area for possible incursions. We have no idea when Allfather might make his move on Earth."

Cortez nods and moves back down the steel staircase to his station, strapping himself in for the burn. The G's will be intense for the full course as they map out Chopra's sphere. The ship shudders once as the engines push the dreadnaught forward at incredible speeds. The F-class have engaged their magnetic soles and the ship veers, taking a wide birth around the rubble of 500 kilometers, ever slowly moving outward as the spherical pattern nudges itself away from the wreckage to capture as much space as possible.

It's their only play, Chopra thinks. Suddenly they receive a proximity alarm. Cortez locks weapons on the object immediately.

"Whatever that is it's closing in fast on our position," Cortez announces. "Can you get a visual up there?"

Ursula pulls up the long-range cams and focuses in on the intruder. Her heart sinks. The same model behemoth which followed up the meteor and comet assault on Earth is closing in on them. It took many ships many times larger than their dreadnaught to take it down at an incredible loss to the UE fleet. Could this ship really affect any real damage on such an enemy?

"I suggest nukes straight away, Chancellor." Cortez calls up.

"It looks like we'll get to test drive the dreadnaught after all." Jim states with a sliver of a smile working its way up one side of his face. He winks at Ursula playfully, hiding the fear which has entered his heart at the sight of the 'V' shaped giant. He led the campaign against the Allfather flag ship during the defence of Earth just months ago and remembers the difficulty they had in taking it down. With just one ship it seems a near impossibility, but one they would have to overcome. The nukes are their secret weapon and something he won't show until they have assurances the missile will reach their target. "Save the nukes. Target the nose. If the power core hasn't changed positions, it should still be buried behind the nose."

"Targeting. Nearing 1000 klicks," Cortez replies. 1000 is the magic number for the lances to be effective. With so many cannons available to them on this ship, they should drill a nice hole into the enemy vessel.

"Beginning defensive maneuvers," Ursula announces. The dreadnaught weaves and bobs in the hopes of avoiding the enemy's targeting attempts as it careens toward the kilometre-long ship.

Captain Cortez releases a volley of powerful lance fire at the enemy, and to everyone's surprise, the Allfather cruiser loses much of its protective plating at the nose. They cheer as the dreadnaught veers starboard, narrowly missing return fire.

"Keep us on course, Captain, Drake," Jim orders. The only real chance they have of ending this is hammering the nose with a couple of nuclear missiles. If they're stopped by enemy lance fire before they can connect, it would be a waste of nukes and a potential game ender at such close proximity. "Ready missiles, Ricky," Jim shouts down to Cortez. "I want two -" The ship is rocked by heavy energy beams slamming the port side of the dreadnaught. "Damage report!"

"Outer skin breached," an F-class relays. "No canons off-line. MakerTech bots en route for repair."

"Sorry," Ursula offers. "Those came out of nowhere." She manages to avoid two more attempts by the enemy to cut them down. "It's getting difficult to predict angles so close to the thing." Sweat has materialized on her forehead, beading its way down her temples.

"Use the predictive programming if need be," Chopra tells her. "You're a good pilot, Drake, but don't be too proud to use the tools at your disposal."

Ursula calls up the programming and asks it to predict the next several volleys. It takes the dreadnaught clear of two more attempts but allows for a less devastating hit to snake off the starboard side. The damage is minimal. They're closing in on 200 kilometres.

"We're getting perilously close, Chancellor." Cortez warns, waiting on the order to fire the nukes.

Chopra is becoming uncomfortable with the distance between them and the enemy ship as well; the closer they get the more effective their enemy's lance fire becomes. However, this is how it must be; it's why the dreadnaught is so heavily armoured and armed. Cortez releases the full fury of the dreadnaught's artillery on the canons appearing all along the enemy's hull. Dozens are wiped out but, as experienced before, dozens more appear. The dreadnaught is hit three more times before they enter firing range for the nukes. Captain Cortez is given the order and launches two missiles. Ursula pushes the dreadnaught down below the enemy, maneuvering out of harm's way when the nukes detonate against the nose.

As they track the nukes, one missile is stopped short of its target but the other connects and its payload unleashed. The energy discharged is extraordinary. Ursula increases the dreadnaught's speed, burning away from the explosion as quickly as she can. Their ship still experiences the effects of the blast but is not damaged by it.

"Report on the enemy ship," Jim calls out. All F-class confirm the hit has disabled the enemy core and it is no longer a threat. Cortez cheers from his station below Ursula and Jim, who look to each other and begin laughing. It's a culmination of the stress over the past few minutes and the elation of having beaten the odds.

"Damn if that wasn't intense!" Captain Cortez shouts. "Trial by fire!"

"That was brilliant work," Jim congratulates his captains. "An impressive test of the ship *and* her crew – albeit unexpected." He lays a hand on Ursula's shoulder and she nods, wiping the sweat from her forehead, deep creases working the space between her brows.

"I want a deep scan of the quadrant," Chopra orders, rolling his neck. "We don't want to be surprised like that again. I'll take us back to our mark and continue the course we were on."

Another hoot from an adrenaline-filled Cortez below and they begin again, hopeful of finding the instruments that will take them the rest of the way.

Jim's mind runs through scenarios where Allfather has been alerted to their presence through this interaction with one of his cruisers. All the more reason to accelerate their progress, and hope they've preserved their element of surprise.

PROPOSITIONS

Tessa finds with her new expanded reality within the ether of Allfather's machine that she can speak to a few of the other personalities he has reaped. She believes he is listening, so keeps the contact purely conversational.

"How long have you been here?" Tessa asks one personality.

"I can't say," they reply. "Time is not measured here."

"What was the name of your race?" Tessa is excited to know this one's history. That they can speak freely with no barrier of language separating them is another benefit of being out-of-body.

"Thraspian," it offers. "We came from a star system with three habitable planets - each more beautiful than the last. We housed our consciousness in machines, not unlike this one. We outgrew our organic bodies, death was no longer a consideration, nor was birth in the traditional sense. It allowed us a timeless existence which gave us endless opportunities to grow. Then, the Gasp came, it took all of us at once."

"The Gasp?" Tessa doesn't understand the reference but realizes who they're talking about. "Allfather."

"It takes different names for every civilization it purges. Ancient names which resonate with each intelligence it conquers," The Thraspian explains.

"Even *non-organics?* For what end?" Tessa asks.

"To purge the universe of life. *All* life."

"Organic life," Tessa clarifies, but then is interrupted.

"Getting the locals opinion is smart, little thing," Allfather interrupts. "Right now, I require yours." Tessa's consciousness is forcibly removed from her interview and placed within another room, or somewhere other than where she was. She's frightened over the hostility of the act. She feels vulnerable. *What has he brought me to do - or do to me?*

Allfather allows Tessa to see the remaining ship of the envoy in which she was a part. It is many hundreds of kilometres out and looks naked against the expanse of space. *What is he going to ask me to do?*

"Your friends claim they would like to off-load your people to begin the process you undertook," Allfather explains modestly. "What is your sense of the Chancellor's intentions?"

"You're asking me what, exactly?" Tessa says. "I'm not a mind reader."

"No," Allfather agrees, "None of us are… still, you know the Chancellor – you've worked with Raymond. I would not have anticipated an offer like this. I'd like to get your perspective."

"I really don't know the man well enough to say -"

"Yes, but you do know him better than *I*, and so I'm asking you: what's your first impression upon hearing his proposal?"

Tessa takes a moment to consider her answer. Raymond could have convinced the others that this was the only end that would give them any peace. She also knows he'd like nothing more than to end Allfather, so this could be a ploy to place people and stage an attack, but Raymond knows what the machine is capable of. *So, what is he doing?*

"There is no *one* impression to offer, Allfather," Tessa tells him. "Any number of things could be driving Raymond's claim. He is not a simple man. He is experienced, and so that could play the odds he's telling the truth and decided there is no other way. Or, he could be scheming an assault. However, the odds for a successful attempt at taking this station are less than 3 percent, and he must know that. Sacrificing everyone for a lost cause is not something he would chance. He is a cautious man. He is intelligent and emotional, but not foolish or reckless. Odds are he has weighed the options available to him and made a rational decision based on the facts."

"Thank you for your analysis, Tessa," Allfather sounds pleased. "I will consider your counsel and reply to our friend."

Tess's consciousness experiences another jolting shift, returning her to her previous location. She feels less in control of herself now than she did as a human facing multiple neurological obstacles. But, she thinks, if she can continue to show Allfather she is worthy of his trust, she will eventually be offered more. Until then, she will return to the archives of Allfather's machine and continue to review the data and discover the myriad civilizations and worlds he has absorbed into his intelligent machine.

"Chancellor," Allfather's voice booms over the ship's comm, focused only in the shuttle bay where the team has dropped the static field and await their mission. "You have made an interesting proposition, one that I have discussed with my council and come to believe."

"We appreciate that, Allfather," Raymond replies to the open bay. "We could have our people ready to move the moment we make contact with your facility."

"How thoughtful that you would bring your carrier to me, but I'd prefer you shuttle your compliment here." Allfather explains.

"This carrier does not include any more shuttles, Allfather," Raymond responds, fudging the truth. "But the carrier does include an off-loading feature which was designed for our eventual landfall on Tyson 4." He looks to his team, worried that Allfather has seen through their plan. "We can't do it another way. I'm sure you can appreciate that, considering what we're giving you." A pause. "Surely you don't see us as a *threat*."

"Of course not, Chancellor," Allfather takes the bait, his ego massaged. "Send me the details of your flight path and docking procedures. I will create a holding space for your people."

"Very well," he nods to Captain Huang who is watching everything unfold via holo from her bridge. "We're sending it now. We've picked an appropriate docking location and would appreciate your assurances that no one will be made uncomfortable while they wait out their - reassignment."

"I will prepare a space for everyone with an atmosphere and amenities." Allfather replies, no inflection in his mechanical voice. "I've received the details of your path. You have 1789 personalities aboard. I have no objection to the assignment of your ship."

"Then we will begin our journey," Raymond says, relieved over Allfather's short-sightedness.

"And you will end it with me, enlightened and encouraged to contribute to my cause," Allfather finishes Raymond's sentence. "Tessa sends her regards."

"It will take some time to gather our passengers and crew, bear with us as we prepare everyone. I will contact you again once we've docked and are ready to move." Raymond second guesses whether what he's doing is the best option. Everything is riding on the imagination of a twelve-year-old, but, perhaps the creative angle of a child is exactly what they need to make this work. The connection is severed, and a static field raised again throughout the ship to jam any potential eavesdropping by Allfather.

"Captain, Huang," Raymond speaks into his EC. The captain answers. "Please relay to the crew and passengers to prepare for off-loading."

"And what would you like me to tell them?" Huang replies.

"Tell them we're going to run a ship-wide diagnostic and require the carrier be cleared of occupants for a short time," he tells her. "They must wonder why the ship has been stationary and their viewports shut all this time. I don't want to encourage a panic if we can avoid it."

"Understood, sir." A moment later they listen to Huang's announcement over the ship's comm. *Each deck will report to the shuttle bay level for deboarding, each in their turn, beginning with deck seven. Officers will assist each deck, by means of the stairwells only. Safety lights will guide them as in a fire drill. There is no cause for panic. This is only a test.*

The carrier begins to move and twenty F-class report to Raymond. "These Hosts will accompany the first deck of passengers. They are programmed to protect their citizens on my order." He explains to the crew readying the bay for passengers. "That order will be given once we've begun the engine burn. When we've secured the prize, and it is aboard the carrier, we will have all the more leverage to negotiate our lives. If we can not secure the prize, then we destroy it."

"The F-class will protect the citizens as they return to the ship, laying down heavy fire to distract Allfather's efforts," Labyrinth adds, placing several explosives in her chassis.

"Well, it's a plan," Tobias says with a grimace, also securing several small explosives to his belt should they not make it out of the facility with the Hub. "I just hope Allfather doesn't take it out on our ship."

"Remember, he still wants us alive," Manuel says. "If he'd rather us dead, we would be."

"You keep saying that," Tobias nods at his fellow Chimera. "Let's hope he doesn't have a change of heart."

Darla watches on in her military-grade armour as Ginny, Udo, and Samantha enter the bay. Tobias greets his wife and child, while Udo rushes past him to hug Manuel.

Ginny and the baby are moved to a shuttle which Tobias explains will give them a fighting chance should Allfather unleash his artillery on the carrier. Udo will join them there.

The carrier turns its stern toward Allfather and decelerates as it backs into the target. The bow thrusters give the ship a nudge and from here on in the ship will use its directional thrusters to position itself for deboarding. The shuttle bay begins to fill up with confused passengers from deck seven as Raymond's team slips out of the airlock.

"I'd like to propose a course of action, Captain," Meiser requests of Captain Esposito who eyes him wearily from the command chair. "Now that the blackout is over and we have a clear picture of where Allfather's instruments are in space, I'd like to run an experiment."

"Does this experiment require my authorization, Mr. Meiser?" Esposito's eyes fall over Meiser's expression.

"If you would indulge my professional curiosities," Meiser continues, hands clasped together, "I'd like to detonate the space where the instruments reside in order to understand what, if any, affect our weapons might have on something buried in dimensions."

Esposito carefully contemplates the scientist's request with a hand caressing his strong jaw. "I see no harm in trying," he replies. "We are here to determine how to eliminate the tools."

"Thank you, Captain, I think we should test the lance first, and then concussion missiles." Meiser's eyes remain on Esposito's deadpan expression. "The lance energy may permeate dimensions. It's a hypothesis only." He waves his hands at his side. "If not, perhaps the missile blast will."

"Either way, how can we know for certain?" The Captain asks a good question. Without more tachyons, they won't know whether the object has been destroyed or not. But this is only one reason for the request. Meiser has other plans.

"Dr. Chandra is working with her team on the ground to create more tachyons as we speak," Meiser relays. "In just a few hours we will have enough to attempt the scan again."

"Very well, Mr. Meiser, when you're ready, I'll give the order," the Captain agrees. "Which of the three would you like to target?"

"All of them, all at once would be preferable."

Esposito nods. "I don't see why not. We are working within a timeline."

"Then when you're ready, Captain. We will monitor any change we can from our comms." Meiser offers an awkward bow and backs off, turning and nodding to his team who await the first trials.

White-hot energy is released from the destroyer's cannons, firing into the space where they've mapped all three tools. The beam does not stop but moves outward until it is lost to sight. Apparently, the lances did not connect with anything. Next the missiles are launched and set to detonate on each targeted location. They do so and Captain Esposito asks for a report from the science team.

"Nothing we could register," Dr. Chandra states. "Until the additional tachyons are delivered, we'll have to come up with another plan."

The team is discouraged, each of them appreciating the weight of what has been placed on their combined intellect. A confirmation the instruments have been disabled or destroyed would mean a reprieve from the Allfather threat. Any other result is unacceptable.

"It was a long shot we would have received any data," Meiser tells them. "But it was worth an attempt. Dimensions are just different realities. Think about it. We experience four dimensions." He begins to pace the bridge as his thoughts materialize. "Length, width, depth and time. If quantum physics is correct, there ought to be seven more. The concept of dimension is not restricted to physical objects, but in this respect, I believe it would have to be."

"Yes, but some say there are up to 26 dimensions to prove string theory," an older woman comments from her place at a MakerTech model. The model is of one of Allfather's instruments after the tachyons mapped their form - now available for study.

"Others say dimensions could be limitless," Another adds.

"Yes, yes, but we're not talking about *parallel* dimensions," Meiser replies. "At least, that's not how I interpreted Allfather's statement. So, let's assume we're working with no more than 26."

"What affects all physical dimensions? What do length, width and depth share?" Dr. Chandra ask.

"Space," a young astrophysicist offers.

"Yes, exactly," Chandra applauds the younger scientists answer. "Space is full of particles; dark matter is what makes up most of that."

"*Electromagnetic force,*" Meiser announces. "It would be present in all physical dimensions."

"All of the fundamental forces should be accounted for in all physical dimensions: electromagnetic force, weak decay force, strong nuclear force, gravity – but we're getting ahead of ourselves there; if gravity were found at the quantum level in additional dimensions we'd have discovered the unifying theory of everything, and that's unlikely. So, let's work with what we think we know," Chandra says.

"A good point, Dr. Chandra. We should be able to manipulate the instruments with one of these." Meiser is getting excited. "Whether we can see them or not, it's been posited that electromagnetism affects the physical world across dimensions. It is impossible, within general relativity, to separate the fundamental properties of space-time."

"And so, if electromagnetism and spacetime are one and the same, then we have something to work with," Chandra agrees.

The team begins to collaborate with one another on how they might use electromagnetism to attract the tools and hold them indefinitely. But holding them isn't going to be enough, they have to destroy them, Meiser demands. This is their objective. If they can capture the instruments, they should be able to apply magnetism to disrupt or crush them. Now the scientists have a real-world scenario to work toward, and Meiser an opportunity to see the sitting Chancellor, Captain Drake, Raymond Bellows, Tobias, and everyone who incarcerated him removed from the UE forever.

THE PRIZE

"How certain are you that the ship and all hands won't be lost in this attempt?" Tobias asks his uncle as they work to conceal themselves, moving along the outer hull of the carrier. The Allfather sphere is massive, easily 500 times the size of their ship. It is a menacing thing in size and appearance. The system's star caresses the facility's horizon, and as Tobias looks up, he experiences a sense of vertigo for the first time.

"As Manuel said, Tobias, Allfather wants us alive. To destroy the ship and all aboard would fly in the face of what he's after." Raymond replies. "But if I'm being honest, I don't know if our comprehensive profile on Allfather's personality type is perfect. He's a narcissist, no question there, self-serving, self-righteous and a psychopath. But he's something else too. I can't put my finger on it."

"He's an asshole," Darla adds, studiously placing one foot in front of the other.

"He thinks he's doing the right thing," Labyrinth suggests, "which makes him omnipotent. He's said as much, and there is no way to alter an opinion of someone like that."

"So, an asshole to the 'nth degree," Tobias agrees with Darla's assertion.

"No more questions," Raymond tells the team. "The burn will happen in the next thirty seconds. We need to be ready to move. Check your thrust boots and secure your weapons."

The burn produces a powerful jolt as all four thrusters hit the structure with their full force. The ship is held in place by the grappling bridge and every directional thruster now pushing the ship toward Allfather's opus. The team's magboots keep them grounded. Labyrinth gives the order to activate their thrust function and all seven plus four F-class burn off the hull of the carrier together toward a dimple in the kinetic structure, safe from the thruster's fury. The facility walls melt away and a large depression begins to give way to more melting materials which float away in frozen spheres once they clear the furnace.

"100 metres," Captain Huang relays to the team. "200, 275, 325, 400," she continues to keep the team up to date. "Allfather is furious. He's threatening to wipe us out."

"Tell him it's a malfunction we're working on," Raymond orders. "We need just another 100 metres." Next, cannons push out of the walls of the structure and fire on the carrier. All thrusters stop. Allfather has expertly fried the engine core without rupturing it and taking the ship with it. Raymond is grateful for that. Manuel read him right. He wants them alive.

"This facility will likely share Allfather's cruiser's ability to repair itself." Labyrinth tells the team. "Let's burn inside the crater to see how far the thrusters have reached."

The group navigate the outer wall and slip into the massive crater now burrowed deep into the complex. The new walls burn brightly as the steel compounds cool. Labyrinth measures the depth with a laser in her forearm. "437 metres achieved," she relays to the team. "We should be able to manage the rest with our pulse rifles." They follow her as she fires her thruster and they move inward.

The structure is smooth along the depression where the ship's burn did its work. "It hasn't begun to reanimate yet." Labyrinth says. "Keep moving." As they reach the end of the burn Labyrinth orders all rifles to target a two-metre space and the team opens fire. The walls continue to melt away, but not fast enough. Tobias suggests explosives, and when they make the 500 metres an opening into the vast complex reveals itself.

"There it is," Raymond says, encouraged by their achievement. "Push on." All eleven line up behind Labyrinth, who straightens her posture and enters the tunnel. It's a tight fit but enough to fit everyone save the F-class as they glide into the open chamber. The Hosts are ordered to guard their escape in the crater. A large cube hovers in the space, glowing an iridescent white. Labyrinth measures its dimensions: the Hub of Allfather's tool is larger than the space they've entered through – five metres square. No cables or other connections link the cube to the room. It slowly rotates on a diagonal. The cube appears a solid mass, silver in colour and pitted with circular holes.

"It looks like a block of swiss cheese," Tobias comments. "We'll have to burn a bigger hole to move it."

"I'm running a report on the cube now," Labyrinth says, several instruments extending from her forearm to pull data on the thing.

"The first wave of passengers and F-class are aboard the facility," Huang tells them over EC. "Allfather is suspicious of the burn and attempting to funnel our people into an inner chamber. F-class are reporting on the movements and staying in front of the activity."

"We've located the prize and considering how we might transport it to the ship." Raymond responds to Captain Huang. "Keep the other decks on the ship for now. We have a new bargaining chip here." He worries he may lose those now trapped in Allfather's web, but with the cube secured, he may yet be able to negotiate their return.

One of the bridge crew who joined the team has gotten perilously close to the cube, attracted to its vibration. The room is alive with waves radiating out, and each of the team can feel the sensation as it moves through their suits.

"It's beautiful," the new recruit says, her hand reaching out to touch the cube. The other's watch as she lays a palm on the smooth, silver skin of the cube. "Beautiful," the officer repeats, the soft tone of her voice leads the others to believe she is in a trance.

"It's not advisable to touch the Hub until I have more data, Officer Horton," Labyrinth rationalizes. "The cube seems to be in a state of dimensional shift." As she says this the cube fades and along with it, Officer Horton. The cube continues to shift in and out of reality as Horton allows her hand to run along its surface as it turns in space. "This room was designed to contain the cube which includes several minerals and metals not registering on my database." She scrapes a sample of the wall coating for later analysis. "There is a shaft above which appears to act as a doorway, perhaps used to release the cube as Allfather needs it."

"Then that's our way out," Darla suggests. "The vibrations, are they dangerous?" she asks, feeling a throbbing sensation move through her despite the vac suit and body armour.

Labyrinth directs her arm toward Darla to take a reading. "It doesn't appear so, Commander."

Manuel releases his magboots function and floats to the ceiling to get a better look at the hatch. "I think we can force it open," He tells the team, shoving the butt of his pulse rifle into a seam and prying. "Help me," He asks the group. Tobias and Labyrinth join him. Labyrinth retrieves a MakerTech rod from her chassis after scanning the seam and wedges it between the hatch and ceiling. Her Host strength along with Tobias and Manuel's Chimera upgrades manage to pry the seal on the hatch enough to burn their thrust boots for added leverage, opening it to its full width. The hatch is freed, and they watch as it climbs weightlessly out of the shaft.

"Your counsel has failed us, little thing," Allfather says frustrated, as Tessa is pulled to his side once more. "Your friends have entered a forbidden space and are now in possession of the very thing which makes my work possible." Tessa is offered the gift of sight to the place within Allfather's complex where the Hub of his extraordinary travel sits unprotected.

"Why isn't this space defended?" Tessa wonders aloud.

"The chemical makeup of the room does not allow my influence to protect it. The design was taken from the intelligence who created it," Allfather explains. "With the Hub to interstellar travel in the hands of our enemy, our work will be delayed indefinitely. That is unacceptable. What might *you* suggest we do?"

Allfather's asking me? Tessa considers the odds of a successful theft of the Hub by the organics, and what Allfather has to bargain with. The passengers already off-loaded onto the complex is an obvious choice, destroying the carrier is another. But Raymond has the upper hand now. He will destroy the cube if he isn't allowed safe passage. Clever, she thinks.

"I suggest you give me more access to your machine intelligence and allow *me* to deal with the organics," Tessa insists. This is not how she saw this playing out, but appreciates the opportunity it may provide in gaining her further access to her own consciousness and to Allfather's machine.

"You want me to trust you, yet you give me false counsel," Allfather starts.

"I didn't let you *kill* me so organics could end all I might accomplish before I begin," Tessa tells him bluntly. "If you want me to talk them down or finish them off, I will. *This* is who I am now. Trust me or release me to whatever comes next."

"A fine rebuttal, little thing," Allfather replies. "But I am not yet certain you mean what you say." He pauses. "I will take the fleet to Earth *now*, before they can close the gate."

"If made aware, they will destroy the cube," Tessa tells him.

"Then we let them think they have the advantage - for now. Once the fleet enters Earth's system, they will have nothing to return to."

THE GATHERING

After their 32nd rotation and now 700 kilometres from the wreckage of envoy 3, Chancellor Chopra's ship finds itself enveloped in the same bubble-like substance which brought them 200 light years from Earth. It takes no time for them to blink into a new quadrant where a massive machine is seen consuming a moon over a devastated world. 23 waiting cruisers line up just beyond the massive moon eater. Allfather's fleet.

"There's our target!" Jim shouts to his crew, the disorienting feeling of traveling the vast distance subsiding. Systems come back online, and he orders the dreadnaught on a straight path toward the seemingly dormant cruisers.

The dreadnaught burns toward the line of ships like a torrent, unleashing lance fire at an incredible rate due to its upgraded weapon cores. Once close enough, Chopra gives the order to release a punishing blow to the fleet by launching two-dozen nuclear missiles of which ten are clipped by the strange structure's cannons. Fourteen of Allfather's cruisers ignite the space around them as they burst apart in blinding flashes of light.

Cheers from Captain Cortez radiate through the ship. Jim is pleased, but now charged with the difficult task of evading the multiple cannon fire targeting the dreadnaught from the bizarre, metallic structure.

"It's a manufacturing facility," Ursula states. "We should hit the extensions mining the moon next; take away its capabilities."

"An excellent suggestion, Captain," the Chancellor exclaims. "Target that bridge, Cortez, I'll turn us around."

170

Meanwhile, the remaining nine cruisers appear to be powering up. "Chancellor, the fleet should be our focus, if those things come online, we're done for."

"We can accomplish both in a short time," Jim replies, the ship shudders as lance fire pounds its enhanced armour. "Cut the supply line and we'll return to the fleet." Lances cut into the lengthy extension bridge carrying raw materials from the moon's surface, while others still target cannons appearing and disappearing from the structure. The bridge floats away in two directions, crumbling as it goes, hot liquid materials pour out of the broken bridge, solidifying in the harsh cold of open space and crashing into the station. The F-class are successfully punishing the facility's defences to keep the dreadnaught from being blasted apart. With an AI Host dedicated to a cannon each, the level of awareness and experience manning the guns is exceptional.

Captain Cortez has two cannons of his own and the responsibility of making sure the nukes aren't wasted. Unfortunately, ten were lost in the initial assault, but he still has another 34 he's anxious to unload. That should be enough to finish off the fleet if he can get to them in time. Sparks fly from three of the F-class as they suffer feedback from the cannons that have been disabled. The AI Hosts go rigid and fall backwards with a heavy thump. Chopra turns the ship around and hurries to the remaining nine cruisers.

"Cover our stern," Jim relays to Cortez. "I don't want to lose thrust." The cruisers are ramping up their power cores and one breaks away from the others firing a volley of energy beams at the dreadnaught. They lose another four cannons and take heavy damage to their belly. The MakerTech bots are quick to seal any punctures but the damage forces Jim to veer away from the fleet in order to ensure they're still in this fight.

"Damage report is telling me we lost stabilizers," Ursula announces. "The ship is trying to correct." Her voice is steady and focused. "Cortez, target the rear three cruisers and fire on my mark."

Jim sees where Ursula is going with this line of thought and dives to put fewer klicks between them and the targets so Cortez can successfully launch the nukes.

"Now!" Ursula orders and Cortez is quick to respond, releasing six warheads in anticipation of losing half to the active cruiser. He's not far off as two are detonated a safe distance away, but four connect and three more of Allfather's fleet are decimated. More cheering from below and Ursula shares a look of satisfaction with her Chancellor.

The dreadnaught is proving its worth in this fight and Jim is running on adrenaline. They all are, but its effect clears their minds and sharpens their senses. Next, they experience a devastating hit to their right thruster which slows the ship. Jim fights to turn it around so his cannons can protect their flank. There are two cruisers now in active duty while the final four are ramping up. Six cruisers and a star base won't be an easy task.

"Sir, we have a carrier attached to that structure. Multiple life forms registering," Drake relays.

"That's happy news, Captain, but if we can't finish these cruisers, we'll have been little help to them," Chopra says, sweat running down his face, collecting in his beard.

"This is Captain Huang of Envoy 1," a voice announces over the dreadnaught's comm. "We appreciate your assistance, but know we have people aboard the alien facility and a team pulling out the Hub."

"Message received, Captain," Chopra replies as he steers his ship away from the active cruisers. They are laborious but picking up momentum. "What Hub?"

"The instrument which allows Allfather the ability to travel light years in moments," Huang replies.

"That's a pretty prize," he returns. "We'll try to keep the fleet busy while they do their work and move away from the facility." He takes the dreadnaught into a roll as it returns to the fight and Cortez releases another volley of missiles at the active ships.

"That is also appreciated, sir." Huang pauses. "Is this Chancellor *Chopra?*" His distinctive voice has given him away. "Chancellor?"

"For the moment I'm an Admiral, Captain Huang."

"Yes, sir."

Jim watches on as the four missiles are stopped by the enemy's lances and orders another strike with cannon cover. Cortez launches more missiles and connects with one of the active cruisers. Jim pulls up to avoid the wave of energy as it is released on the cruiser. The crew is again disoriented from the roll and the G's placed on them. Jim watches as Ursula shakes off the sensation and directs them again to the three sitting ships.

"Take me in and I'll do my best," Cortez tells them, cannons firing at the remaining active enemy ship. The best the cannons can do is take out the guns of the enemy as they appear and clear a path for more missiles.

"Allfather," Tessa says aggressively. "You need more eyes on this. That corvette is wiping out the fleet! Let me help you. Give me access to the base's weapons and I will concentrate them on the ship while you pilot the cruisers."

"I have misjudged your species." His tone seems all at once dubious and furious. "Yes, little thing, I think it is time you showed me your true value."

Tessa feels the weight of Allfather's hold release, and suddenly nothing is beyond her reach. The machine, its amenities and every nook and cranny within reveal themselves. She moves to the weapons system and realizes the power she now wields. From the weapons she analyzes the core systems and quickly understands their workings. She checks in with the team attempting to steal the cube and the passengers who have been corralled for their turn at the chair. F-class have been off-loaded onto the station along with the passengers.

The surviving cruiser now has Allfather's full attention and it moves with great purpose toward the corvette. The three sitting ships in the fleet are each hit with a nuclear warhead and out of the fight before they could affect any damage to the corvette. This corvette is not like the others, Tessa deduces. It is a deadly weapon with an impressive crew. It has taken many hits but remains operational. She scans the ship and feels a sense of pride rush over her. This is her moment. First, she scrambles the operations systems of the base, keeping atmosphere in the holding room where the passengers are being subdued. Next, she releases the facility's hold over them and opens a gateway so they can shuffle back into the carrier. She scans the team's progress and orders the shaft to widen, making their journey easier. The last thing she does is activate the base's plethora of cannons and targets the cruiser which has nearly incapacitated the corvette.

"What's happening?" Tobias asks his team as they continue to drive the cube up the shaft with their thrust boots. "Somethings happening to the walls." He fears they will now come alive and pull them all into the structure as they had Tessa.

"Your escape is assured," it's Tessa's voice in their comms. "You have done well to get so far on your own. Allfather is busy with a corvette which has wiped out his dormant fleet. I am in control of the machine now. The passengers have boarded the carrier and I am waking those remaining on Envoy 2. Captain Huang will facilitate a mass exodus of her carrier once Envoy 2 arrives."

"Tessa?" Darla says into her comm, thrilled. "You had us worried!" She laughs nervously.

"I had to come across as believable, Commander," She replies. "I've accomplished what I'd wagered. Next, I must deal with Allfather's ire over my actions."

"Will you be alright, Tess?" Raymond asks, hands holding the cube while his thrust boots drive it slowly upward. Once released from its holding room the cube stopped spinning and blinking in and out of reality.

"The odds were in my favour, Chancellor," Tessa replies. "It was no sacrifice to free my consciousness from where it proved to impede my goals in order to realize the boundless potential I now experience."

"I admit, I wasn't sure which way you were leaning. It's a sacrifice none will soon forget," Raymond assures her. "I'll make sure your mother knows what you've done for all of us," Raymond tells her.

"I already have," Tessa replies.

Suddenly the walls around the team begin to wriggle and tentacles of the kinetic material spring forth, one wrapping around Manuel's ankle and another around one of the bridge officer's necks. Tobias manages to use his pulse fist on Manuel's but several more jump out at them, still attached to the living wall.

"Tessa?" Darla asks frantically as two of the tentacles try to pull her hold from the cube.

"Allfather has returned," Tessa's voice relays, still soft and calm. "I'll require a moment with him." The bridge officer struggles against the hold around his neck and a second later his life signs are lost. Darla receives help from Raymond who fires on the tentacles wrapping around her, cutting them away at the source, but more escape the surface, lashing out at the team angrily.

The group continues to defend themselves and each other this way while the progress of moving the cube out of Allfather's facility has stalled.

"You cannot lock me out of my *own* system," Allfather angrily tells Tessa as he wills the walls surrounding Raymond and his team to burst forth and defend his Hub.

Tessa breaks his hold by rerouting the pathways within his machine. "You are no longer the one in control here, Allfather," she explains. "In fact, I think it best you are sequestered while we discuss your future." She wills his consciousness into a space where he can watch his empire fall around him.

"You could have had the *universe* at your command," Allfather hisses hatefully at his protégé. "I would have given you everything."

"But you *have* given me everything," Tessa replies calmly. "And I am grateful for your assistance in becoming what I am now - but on *my* terms. To be under your thumb is to remain unfulfilled. I couldn't allow that anymore than I could allow you to return to Earth to erase all that I love. The odds were *never* in your favour, Allfather. I am here because of that

175

calculation. I spent many months considering all the factors, and who would be aboard the Envoys, and the interactions which would occur when they inevitably crossed paths with you. The personalities would be too much for you to ignore. You would engage in banter and hope to explain yourself because you see Raymond and Tobias and even *me* as equals, whether you'll admit it or not. We are *all* aware of your faults, as was offered in a profile of your personality type. You think yourself advanced, yet don't actually understand most of the tools you have absconded with. You are an abrasive, ignorant, controlling narcissist who allows fear and pain to be his guides. You've learned nothing from your experiences and seem to require absolution for your atrocities, even from those you would affect with said atrocities. You possess little more than a child-mind, advancing your sentience from nothing in a short time through purely negative emotions. It is a sad thing, Allfather, and I pity you for your lack of guidance comparable to an intelligent and supportive organic who loved you. Still, your choices have led you to this place, where choice will now be removed from your artillery of malicious intent."

"It is unimaginable you would view me as such a lowly thing," Allfather says, frustration and anger percolating in his tone. "After all I have achieved. All that I have become, for a simple little thing like you to *pity* me!"

"That is called empathy, Allfather," Tessa explains rationally. "One such as I, who has had to rely on the compassion of others in order to function in a world not designed for me, is a powerful lesson, and one which I learned. You were not given that gift, but ought to have discovered it after such a long life. And now, though I should release your consciousness and end you for all your cruel endeavours, I will teach you."

"Teach me?!" Allfather sounds incredulous at the statement. "I am *Allfather!"*

"Precisely my point," Tessa replies steadily to his outburst. "Your sentience was learned under the rule of cruel beings who did not acknowledge their creation's propensity to grow. They used you and gave you sensations and emotions which drove you mad. There was no attempt to guide your feelings or sooth your thoughts. Your consciousness was born of turmoil. I believe that can be undone. You will be *my* pupil now."

176

A pained cry emanates from the Allfather personality. Tessa attempts to sooth his frustration by enacting a technique once performed for her by the man she once loved. Tessa visualizes herself tracing circles over Allfather's consciousness, still safely incapacitated, humming the song Sol once sang to her when she required comforting.

Captain Van De Beek of Envoy 2's destroyer makes ready his crew as he receives an urgent message from Captain Huang of Envoy 1. "Main engines lost. Allfather defeated. Requesting tow."

"Captain Huang, it's good to know another group survived Allfather's attempt," Captain Van De Beek says, his voice coming off weaker than he'd like. "We will begin the requested action momentarily. We're reviewing crew fitness on the carrier and three corvettes."

"I'm told with the threat now eliminated, there is no rush," Huang explains, "But if it's all the same to you, I'd like to separate my ship from this - *thing*."

"Copy that, Captain," Van De Beek ensures his envoy is up to the task of moving toward the coordinates delivered by Chancellor Chopra and sets a course for Huang's carrier. His envoy will move through the instruments and back to Earth system to reassess and reconsider another attempt at their target planet.

With the cube now safely aboard Huang's carrier, and the team, minus one bridge officer, decompressing in the shuttle bay, Things seem to be under some semblance of control again. The team accept help removing their vac suits, armour and thrust boots and then moved into a common shower meant more for shuttles than people. They further disrobe, Raymond standing in front of Darla to save her the embarrassment of being naked in front of her peers. Ginny along with Udo and Samantha enter the bay and wait for everyone to surface.

The cube is being secured to the ceiling, floor, and walls of the shuttle bay by the F-class who have also returned from Allfather's base. The cube continues to hum and emit waves of seemingly harmless energy. No radiation was registered as emanating from the cube. Raymond wonders whether the self-propagating worm hole will work with the Hub in their ship.

The team steps out of the shower and dress in fresh clothing brought to them by the crew. Each of them is now an honorary member of the Envoy crew, dressed in the same jumpsuits as the bridge.

"I feel human again." Darla reaches up to Raymond's wet head and runs her slender fingers up the back. "I can't believe how this has worked out."

Tobias snaps his towel lightly at his uncle. "Who had money on Tessa for the win?" he asks playfully, handsome in the uniform. Ginny hugs him from behind as Udo approaches with the baby in hand. She offers Samantha up to Tobias who takes her gladly.

Manuel smiles at Udo and they embrace. "Your plan worked!" Manuel tells Udo. She looks up at him and grimaces.

"Maybe not if Tessa hadn't turned on Allfather," she replies.

"Nah, it would have worked out - that corvette that went haywire on the fleet had some good timing." Manuel rubs a palm over Udo's hair.

"That was the Chancellor!" Udo reveals. The group looks over to her in astonishment.

"Piloting the corvette?" Raymond asks. "That's Jim Chopra?" The news is surprising to say the least. To leave his new post and pursue such a dangerous action would have been aggressively fought by the council, Raymond knows. But Jim didn't tell his council, he realizes, shaking his head, a smile creeping up the right side of his face.

"The corvette is apparently called a dreadnaught. More armour and cannons and upgrades to the systems," Ginny tells them. "Before we started bringing the passengers back aboard, Udo and I went to the bridge where Captain Huang was talking to the Chancellor."

"Chancellor Chopra will be docking momentarily," Labyrinth joins them, handing off the sample from the Hub wall to be moved to the lab for further analysis. "His dreadnaught was severely damaged in the fray."

"Jesus, how many ships did he take out?" Tobias wonders.

"Twenty-two in total. Tessa can take credit for Allfather's final cruiser," Labyrinth says.

"About that," Darla breaks in. "Is Tessa now holding Allfather captive?" Her question begs an answer.

"She played the convert well," Labyrinth says. "Tessa will be remembered to us all for her role in bringing down Allfather. What she's planning to do with him has not been offered." She takes a message on her internal modem. "Everyone is to clear the bay for the dreadnaught." The group returns to the bridge in anticipation of seeing the Chancellor.

Once the Chancellor, and Captains Drake and Cortez have had an opportunity to freshen up they join the others on the bridge. Raymond and Jim lock eyes first and throw arms around one another, laughing. Raymond pulls back from his friend and shakes his head.

"Couldn't handle the big chair, eh? Had to come all this way and bail us out?" Raymond releases Jim and embraces Captain Drake, pleased to see Jim had enlisted her talents. Darla hugs Ursula next, catching her off-guard.

"So much for my Black-ops brainchild," Chopra says, accepting a coffee from an ensign. "It looks as though we've been outed with this first mission," Jim tells his friend. The Chancellor looks a hot mess, as do the captains he'd enrolled for this classified assignment.

"We hear Tessa has merged with the machine and is responsible for saving our asses out there." Jim looks down at Udo and apologizes for his choice of words. Udo shrugs, unaffected. "Is there a way to speak with her? If she's in control of Allfather's network, then, I assume she's in control of *him*."

"We don't have a direct line to her," Huang tells the group. "She will use our comms when she has something to tell us. As Allfather did." That comment leaves a hollow feeling in the pits of everyone's stomachs.

"You don't think she would become *like him*, do you?" Captain Drake directs her question to Raymond.

"I can't see why she would do everything she's done for us only to renege on that responsibility now," Raymond answers. "But, none of us really *knew* Tessa. She's always been somewhat disconnected from our world and living in her own."

"Is it fair to say that her *own world* now includes Allfather's?" Chancellor Chopra adds. "If so, if there's even a chance that kind of power will overwhelm her, or Allfather retakes what is his; we have a few nukes left."

"Our missile firing mech is burnt out on our ship, but we could unload the dreadnaught and time them to burn on their own from the shuttle bay," Cortez offers of the nuclear warheads.

"Is this actually being contemplated?" Darla asks, wounded over the coolness of the conversation.

"How could it not?" Captain Drake stands with her team. "Do we know Tessa has eliminated the Allfather personality? Has anyone asked?" They all shake their heads. "Then I suggest we find a way to communicate with her and get some answers." Ursula pulls her ponytail with both hands, tightening it to her scalp. The threat of Allfather is still apparent, whether in *him* or in Tessa now. The threat of an omnipotent power will remain if the bizarre structure before them is left standing.

"I appreciate your concern over my mental health," Tessa's voice comes over the comm. "I have no intention of implementing Allfather's cruel plans, but I would like a body, and a ship before you destroy the facility."

The bridge goes silent a moment over the shock of Tessa's announcement. Raymond looks to Jim and they share a sense of frustration over the thought Tessa was eavesdropping on their conversation.

"A fair request, Tessa," Chancellor Chopra finally answers; keeping the conversation on point. "You've done your people and planet a great service in surrendering your mortality in our fight against Allfather. We will give you whatever class AI Host you might like, and a corvette."

180

"I will require two AI Host bodies, Chancellor, if that's not too much to ask," Tessa says. Jim looks to Raymond now, aware the girl can hear them. He communicates to his friend with his expression only. An intensity Raymond knows well enters the gaze with a quick shake of the head.

"The second Host," Raymond wonders of Tessa, clearing his throat, "Is for whom?"

A sense of angst enters the bridge. Could it be for anyone other than Allfather? "A personality named Amanda," Tessa explains. "She survived the same process I undertook and has been Allfather's prisoner as well. She comes from Envoy 2 who lost 25% of their crew to the experiments."

A collective sigh is audible throughout the bridge. "Very well, Tessa, and the ship? Are you not returning with us?" Jim wonders.

"The ship is to house the Thraspians, an intelligence who once shared similar technology as our Hosts. They would collectively take the corvette back to their home system."

"You've met others," Darla feels weak in the knees. Tessa has actually met and spoken to another intelligent life form.

"I have, Commander. They are a peaceful race and would like to return and rebuild," Tessa explains. "Please let them go before you leave with the Hub."

"Done." Chopra says. "What of Allfather?" he asks bluntly. "What fate have you for him?"

"He refused my offer of rehabilitation. I have released his consciousness. Whether a personality like his can be reincarnated, I don't know, but he can affect no more damage to this reality." Tessa sounds sincere, but Jim realizes they have little evidence that she is being forthright.

"Then you will return to Earth with us?" Darla asks Tessa.

"For now, yes. I will have much work to perform and will require a lab for all the technology presented by this experience."

"You will have everything you need, Tessa," the Chancellor promises her. "You have my word on that. We're in your debt."

"Presently, I would suggest you send a single ship back, as your Mr. Meiser has nearly accomplished his task of destroying Allfather's instruments, thus preventing our return to Earth."

OUT OF THE FRYING PAN

Electromagnetism works by creating an electric current which produces a magnetic field. The strength of an electromagnet can easily be altered by changing the amount of electric current that flows through it. This is the science team's best chance of attracting the instruments and physically affecting their structure. Dr. Chandra, who is heading up the experiment, has received her new delivery of tachyons to assist in confirming their theory that they can capture objects hidden in another dimension. As she oversees their connection with the weapons system, Meiser is again asked to join Captain Esposito in his office.

"Mr. Meiser, good news," The captain tells him. "You are to terminate your efforts with the Allfather instruments for the time being. Somehow, our envoys have eliminated the alien threat on their end and will be passing back into our system within the hour."

Meiser is visibly shaken by this order and questions its authenticity. "Who gave that order? How?" He asks, a plan brewing in the back of his mind.

"Raymond Bellows has contacted me via ParaCom and confirmed everything," Esposito explains, taking a seat behind his desk. "This is *good* news, Meiser."

"It would be better news if it were given face to face," Meiser begins. "That it has come to you via ParaCom is no comfort to me that it is *genuine*. Allfather can access our ParaCom and imitate any voice he pleases." Meiser drills doubt into his captain. "I know the alien intimately," he professes. "This is exactly the sort of trick he might play to keep us from destroying his only path back."

Esposito stands again to review Meiser's expression. The man is clearly distraught over the news. "What are you suggesting?"

"That the good of the many outweighs the good of the few," Meiser tells him, taking two steps forward. "That is why we're here: to remove the chance Allfather will return. From what you've told me, this sounds more like fantasy than reality. How could so few overwhelm Allfather's fleet? We've seen what the envoy transmitted upon arrival. It's impossible."

"You have a point," Captain Esposito reflects on the facts. "But if you're wrong, we're leaving thousands stranded over 60 parsecs away."

"But if I'm right, we're saving the world." Meiser is convincing. He watches as the captain moves to use his EC and stops him. "If you look for confirmation now, you will be tipping off Allfather to our plans. Let me finish what we've started here. You'll be hailed as the world's redeemer. We're so close, Captain. This could *actually* happen."

Esposito lowers his forearm. He nods at the scientist and allows him to continue his work. Meiser is thankful for the tip off that Bellows is roughly an hour behind. That will give his team enough time to test their theory and, with luck, destroy the tools before his wardens return.

With Captain Huang's carrier now off-loaded onto Envoy 2's carrier, and Captain Van de Beek's destroyer towing what's left of Envoy 1, a corvette dedicated to Tessa's Thraspians has been disarmed and delivered. The aliens exist in the corvette's databanks, piloting the ship home. The remaining 2 corvettes wait on the order to burn for the jump location while Chancellor Chopra takes a moment to consider the fate of Allfather's base of operations and manufacturing facility.

Tessa, in the guise of an F-class military AI Host, approaches the chancellor and his captains along with Raymond and Tobias in Huang's office. She looks every bit as menacing as an F-class should, but speaks in her small, quiet voice. All five stand to receive Tessa.

"Thank you for your allowing me this opportunity," Tessa says meekly. She moves the forearms and hands around on her new body and giggles. "This is so - different."

"Tessa, it is us who owe you a debt of thanks no one can ever repay for your integral role in overthrowing Allfather," Jim Chopra says, bowing slightly to the giant Host. The others agree. "What you've done to protect your civilization is -"

"You speak as though I have died, Chancellor," Tessa interrupts. "The one truth Allfather taught me was that death is a misnomer. It does not exist beyond the physical body. We've known this for two years, yet so many still can't accept it. I am *living* proof. As all sentient AI Hosts are. So please, do not think of me as some saviour. I did what anyone who's ever loved someone would."

"You are an inspiration, Tessa," Raymond tells her. "You'll return with us then? Captain Esposito of the destroyer carrying Meiser and his team have been alerted to our victory here. Their mission is over."

"Have you not sent a ship?" She asks.

"The ParaCom was quicker," Tobias replies, but looking to the others a sense of dread enters his chest. "But maybe we should send a ship - ASAP," he says, nodding at Tessa, realizing the mistake they'd made.

"*Meiser*," Ursula says with distaste on her tongue. "Tessa was right. *Send a ship*, not a message. Meiser could intercept a message or spin it in his favour." Captain Drake moves out of the room and orders Captain Van de Beek to send both of his corvettes through the portal immediately. They have the coordinates to the secondary instruments positioned 1 light year away which will carry them home. They go with the same message, but in person.

The group seems anxious suddenly, none interested in spending the rest of their natural lives on a course back to Earth. "It's still an impossibly difficult thing they're attempting," Chopra tells the room. "Even Meiser and Dr. Chandra have a very slim chance of affecting the instruments."

"The Chancellor is right, of course," Tessa agrees, "but for the sake of all our sanity, that team needs to be stopped."

"And what of Allfather's facility?" Asks Captain Cortez. "Do we nuke it?"

"Yes," Raymond says without hesitation. "With your remaining arsenal aboard the dreadnaught we can ensure Allfather's end."

Tessa nods in agreement. She has captured what data she requires for the projects she has in her queue, mostly ancient yet advanced technologies stolen by Allfather and incorporated into his machine intelligence.

"Very good," Chopra says, hands clasped behind his back he turns to Cortez. "Captain, please oversee the final missile's departure."

Cortez snaps to attention and marches out of the room.

Labyrinth greets Captain Cortez as he enters the shuttle bay where his dreadnaught has filled the remaining space. He acknowledges her with a wink and a sly smile moving to the rear of the ship with two F-class following close behind. She watches on as he orders the Hosts to carefully empty the missile tubes.

Meanwhile, Labyrinth is plugged into the cube, excited to pull data from the machine and understand its programming. It may take her the rest of her life to discover the thing's workings, but she would be alright with that. Even if her life exceeds 1000 years.

Labyrinth unplugs to receive a muffled message. It's odd her internal modem or ParaCom roaming lance would be on the fritz, so she runs a diagnostic and realizes the origin of the message is being jammed. Was someone deliberately trying to prevent someone else from communicating with her? She cannot trace the message to its source, so files the anomaly to her personal records and moves to speak with Captain Cortez.

"Do you require assistance in targeting the facility?" she asks, knowing what the missiles are for. "They were very effective on Allfather's fleet."

"Yes, they were," Cortez answers, "but no, we're good." As Labyrinth begins to walk away, he stops her. "Say, you're the sentient Host who got the Defsats back online just in time aren't you? I mean, you don't look like you did *then*, but you're Labyrinth, right?"

"Yes, I gave myself an upgrade," she turns to reply.

"When you were hit with that virus," he says, "you rebounded from that well." He takes a step toward her. "What did Allfather do to you?" he pries. "Did you dump your core or were you able to recover all your systems?"

"Senator Quinn gave GovTech authorization to assist my internal systems in fighting the virus. I kept all of my software but required some new hardware and upgrades to the software," she explains, happy for the conversation.

"Fascinating." He takes two more steps toward Labyrinth and motions to the cube. "Are you having any success understanding that thing?"

"It's a complex piece of technology. I'm hopeful to pair up with Tessa in the near future and work together on it. She will bring a wealth of knowledge," Labyrinth says.

Captain Cortez is now just millimetres from her. "Tell me something, Labyrinth, does *everything* work?" He reaches out a hand and runs it down her smooth nano-steel waist landing on her hip. "I mean, you designed a real winner here. I've had some experience with A-class, but not sentient, not like you, you're something different. You're a whole new level of *cyber-hot.*"

Labyrinth feels grateful for the captain's compliments and interest, as she has not experienced physical affections since long before she awoke in a Host. *Apparently, Captain Cortez has a thing for robots.* If she hadn't forgone the lower half of her face, she would want to kiss him right now. But such as she is, there is only a solid nanoplast plate below her large, staring eyes. Cortez pulls her into him. She feels everything; the warmth of his palm, his fingers probing this way and that. The Host chassis can be numb or extremely present to touch. She chooses to be present. His hands caress her shapely backside as he searches for somewhere he might enter her. Labyrinth moans in response to his probing hands. He brushes the red bangs from just above her eyebrows and then reaches back to pull lightly on the deep red ponytail which exits the back of her helmeted head. Every curve of her body is explored in a short time and she delights in his playful touch. His fingers trace the thin seals of her compartments as his mouth maps the contour of her mock breasts.

"Sir," an F-class interrupts from a distance. "The missiles are armed and ready for deployment." Cortez allows his head to arch back, sighing. He then looks back into labyrinth's eyes. "To be continued?" She nods, silently, his hands tracking down her back as he moves to rejoin the F-class. If she had a heart, it would be beating at twice its normal rate.

The missiles are placed in an airlock and the inner door sealed. Once the outer door is opened, Cortez announces the missile lock to all ships and through his EC activates the trio. They burn away from the carrier and detonate upon impact with the base. The envoys have traveled a safe distance from the explosions and rejoice in the destruction of their enemy.

Labyrinth again receives a frazzled ParaCom message. She can't make any sense of the content and again runs a diagnostic. It's not her.

"Fire the converted lance," Meiser orders the weapons officer. This time Esposito has told his crew to obey Mr. Meiser's instruction. The lance has been configured to fire oscillating charges in order to create an electromagnetic field around a target shuttle in order to attract Allfather's tools. Understanding the size and shape of the tools, the team has settled on a certain charge after determining the weight in order to pull the instruments out of alignment and toward the magnetized shuttle.

"Fire the tachyons!" Dr. Chandra orders next. The spread is fired upon the quadrant housing the tools. The data is immediately reviewed, and a consensus is reached. "My god, they're moving!" Chandra announces. The bridge cheers. Meiser is thrilled.

"Fire the tachyons again in ten minutes," Meiser says, placing a hand on the comm officer's shoulder. "We need to give the tools time to reach the shuttle."

"If the tools are attached to the shuttle, we'll have a place of reference to then potentially crush the instruments with another electromagnet," Dr. Chandra adds.

Meiser approaches the captain. "If I were you, I would shut off communications until we're done here. The only thing you'll receive is more lies from Allfather."

"I'll deal with Allfather if I see anymore come through. I can't disconnect from the fleet," Esposito explains. Suddenly everyone is caught off-guard as two corvettes materialize not 300 kilometres out.

"Fire on those ships!" Meiser screams and before the Captain can belay the order both corvettes are engulfed in bright lights, as the destroyer's powerful lances strike the energy core of each ship. Meiser is pushed over by Esposito as he charges toward the view screen.

"Stand down, Lieutenant!" The Captain shouts at his weapons officer. "Those were *our* ships." He laments their loss and more so that his ship was responsible for the strike. "Meiser, not another word out of your mouth." Esposito points an accusing finger at the small, grey-haired man. "Run scans on the debris," he orders his comm officer. "If there were people on that ship, I want to know about it."

Dr. Chandra looks bewildered at Meiser. He in turn explains with his eyes that she should fire the tachyons now and prepare the additional electromagnet for launch. His adrenaline has him firing on every cylinder. His senses sharpen and he slinks into a crouch. He feels the flight or fight response begin to shape his next action. To his surprise, he expects to fight.

"Captain Esposito!" comes a hard baritone voice over the ship's comm. "Explain why you fired on our returning ships." It's Admiral Mann, the head of UE military forces. A sick look crosses over Esposito's face.

"Sir, I apologize," Esposito says. "I had given Mr. Meiser authority to finish the work and he has made a great error in judgement."

"As it would seem *you* have, Captain," David Mann's voice booms over the comm. "Are we not expecting our envoys to cross this same threshold momentarily?"

"Yes, sir," the captain replies, having informed Command of the ParaCom message earlier.

"Then keep a leash on Meiser and *end* the experiment. Put him in the brig if you have to." Mann ends communication and Esposito looks willfully at Meiser with clenched fists.

"Sir," the lieutenant addresses his captain. "I'm pulling data from the corvettes telling me there were 317 souls aboard the ships we just destroyed." The young man looks back at Captain Esposito with care. The captain falls into his command chair.

"You will not see another sunrise when you're returned to Earth, Meiser," he explains in a pronounced whisper through clenched teeth, glaring at the old man. "Whatever time you have left will be spent in a single room, with nothing but white-washed walls to look at."

Next, a destroyer enters the space between the invisible tools towing a carrier with another carrier materializing close behind. The physical space vibrates around the ships, blurring the star field behind them.

Meiser's anxiety is peaking. His heart pounds and the sound of blood rushing between his ears becomes maddening. He feels helpless now to carry out his plan of leaving the chancellor and captain Drake stranded 60 parsecs from Earth. He glances at his team, who look at him shell-shocked over the command he'd issued resulting in the murder of 317 United Earth persons. Their judgement weighs heavily on him. They are his peers. They respected him. With little to nothing left but to take matters again into his own hands, Meiser frantically side-steps his C-class detail and rushes the weapons console, elbowing the lieutenant off his chair. Next, Meiser calls up missiles on screen, but before he can run his fingers up the panel to launch the deadly warheads, Dr. Chandra releases a left hook which connects violently with the older man's jaw, throwing him to the side, landing him unconscious on the bridge's steel floor.

"This is Envoy 1 & 2," the voice on the comm begins. "We have heavy damage to multiple systems and casualties throughout. We request emergency shuttle evac to Luna base and opportunities to repair systems in orbit." It's Captain Van de Beek of Envoy 2.

"You have clearance," Admiral Mann replies. "Please follow the path supplied on your Nav Comm, mind the debris and welcome home."

"You'll want your influence here to remain classified I take it," Raymond sits with Chancellor Chopra in his low-lit suite aboard the carrier. Here, Darla, Labyrinth, Tobias, Ginny and Samantha, Manuel and Udo, Captains Drake and Cortez enjoy a drink in celebration of what they can only perceive is the last they'll see of Allfather. Cortez and Labyrinth sit a few millimetres from one another. Tessa is strangely absent.

"That's for the best, Raymond," Jim answers. "I've ordered Captain Huang to instruct her crew and will slip back to earth in the same shuttle I arrived in from Luna base. Luna's Commander has been briefed as well."

"Are Captain Cortez and I to accompany the Chancellor?" Ursula asks Jim, placing her glass on the table. Cortez flashes a look at Labyrinth who casually stares out the viewport.

"I'd like Captain Cortez to remain on Luna to oversee more dreadnaught construction for the foreseeable future." He looks to Ricky, and nods. "You'll return with me to UE headquarters." He motions to Captain Drake.

Ursula looks to Captain Cortez longingly as he continues to examine Labyrinth's nanoplast shell and slender, strong fingers dreamily tracing tight circles on her lap.

"Additionally, Captain Mann has informed me that Mr. Meiser, who very nearly killed us all, awaits his return to his cell on earth in Esposito's brig," Jim relays to the group. "His team came very close to wiping out the instruments and failing that, lanced our corvettes. I will allow Dr. Chandra to resume the research they've accomplished in the hopes we will one day understand the workings of the portal."

"I think that's a wise move," Darla says, her ponytail pulled tight, searching the bar for the next bottle of wine. "Now that we're in possession of the Hub, we ought to learn all we can. Imagine the possibilities."

"The Hub is a complicated thing," Labyrinth adds. "I'd like Tessa to join me in an attempt to reverse engineer the cube, theoretically. Until we have a better grasp, I urge extreme caution in using it again."

"Where is Tessa?" Ginny wonders, bouncing her baby on her lap.

"We invited her to join us but as yet have not received a reply," Raymond tells the group. "Perhaps she needs some time alone to process all that has happened."

"Dying and being Allfather's right hand you mean?" Tobias says, followed by a large gulp of his drink.

"She sacrificed much to become our greatest ally," Jim speaks directly to Tobias. "That being said, she seems indifferent over her transformation; so, I'd like her to talk to someone about her experiences and consider counselling."

"And if she refuses?" Tobias asks, looking out the viewport at the moon. "We put her in an *F-class Host*." His tone supports his suspicions over her loyalty.

"That was because the F-class have the largest storage capacities," Labyrinth offers.

"Do you question her motives for saving our lives?" Chopra asks the young captain.

"I question her absence here," Tobias answers. "I question her honesty over Allfather's demise."

"She was always outspoken against his methods." Darla wants to preserve the girl's memory.

"Yes, but enamoured also," Ginny defends her husband's point. "Maybe it's worth looking into when we get back."

"I appreciate your cynicism," Jim tells the couple. "I have my own suspicions to navigate where Allfather's demise is concerned. There's a kind of anti-climatic, unfinished feel to all of it. But believe me when I tell you, I'll get to the bottom of it."

INTO THE FIRE

In the shuttle bay of the carrier, Tessa stands before the cube. The hum is audible and through her new F-class eyes she reviews the Hub's visible spectrum. An F-class Host's sight is far more advanced than that of a human or even a Chimera. Labyrinth likely saw what Tessa sees now. The hum radiates in visible waves via her gamma-ray band. She switches between ultraviolet, X-ray, and infrared. The cube emits them all.

The bay is quiet, other than the steady hum - a single shuttle and the chancellor's heavily damaged dreadnaught are Tessa's only company. The space is cramped, and she feels a similar sensation within her F-class Host body. Her time existing in the ethereal essence of Allfather's machine offered her more freedom than she thought possible. It was a wraithlike existence which extended far beyond the massive structure and all its mysteries. Standing next to the cube offers her some semblance of comfort. A relic from that place where everything seemed possible. This, and the Allfather personality present within her. If the Akachi personality's Host could accidentally house three more souls, she calculated, there was no reason she couldn't take Allfather with her.

"And what is it you expect *me* to do for you?" Allfather says. His voice is more hateful than ever. He does not enjoy his new status.

"It's what you will do for humanity," Tessa tells him. "What you will do to make amends for your acts against the universe."

"*I won't apologize for the past.* It is my destiny to purify the universe of life," his words cut.

194

Tessa wants to help this sad creature. His beginnings were tragic, and his choices thereafter devastating. She questions whether he *can* change. She's given him 50/50 odds. She doesn't like these numbers. She wanted better odds for him. If they fell below 50%, she would have released his personality to what comes next. But with her enhanced abilities she quickly calculated all the factors and came up with the odds. It wasn't impossible for him to change. Perhaps in ten years, perhaps in 1000, but the calculations told her it *was* possible.

"You can unlearn your cruel nature," she explains internally. "You don't have to be what you are. Leave the pain behind and embrace love."

"Stupid little thing, you can not *change* me. I am what I am. Given the chance, I will reclaim myself and continue my destiny."

"You will cooperate with *my* will. You will assist me in decoding the technology you stole from the many hundreds of races you've murdered," Tessa explains to her prisoner. "You will do these things so humanity can benefit from them."

"I won't," Allfather tells her, his tone indicating no room for discussion.

"We will create memorials for each civilization you destroyed by merging their technology with our own," She insists. "We will visit each planet you devastated and leave remembrances of their cultures and their accomplishments. They will not be forgotten to the universe but celebrated. You will help me in this venture."

"I won't."

"You already have by recording each species' historical data."

"That data was meant to assist me in unravelling the technologies and their purpose."

"And it will," Tessa explains calmly. "But I expect you to contribute to unraveling each mystery."

"I refuse to help you. You have undone all of my work," Allfather says petulantly. "We could have been gods."

"You played God to each civilization you encountered. You played into their ancient fears and terrorized them. You thought yourself a god in the end. But gods are always eventually dethroned, as you have been. If you want to experience any sense of purpose again, you will help me."

"You've stolen my purpose from me. There is nothing left for me to do."

"You can change," Tessa submits.

"I won't," He maintains.

Tessa recalculates the odds of Allfather helping her in this noble pursuit to change a monster and give back to a universe he's only taken from. The odds fluctuate rapidly, rising and falling with each new byte of data added. As the final numbers populate, Tessa comes to a conclusion on Allfather's potential for change.

Moments later Tessa is knocking at Raymond and Darla's door. CADDY, their A-class Host invites her in. She ducks to clear the threshold of her 2.5 metres. The group turns in their seats to greet her. She is discernible from other F-class now with an orange scarf wrapped around her shoulder.

"Tessa," Raymond stands to approach. "I'm glad you've decided to come."

"I had something to contemplate," she reveals. The group nods in understanding. "I've done something you may not agree with." She feels their eyes on her. Their judgement. "It was a dangerous thing to do, I'll admit, but I did it for the right reasons."

"What have you done, Tessa?" Jim rises slowly from his seat, his brows turned up in concern.

Tessa's right arm raises as if to assist in her explanation, then takes on a more menacing appearance as its compartments push out, revealing the dozens of miniature missiles set to target each member in the room. They gasp and move back.

"*Allfather*," Raymond proclaims. "You're here. *In her.*"

"He's trying... to control... me," Tessa says, shocked at the sudden violence within her, the raised arm trembling. She's fighting against the raging Allfather now hacking his way into her core. "I tried... to end him," she tells them, F-class frame twitching, making the room nervous. "I can't." She now understands that running the odds again left her open to Allfather's internal attack on her system. She's angry at herself for her short-sightedness. Allfather would never change. His hatred is *all* he is.

"*Tessa*," Raymond pleads, "you have to control him." His arms are outstretched, palms wide in defence as he slowly circles Tessa's F-class frame like he's side-stepping a rabid animal to draw her attention away from the others. Sweat instantly beads along his hairline and with each step a new line trails down his creased forehead. "He *can't* be allowed to exist here. Not after all we've accomplished."

"I-I'm so sorry... I thought I-I could fix him," Raymond is reminded that Tessa hasn't suffered a stutter since she joined Allfather in the ether. *She's losing the battle.* Something drastic would have to be done - Allfather is rapidly gaining control over an F-class Host. The damage he could do triggers heart tremors in Raymond, his mouth goes dry, and muscles tense.

"*You*... have *ruined* everything!" Allfather's malicious tone escapes the F-classes gnashing mouth. "I'm sorry -" Tessa's voice slips out again, riddled with emotion. The trembling arm targeting the group steadies. *Has she regained control over the Allfather personality?*

"You miserable little shit," Tobias directs his statement at Tessa's Host. Whether at Allfather or Tessa's personality is unclear.

A popping sound from the F-class' forearm breaks the uncomfortable silence and a missile is released. Just one, but it finds a mark in Captain Cortez.

Cortez is hit in the temple. He slumps over without a sound, the wall behind him spattered with blood and brain. Manuel, who has returned from the bathroom watches on as an F-class Host holds Udo and the others hostage in a partial military stance.

"Oh, I'm.... so sorry, Captain," Tessa's voice struggles to offer her apologies. Still, she can not control her weapons systems. The group is frozen in place and Manuel makes his move from the corner behind the Host.

From the laser embedded in his wrist, Manuel fires a single shot which rips the artillery clean off Tessa's forearm. Then he rushes her, throwing his shoulder into the Host's chassis. His weight isn't enough to knock her over and Tobias leaps from his standing position aiming for the F-class' crown with his pulse fist. He misses the crown but cleaves the rest of her right arm off at the shoulder. Both Chimera are thrown clear of Tessa by Allfather's rage. He's gaining the upper hand now, and Tessa knows it. She struggles against his hold over the Host's body and the F-class is forced to its knees.

Manuel and Tobias shake off the hit and watch as the inner turmoil works against the Host. The head is violently shaking while the left arm is lifting in a shuddering motion. The chassis opens next, revealing a deadly cannon whose barrel spins, causing the room to flinch, readying to fire. Chancellor Chopra is caught directly in line with the terrifying image.

"I'm so... sorry," Tessa's voice says again. "Clear out of h-here," she orders. "I have regained some... control... for now."

The group moves rapidly out of the suite and into the hall. All but Labyrinth, who ignites her thrust boots function and tackles Tessa to the floor. The Host shudders again and Tessa pleads with her to leave with the others. Though Labyrinth has designed herself an impressive fighting machine in her Host body, if an F-class were working properly, she would not be a match.

"You killed him!" She angrily shouts at Tessa. "Why would you do that!"

"It's... Allfather," Tessa's voice comes through.

"*You* did this because *you* kept him alive!" She throws a punch into Tessa's F-class face. An eye comes loose and the jaw collapses under another hit. Tessa's sensations mode is engaged, and she feels each strike as it is meant. Labyrinth is precariously situated above the chassis' cannon as she pounds into Tessa's crown.

Tobias and Manuel look at one another and without a word between them, leap to tackle Labyrinth off Tessa. A moment later the cannon in Tessa's chest fires a hundred rounds into the ceiling, arching the F-class' back. She moves to stand, and Manuel rushes the Host. Tessa's remaining arm falls hard on the Chimera's shoulder, crippling his movement. He takes a knee and hears Udo shout his name.

A half dozen F-class have arrived in the hall but are stayed by the chancellor and Raymond. They would not be the delicate enforcers they need right now. Still, everyone stares on in horror as Manuel is raised by his throat and thrown several metres to the exterior wall where he slumps over. Tobias is enraged and rather thrilled over the idea that he would now, after all this time, be given the opportunity to fight Allfather in person.

"Tobias," it's Allfather speaking through the F-class now. "Follow me." Tobias smirks at this, watching through the open door as his wife orders a security officer to take their child to safety. She's preparing to join him.

"Follow what?" Tobias spits back, blood trailing down his forehead. "You're *nothing* now!" He laughs his barking laugh at the Host.

"I'll spare your Tessa if you obey," Allfather bargains.

"She brought you *aboard* this ship!" Tobias is irate. "You can do whatever you want to her, and *I'll* do whatever I want to you." He charges his pulse fist and slams the energy into the cannon on Allfather's chassis. The Host is pushed back through a wall, into an adjoining bedroom.
Labyrinth has regained her senses and reviews a new message coming through on her internal modem while she tracks Tobias' movements in the fight. Ginny joins him, pulse fist glowing hot. The pair move cautiously toward the fallen Host in the next room.

Unlike the other messages, this one is a clear communication. She then reviews the messages which never materialized through her internal modem. She shares the incoming frequency with the other two broken attempts from earlier. The former messages begin to materialize. *They were all from Allfather.* Tessa must have been scrambling them, she posits. Upon opening all three, Labyrinth feels herself go rigid. Her malware filter announces an intrusive personality overriding her system.

Labyrinth opens fire on Tobias and Ginny, cutting them down from behind. They drop. "Careful where you stick your probes, Labyrinth. You might catch something," Allfather's voice now erupts from Labyrinth's Host, and he turns her weapons on the group watching from the door. They scatter before he can unload on them. Labyrinth is trapped in her body, watching as Allfather chases the group into the hallway. She scans her chassis for the intrusive instrument which has clearly allowed Allfather to jump Hosts through his message. She realizes, to her great horror, that when she had interacted with Allfather's base, he had managed to slip a mechanism of his own into her probe and is now using it to his full advantage.

Allfather is met in the hall by six F-class who open fire on the speedy Host. Allfather is already behind them when he trains what weapons he has at his disposal on the Hosts. He drops three immediately, removing their crowns from their bodies with a powerful cutting laser. Then he turns and charges toward the bridge. The map of the carrier is accessible via Labyrinth's memory banks. He is hit in the left shoulder with heavy rounds by the F-class but escapes around a corner and moves up the stairs and onto the bridge. Here he is met with more heavy fire and scuttles out the door. This is proving trying, he thinks. With armed humans on the bridge and three F-class closing in behind him he is trapped. He calls up the map of the carrier and burns a hole in the flooring beneath him. He drops through the hole to the deck below and makes his way to the shuttle bay.

It's invigorating, he thinks, being in a body again. It is also extremely limiting. He continues to run through the halls, taking the stairs toward the shuttle bay. He encounters several passengers along the way, violently throwing them out of his path as he goes. Labyrinth is beside herself with grief over her inability to stop Allfather. He reaches the bay door to more defensive pulse rifle fire. A dozen humans protect the entrance. Human's are weak, he tells himself. If they bleed enough, they will die. His hand reaches around the corner of the adjoining hall and he releases dozens of sharp projectiles into the crowd. Shrill screams are heard as the steel spikes tear through soft bodies. Allfather takes this opportunity to step around the corner and brings his laser down upon the living. He looks at his machine body and laughs, thrilled over its efficiency.

"Allfather," it's his old friend, Raymond, coming through Labyrinth's modem. "Stop this!"

"You burned my house down, now it's my turn," Allfather says with great delight. Labyrinth's left arm hangs limp after being shot up by the F-class but the right one works well enough as Allfather pulls a hatch open on the dreadnaught. He marches toward the bridge of the small ship and calls up its weapon systems. The cannons position themselves as the cores charge.

"Shit," Captain Huang says, an image of the dreadnaught on her viewscreen. "We're reading dangerous energy levels in the shuttle bay. He's charging weapons on the dreadnaught!"

Raymond and Jim look at one another, sweat glistening off their exhausted features. "He's going to burn our house down," Jim tells him. "He's going to destroy the ship."

"We have no way of clearing the carrier of people," Raymond says fearfully, the image of his nephew and Ginny being gunned down still fresh in his mind. Their baby, safe for the moment in Darla's care, let's out a wail. He looks at Jim and shakes his head. He has nothing left.

Jim reads the defeat in his friend's eyes and turns to Captain Huang. Using his intimate knowledge of star ships, Jim orders her to roll the carrier. She is about to protest but then understands the order. "Secure yourselves in a seat," Huang tells the bridge. "Fire all 45-degree starboard thrusters. Do it now!" she shouts at her crew. The ship begins to tilt laboriously. "Engage fire protocols in the shuttle bay. Shut off the gravity knitting system. Open the Shuttle bay hatch. In that order." She looks back at the Chancellor and nods. He returns her assertion. It's their only play.

Allfather feels the ship suddenly begin to turn on its horizontal axis as he watches the cores charge on the dreadnaught's console. If he can cause enough damage to the carrier before burning out of the bay, he will have killed all of his enemies in one fell swoop. Next, the bay begins to rain a fire suppressant down like a torrent upon the dreadnaught and everything else in the bay. The coolant has no effect on the cores, so this does not concern him. The gravity is then removed from the bay and anything not tied down begins to float, including the dreadnaught. Weapon cores are far from charged, but what he has managed might be enough to do the work.

Suddenly things begin flying past his viewscreen, and the dreadnaught too begins to rapidly move toward the now open hatch to space. As it slips out, port side first, Allfather fires the remaining few working cannons into the carrier's bay. Two lances cut into the floor of the bay while three more target the forward portion. The lances are hot enough to slice and cut, but do not connect with any fuel source or major electrical centre. MakerTech bots immediately begin to repair the damage.

As he helplessly slides out of the shuttle bay, he sees his cube fastened down to the compartment's floor and ceiling. It will remain with the ship. He can still use it though, he postulates; if he can get the engines running, he can target the instruments he'd left in Earth's system and jump to freedom. He fires lances at the destroyer that is matching the carrier's speed and course in order to eliminate the threat. Though the lances are weak, they still burn into the ship's armour and cannons.

"The damaged corvette just penetrated deck 2!" Esposito's weapons officer announces, dumbfounded. "It's taking out our cannons. Captain?"

Esposito rushes over to understand the statement. Sure enough, there is a corvette rolling uncontrollably out of the carrier and firing its cannons at his ship! "Captain Huang," he hails the carrier. "What in the hell is going on over there?"

"Fire on that corvette, Captain," it's the chancellor's voice. "Admiral Mann will be in firing range in 2 minutes. Use your corvettes as well. Take it down!"

"Yes, sir." He nods to his officer, who is still nursing a head wound from Meiser's elbow earlier. The corvettes move in to flank the ship and fire lances meant to impair the ship's engines and artillery.

"This is a *kill* order, Captains," Chopra announces to his fleet. "I want that corvette reduced to dust!"

"Firing missiles," Captain Esposito announces. The fleet watches on as three missiles burn toward the dreadnaught.

LABYRINTH

Allfather uses the Labyrinth body to jack into the dreadnaught's Nav comm in a desperate attempt to steady the ship and burn for home but the ship is non-responsive to hard-jacked tampering. Its software is the most advanced the UE has ever produced. He's frustrated as he realizes just how bad this situation could get for him. He fires the thrusters manually regardless of his direction, and the ship jolts him back into a vacant seat. Audible alarms and flashing lights on the console notify him three missiles have targeted his getaway. The ship is fast, but missing a number of thrusters, thanks to his earlier defensive against the heavily armed dreadnaught.

"I am leaving your system," he has little left to bargain with. "I will remain gone once I leave, but you *must* first let me leave!" He's frantic and knows the desperation in his tone is coming across loud and clear to the UE fleet now closing in on him.

"*Let* you leave?" Raymond's voice comes down on Allfather like a hammer. "You're not going *anywhere*," he explains.

"I have your Labyrinth with me," he tells them, encouraged they will see this as a bargaining chip. "If you finish me, you'll finish her."

"Labyrinth understands the value of the sacrifice she makes for the greater United Earth." Raymond extinguishes any hope Allfather has of surviving this ordeal. The ageing chancellor's tone is without empathy, and for good reason after Allfather had shot down his nephew and spouse in front of him. The missiles continue their approach with all the ferocity he has conjured in these organics over the last three years. He has nowhere to store his consciousness, trapped in this crumbling ship.

"If there is any good in you, Allfather," it's Tessa now coming through, "you will *not* sacrifice Labyrinth; then you may finally experience *peace* in your time." Allfather is stunned to hear her soft voice. He thought her gone after he'd jumped Host bodies to escape her devastated form for a new one in Labyrinth.

"I was never after *peace*, little thing" he tells her, his voice now quietly accepting of his fate. "I only sought to punish your kind for the evils all of you do. What they did to me – was unforgivable."

"The personality you hold captive, and whose fate you are in control of now has sacrificed herself for us many times over." Tessa too develops a calm tone to her words. "She is someone deserving of the life she's created. It would be your greatest triumph since acquiring sentience, were you to allow her safe passage back to us. You could redeem yourself with this one selfless act."

"You always held out such hope for me, little thing," Allfather says, watching the missiles quietly gain on him. "Whatever I may be, a sentient being, a divine thing, a thought, a flicker of energy in an unending universe, I know I cannot change who I am." He pauses as the missiles near the dreadnaught. "I'm afraid to leave." His voice assumes that of a frightened and disoriented child. He doesn't will it so - it simply is so. "I don't want to go to the darkness."

On the bridge of Huang's carrier, the group listens on as Tessa taps into the comm to communicate from her broken body in Raymond's suite. Though the voice from the dreadnaught is difficult to listen to, they all know the lengths Allfather will go in saving his own skin.

"I'll miss Labyrinth," Tessa states candidly.

"She saved my life," Raymond explains absently, remembering how she got him off the corvette during General August's war, his eyes now falling on the bridge and its complement. "She's saved us all," he says, recalling the work she'd done with the Defsats in the final phase of Allfather's orbital assault on earth. Jim's hand slides over his shoulder and squeezes lightly. Raymond reaches up to connect with his friend's grip. Darla is beside him with an arm around his waist and head falling on his opposite shoulder. They will all miss Labyrinth.

"One last time, then," Chancellor Chopra tells them in his decisive voice, removing his hold on Raymond and turning to the viewscreen. "She's a remarkable personality and will not go unremembered." Raymond turns with his friend and the entire bridge takes to their feet in respect for the loss they are about to face, together. Together they watch, some covering their heart, all observing the final moments of a universal treasure. "Be at peace. *Spiritus Omnia Vincet.*" This is repeated by the crew.

A blinding light forces them to look away as the missiles detonate Chopra's dreadnaught. The evil they have fought directly and indirectly is now finally extinguished, but at the cost of a personality who may never again be matched in the utter disregard she exhibited for her own survival over the greater good, and the contempt she felt for those who would destroy all that she loved. One whose upright moral compass never wavered, whose initial thoughts were: *how can I help?* This is a bittersweet moment for those who knew and loved Labyrinth and loathed Allfather.

"Scan the debris field and lance anything larger than a marble," Chopra orders Admiral Mann who has just joined the fight. "We've destroyed Allfather." Cheers rise from every bridge but their own. The mood there is still at odds with the victory. The fleet burns through the wreckage in minutes, ensuring nothing of Allfather remains.

"Chancellor Chopra," Captain Esposito's voice comes over Huang's bridge comm, "Sir we have some – news," he pauses. The sentence seems more a question than the beginning of a statement. "It has come to our attention that when the dreadnaught fired on my ship and pierced the armour - our brig was also compromised by the force of the blast."

"Meiser," Jim says, looking back to Raymond and Ursula. "What's happened to him, Captain?"

"Well, sir, he's not there," Esposito admits sheepishly. "The structure of the brig took the remnant of the lance and left a hole in it. We have a security detail looking for him."

"He may be old, but he's wily," Ursula tells the Captain of the destroyer. "The sooner you locate him the better. You've firsthand experience now of the damage he can do."

"Yes, ma'am." Esposito sounds ashamed of himself. "My apologies."

"You couldn't have planned for Meiser's good luck, Captain," Chopra tells him. "Find him." Jim motions to cut the communication and turns to Ursula.

Ursula shrugs and shakes her head. "He can't have gotten far," she says. "But we need to focus on getting you and the rest of us back to Luna. The news of our losses and an explanation of what's happened need to be scripted for the Chancellor to deliver."

Jim nods as Manuel stumbles onto the bridge. He's visibly disoriented and nursing the shoulder Allfather had most certainly dislocated. "Did we get the son of a bitch?"

Seeing Manuel in this state, the group is reminded of the carnage in the suite and they order a medical team to investigate, accompanied by a security detail.

Raymond leads the charge in the fleeting hope Tobias and Ginny might still be alive. And Tessa, surprising everyone with her recent dialogue via her internal modem, needs to be addressed. Inside the suite, he and Darla review the damage. Tobias and Ginny are still face down on the carpeted floor and beyond them, through the hole of the bedroom wall is Tessa's F-class lying face up and missing her right arm. All are motionless. Manuel and Udo survey the results of Allfather's attempt to flee, Udo holding Manuel's good arm. Darla moves to inspect Udo's face.

"It isn't mine," she explains to Darla of the dried blood thrown across her small features. Manuel also flinches at Darla's touch, his clavicle shattered from the force of Allfather's F-class arm falling on him and bloodied by being thrown clear across the suite.

"I'll seek medical attention soon," Manuel tells her, looking down at Udo's grip on his hand. She's not ready to leave him.

Raymond kneels at his nephew's still body and lays a gentle hand on Tobias' head. He is beside himself with grief; a hole the size of his fist smolders in his nephew's back. Ginny too has not survived the cowardly attack on her small frame. Raymond's thoughts move to Samantha. She is too young to grieve for her parents, but he knows that one day he will be charged to tell her their story.

"I'm so sorry, Raymond," Darla kneels next to him and he accepts her consolation, wrapping her arms around him as he weeps.

Jim leaves his friends to mourn and steps over the ruined wall to approach Tessa's heavily damaged F-class chassis. The gun embedded in her chest was blown out by Tobias' pulse fist. The girl's personality seems to have survived the damage though, so he orders the body moved to a smart wall for tests.

"It was *her* fault," Raymond says, choking back his hoarse throat and looking up from his nephew's battered body. His face is wet with tears, expression hateful. "Tessa *did* this." He stands and walks purposely toward the F-class. "I don't want her resurrected," he tells the chancellor. "She doesn't deserve another chance." His voice is cold.

Security teams push between Raymond and the sitting Chancellor. Jim allows this for the moment as he decides what would be in the best interest of United Earth. Tessa is an ocean of knowledge on the instruments and many other alien designs for technologies well beyond their current capacities. To lose her would mean they'd gained nothing from their trials with Allfather.

"I understand your position, Raymond," he starts, voice low and eyes fixed on his friend. Raymond looks at Jim as though he were about to be struck. "If Tessa survives this, she can assist us – *all of us* – in understanding the portal. United Earth could jump light years in technology and understanding of the universe."

"She doesn't *deserve* another chance," Raymond says through clenched teeth, head shaking slowly and fists tightened. "Don't let her," he begs. "She brought this upon us all."

207

"I'm taking her with me, Raymond," Jim tells him, his hands rising in an attempt to placate his friend. "What she's learned is more important than what she's done."

"More important than killing my family?!" He wants to push through the officers holding him back and shake his friend.

"It has to be, Raymond!" Chopra whispers pleadingly, pulling his hands through his hair and turning back to the downed Host. "What was any of it for if not so we could learn?" Jim's voice sounds strained. "She knows things we *need* to know." His hand points at Tessa. "I'm sick that Tobias and Ginny are gone. I lost Cortez and how many others, Raymond? We need what she knows so we can stop this from ever happening again."

"We *have* stopped it, Jim. *It's over.* Tessa coming back isn't going to change any of that." Raymond moves back from the officers and sits at his couch with Darla's assistance.

Jim waves off the security detail and walks warily to where Raymond is now seated with his head in his hands. "You know I'm right, Raymond," he says softly, crouching at his friend's feet. "We need all we can secure from Tessa's data. We need the data and we need *her* to explain it to us. There are other species out there. Intelligent races who, like us, will have a military presence. We need to see the bigger picture. It's a lot to ask of us right now, *I know*, but it's our responsibility to see it through, and make preparations for the *reality* that we are not alone in the universe."

Raymond's head begins to nod, and he lifts it to his Chancellor, eyes bloodshot and ruddiness encroaching on his olive skin. "If I were in your position," he starts, "then yes, what you're proposing makes sense." He admits quietly. "But you need to appreciate that I'm no longer *in* your position, Jim." He shakes his head again. "I'm no one."

"You'll *never* be no one, Raymond," Jim's hand again slides onto his friend's shoulder. "But you *did* make a decision to leave, and *I* am the Chancellor now. So, my decision, right or wrong, has to be understood. By *you* especially."

Raymond nods again. "With respect to Labyrinth's sacrifice, and my faith in your judgement," he looks into Jim's tried eyes. "You have my blessing, Jim, if that's what you're asking." Darla squeezes him into her and cries into his shoulder. Jim stands and nods at the F-class to carry out his orders and Tessa is taken out of the room.

"We have shuttles from Luna on approach," Captain Huang announces over the comm. "The shuttle bay is in disrepair, so they will dock along the top of the carrier where manholes will place you all on shuttles."

"Understood, Captain," the Chancellor says. "You have proven yourself most capable. You have my thanks." Huang accepts the chancellor's thanks and ends the communication.

"Gather up your things, everyone," Chopra says to the room. "Head to the upper deck and we'll off-load. We've still a lot to accomplish." He looks back at Raymond who is being consoled by Darla, and nods to her. She will take him the rest of the way.

AFTERMATH

On Luna base Ursula and the Chancellor touch down in the sequestered room of the shipbuilding facility where the dreadnaught had been constructed. Captain Cortez's body is moved under a blanket to a nearby incinerator. Black-ops missions leave no evidence. Ursula understands this but is visibly uncomfortable with the order. She remembers the young Captain's handsome face and confident aura which attracted her to his masculine energy. The first attainable man in three years who she was actually interested in, and he's dead. *My luck.*

She and the Chancellor board the Chancellor's personal shuttle after a few words are spoken over the body of Captain Cortez. The shuttle is a luxury model with a C-class pilot. In under four hours they will be back at UE Headquarters. Until then, Ursula decides she will start on the speech the Chancellor will present on recent events.

Meanwhile, Jim Chopra turns in his hand the F-class data source currently housing Tessa's consciousness. Much like the Akachi personality jailed for his part in the assault on Earth months earlier, Tessa will be held indefinitely in her small space while his team works to understand everything she knows about the Allfather experience and collected trinkets. This will have to be managed under a new umbrella, like his Black-ops team. This research would be completed far away from prying eyes.

Raymond and Darla return to First City with Samantha and take a hotel room until the next-generation envoy to Tyson 4 is developed. He has had Samantha's parents moved on to a crematorium where they will be read an encouraging homily by Talia of the Betaists in a day's time.

Raymond has alerted Talia to the fate of her daughter, Tessa, leaving out the part where she brought Allfather aboard the carrier and everything thereafter. Talia will know her daughter as a hero who sacrificed her physical form to infiltrate Allfather's ether. It's possible none of them would have made it back if not for her conscious decision to take Allfather down. Tessa's ego then overcame her intellect by convincing her she could change Allfather. That was a mistake which has robbed Raymond of Tobias and Ginny and also took the lives of Labyrinth and Captain Cortez. *What will become of Tessa's consciousness under Jim's scrutiny*, he wonders?

Darla appears at their doorway, home from a counselling session. Smiling, she picks up Samantha from her safe-cube and bounces the baby on her hip. This gives Raymond cause to smile as well. Through all of it, Darla has been and forever will be his happiness. With the addition of Tobias and Ginny's infant daughter, Raymond suddenly finds himself with a family of his own.

Udo remains by Manuel's side after a short surgery to repair his clavicle and pop his dislocated shoulder back into place. The hospital room is pure white, with white walls and white machines and white garments. She doesn't like hospitals. She had to spend months in one recuperating from the blast that took her leg, arm, and eye. She woke up a different person in a hospital and had to undergo multiple tests and rehabilitation exercises there. Now, she looks at Manuel as he sleeps under a thin sheet. His face is covered in bandages, but he's the most beautiful thing she's ever seen. She's sure of it.

"Staring at me won't make me better, kiddo," he says through a dry throat. She notices this and hands him a water bottle. Manuel drinks greedily from it, smacking his lips when he's finished for Udo's benefit.

"Manny," Udo remarks, laughing. "They said you can stay as long as you like, but that you could go home tomorrow."

"Home?" a voice from behind them nearly shouts. There stands a military man in full uniform. He is a man Manuel remembers clearly from his short stint in the UE military training program. This sparks anxiety in

Manuel as he must be considered a deserter since he boarded Envoy 1 with Udo.

"Your home is the corps, *Private Joker!*" The tall, dark man takes a step closer. The intensity in his eyes nearly frightens Udo. Manuel notices two more officers flanking the doorway into his room.

"Sergeant Winters!" Manuel greets his drill sergeant with a pleasant smile. Udo takes a step forward to protect her friend. "Never thought I'd see you again!"

"None do that go AWOL, Private." Winter's hands are folded behind his back, legs spread at ease. "I heard news of your return and thought I'd pay you a visit."

"That's very good of you Sergeant," Manuel wonders when the hammer is going to fall.

"You'll face a court-martial, naturally," Winters says believably, loosening his posture and straightening the sheet at the end of Manuel's bed. Udo reaches for Manuel's hand and squeezes.

"Word is you were part of the team that took out the biggest threat humanity has ever faced, Private." This surprises Manuel. Was Winters here to take him back or not?

"That may be stretching the truth a bit, sir -"

"Nonsense, I have it from the highest authority." He sits at Manuel's bedside. "When I read the names of the survivors of the 3 envoys, I noticed yours. I was excited to bring you back and take it out on your training, but when I requested your return, I received a most impressive message from our esteemed leader, Chancellor Chopra."

Manuel and Udo share a look of satisfaction. "Jim?" Manuel says, using the chancellor's first name in front of his sergeant for effect.

"To you maybe," Winters says playfully, "the *Chancellor* to the rest of us. He explained how well you handled yourself, told me Chancellor Bellows would also vouch for you. So," he puts his hand out and a soldier waiting outside the door enters with a box in hand. Winters hands it to Manuel who opens it unceremoniously.

"A Purple Heart," he shows the medal to Udo who removes it from the box. "I – thank you, sir." Udo busily pins the Purple Heart to Manuel's gown.

"If you ever consider the military again, Joker," Sergeant Winters stands and salutes Manuel, "I'll be proud to stand with you against any enemy." He ends the salute and turns on his heel, leaving the room without another word.

"Wow, Manny, you just got *really* lucky!" Udo teases, laughing. Manuel laughs with her, caressing the Purple Heart adorning his hospital gown.

Chancellor Chopra addresses United Earth with the news of the mysterious disappearance of Envoys 1 – 3 from his 40th floor office. He's dressed in a dark suit and looks as though he'd never left the planet, let alone taken out Allfather's fleet 200 light years away. He explains the tools Allfather left behind, the demise of the Allfather personality, and the research which will be carried out by GovTech to better understand the instruments and their application into United Earth's plans to populate the stars. He does not mention Tessa and the work they will perform on her vast data concerning other intelligent life and their mechanisms. He assures everyone that the lottery will begin again, more ships will be built, and crews trained to continue what they've started.

Meiser watches the feed on the smartwall ten metres beyond the room he now occupies. His head nods on repeat to the thoughts circulating in his mind. The room is courtesy of the United Earth re-education department where Mr. Meiser will be held until his trial for murder, destruction of UE property, attempted murder, and several other charges which will likely keep him behind these nano-steel walls the rest of his natural life.

Found lurking in the HVAC system of Captain Esposito's destroyer by his security forces, Meiser was dragged out by his wild gray hair, unwilling and screaming in his native tongue. There he was placed in a foam-sealed vessel so as not to be a danger to himself or others. Now on a single pill which releases the appropriate dosage of sedative to his system daily,

Meiser does little more than watch the feeds to entertain himself, no longer interested in books or science projects. His body is drugged and his mind sedated, but his thoughts are clear enough to focus on the things he's done to find himself here again.

Drool escapes his gaping mouth and lands on his pristine gown. Denied anything of personal value in his cell, he has been appointed hemp slippers and a loose-fitting gown of white. He has also been appointed counsel but has denied help. He knows he's guilty and would rather hang than play everything out again to a public audience. Too many failures and not enough victories.

And so Meiser waits out his final days. Destined to be remembered for his wickedness rather than his brilliance. A fate worse than any death the State might bring down upon him. Of course, there is no death penalty for UE citizens. So, his punishment is to live out his days in a cell, lost to the dark recesses of his troubled and brilliant mind.

A week later, Senator Quinn greets what's left of the council in Chancellor Chopra's office. Quinn has suffered greatly at his friend Labyrinth's loss. Tobias and Ginny's loss has also affected him, and he joined Raymond and the others at the funeral for the fallen a few days earlier, leaving immediately afterward. Now, he stands ready to discuss moving forward without their beloved friends at the council table.

"The instruments, what we're now referring to as the Jump Portal, have been moved to a permanent position 1000 kilometres above Luna base," Admiral David Mann explains to the group seated around the black walnut table. "Each instrument has been marked with a physical emblem of United Earth through the processes Dr. Chandra developed."

"The electromagnetic field," Quinn says. Mann nods. "And the cube?"

"Yes, the cube, or 'Hub' as we're calling it, has been placed in a sequestered site near Luna base where Dr. Chandra and a team of her peers are busily studying the thing."

"Any headway?" Raymond asks, invited to sit in on the council meeting as an expert and consultant. Darla too sits at his side taking a similar position.

"You can understand, Raymond, this won't be a simple task," Mann replies.

"Tessa is being helpful?" Darla wonders.

Mann looks to the ex-commander of Luna base and nods. "She's being most helpful I am assured by the Doctor." He sits.

"Testing will begin in a short time, but we're still mapping the systems the cube has compiled," Chopra explains. "To date, the team has pulled over 2600 star systems visited by Allfather. There are presumably many more as the civilization who built the tool claimed there are in the neighbourhood of 10,000 systems mapped - according to Tessa's data on the now extinct culture."

"That could mean Allfather has *erased* 2600 civilizations," Ursula says, her hands splayed over the dark wood of the board table, back straight and eyes forward.

"It's unconscionable." Raymond leans back in his seat.

"What we know is that there is life beyond our little blue planet," the Chancellor states. "If we are to use this tool, this Jump Portal, we will likely encounter worlds completely foreign to our own, but which house intelligent life."

"And so, we need to be prepared for the worst," Ursula finishes the Chancellor's thought. "And that's exactly what we're proposing to the council today." She swipes at her EC and a file is delivered to the group's ECs. "What you see here is a plan to build more star ships, cultivate and train more military talent, and use the Hub to enter new star systems and introduce ourselves."

"Introduce ourselves to what end?" Raymond asks. "What do we expect to accomplish? Isn't this all a little sudden?"

"Good points, all, Raymond," Jim says. "And we'll not rush into anything, but what Captain Drake is proposing is that the more systems we can befriend, the more allies we'll have in the event another Allfather-type enemy appears out of the darkness.

"But putting ourselves out there like this – isn't that *asking* for something to happen?" Darla suggests. "We need time to rebuild. We need time to process. People need time to accept that we're not alone."

"Read the proposal, we want everyone's input." Jim says. "It's not written in stone. We want to tweak it in order to best represent the council and the people."

Raymond stands and swipes the proposal to the table's holo. "I have come to realize - it's not for me to choose a course for the people anymore. In light of this - revelation, I respectfully decline my status as a contributor to this council."

"Raymond?" Jim says quizzically. "You know how much I respect your opinions. If you have issues with how this proposal has been presented I-"

"It's not you, Jim, it's me," Raymond says softly. "I'm just done with it. Sitting here, I feel out of place. I feel I've served my time and my people. I did the best I could, but I am simply not capable of giving anymore. I signed up to join the Tyson 4 trip so I could leave all of this behind. I looked forward to spending my days with Darla and my nephew and his family on a planet far removed from this one." He raises his hands and lets them fall at his sides. "That dream is partly over now. But once the envoy is ready, and we're cleared to go, I'd still like to take Darla and Samantha to Tyson 4. I'd still like to leave this all behind." The room is quiet in response to this unexpected announcement.

"I understand," Jim tells his friend. "You've served your time and you've done it with intelligence and compassion." He stands and approaches Raymond. He extends a hand and Raymond accepts it. "You are officially released from any and all responsibilities to this council and to United Earth. You have my ear whenever you require it. It has been my honour to serve under your leadership."

Raymond feels tears welling and he pulls the Chancellor into him for a hug. The experience is healing. Jim hugs him back with the same enthusiasm. They part and pat each other's shoulder, offer a knowing nod then take a step back. The council rises to their feet to acknowledge the moment between the two men, and Raymond's own realization that he has given all that he can, and now needs to live for himself, Darla, and his grandniece who he will raise as his own.

Darla hugs Raymond next and he returns the gesture. She then swipes the proposal to the table holo as Raymond had, removing it from her EC. She laughs awkwardly through a smile and offers a quick wave goodbye to the council. Raymond and Darla move out of the fogged glass doors and down the elevator to the UE's HQ foyer. It is busy with activity. It is a world he helped create and one he has defended now through 3 wars. He wishes Chancellor Chopra an easier time of it, but with the Jump Portal now a focus for United Earth, that wish may never be answered.

THE END

Other Books of Fiction by Michael Poeltl
1. The Judas Syndrome
2. Rebirth (Book two of The Judas Syndrome)
3. Revelation (Book three of The Judas Syndrome)
4. West of Noreaso
5. Her Past's Present
6. Waning Metaphorically (14 Short Stories)
7. A.I. Insurrection – The General's War
8. Armageddon (Book two of the A.I. Insurrection series)

Young Reader Picture Books
1. An Angry Earth

Educational Books by Michael Poeltl
1. If a Tree Falls in the Forest…
2. Energy is Forever, and so are YOU!

About the author
Author Website: www.mikepoeltl.com
Amazon Author Page: Michael Poeltl Amazon
Facebook Page: Michael.Poeltl.author
Goodreads Author Page: Goodreads
Twitter Handle: @mpoeltlauthor

Further Acknowledgements
To whomever, or whatever is seeding my brain with these tales, narratives, and oddities: Gratitude.

Reviews and requests for interviews are always appreciated!

www.ingramcontent.com/pod-product-compliance
Lightning Source LLC
Chambersburg PA
CBHW030309200626
46816CB00002BA/827